Elite Bomber Command

Stark in its realism and authenticity,
this novel is set against
the background of
Bomber Command's saturation
raids on Germany.

It is the story of the loves,
the fears, and above all,
the courage of
the elite of Bomber Command
and the German
Night Fighter Force.

It is a novel
which commands attention
for its accuracy of detail
and its characterization of men
keyed to the breaking point.

BOMBER RAID

James Campbell

BELMONT TOWER BOOKS · NEW YORK CITY

A BELMONT TOWER BOOK

Published by

Tower Publications, Inc.
Two Park Avenue
New York, N.Y. 10016

To
Douglas and Lorene
also to
Those Who Knew Them and
Never Saw Them Again

Lovers in peace-time
With fifty years to live,
Have time to tease and quarrel
And question what to give;
But lovers in war-time
Better understand
The fullness of living,
With death close at hand.

from *The White Cliffs*
By Alice Duer Miller

(by permission of the Estate
of the late Alice Duer Miller)

Chapter One

The girl in the yellow beret fingered the glass in her hand, sipped it and savoured the tartness of the drink. She placed her heel on the step of the stool and eased herself into a more comfortable position. She rummaged in her handbag, pulled out a packet of cigarettes and leisurely lit one. Ilona Stroheim glanced in the long mirror behind the bar and approved of what she saw. Her long dark red hair hung loosely over her shoulders and accentuated the wide-set green eyes. She had tawny eyebrows which she refused to darken and she always used the palest of lipstick when she could get it in bomb ravaged Berlin.

Firm breasts thrust out beneath her thin forest-green blouse. Her knee length black velvet skirt clung tightly to well formed thighs. She crossed a long, shapely leg. It was marvellous, she thought, to get into civilian clothes again, although Johan had told her she looked equally elegant in uniform. She had never decided whether she was beautiful or not. Werner had told her. The last time she had seen him, over two years ago, was shortly before her marriage to Johan. He had placed his hands on each side of her face and whispered that her grace and charm had made the question of her beauty irrelevant. Her figure was appealingly trim and she was tall enough so that both Johan and Werner felt at ease holding her close, dancing with her, or walking in the forest glades which surrounded the little Bavarian village of Feissendorf, ten kilometres from the suburbs of Nuremberg.

A prickle of tears stung her eyes as she reflected on those days. Skiing in the mountains, skating on the frozen lakes under the stars, and listening to the crash of water from the falls high above the village. They had all gone to the village school, Johan, Werner and his brother Wolfgang. Now Johan was dead, killled a month ago in the frozen hell of the Eastern Front. The official communication that Leutnant Stroheim had been killed in action had reached her the previous week.

But the message of those cold words was only seeping through to her now. And with it came the realisation her heart had always known, that although she had been immensely fond of Johan she had never really loved him. It was Werner, always had been, always would be. She bitterly regretted the stupid row they had the day before he was due to return to his night-fighter Staffel. Just then Johan had asked her to marry him and this time she had accepted. She was sitting on the same stool as she was that afternoon he had brought her the yellow beret. There was little to buy in a city under constant attack from the air but in a little shop she saw the beret and paused. Johan had looked at it, then at her, and strangely it was her size.

She opened her bag and read again the posting notice sending her as communication plotter from the Supreme Luftwaffe Command position of the 1st Night-Fighter Corps at Treuenbrietzen, south of Berlin, to a sectional control centre near Nuremberg. The centre, she knew, came under the overall control of Schleissheim and she would be doing the same work as before, placing on an illuminated glass map the positions of the bombers as the plotters pin-pointed their course. She was coming home and was elated. A happiness made fuller by the thought that she would be seeing Werner before she left Berlin. She had written saying that Johan was dead and he was

8

genuinely upset for they had been childhood friends. Werner's letter had come by return and she was pleasantly surprised. She checked her watch. Feldwebel Horst Munzberger was late for their farewell drink.

On 187 Halifax heavy bomber squadron, based at Merton Wold in East Yorkshire, Warrant Officer Innes Mackay, the six-foot bomb-aimer of S-Sugar, downed the remnants of his half-pint tankard and said to the rear-gunner of Q-Queenie, with studied sarcasm:

"You're seriously suggesting that a clapped out aircraft like Queenie got to twenty-thou' on the last Berlin 'do'?"

"We bloody well did and what's more we got an aiming-point on our camera, more than you sods did," Sergeant Orly said heatedly.

Mackay surveyed the crowded Sergeants' Mess and shook his head. "Come off it for Cri'sake. There weren't any fuckin' aiming-points, just trace on the pictures. Anyway, you wouldn't recognise an A.P. from a light ale label. So belt up."

Sergeant Fred Hopkins, Q-Queenie's mid-upper gunner, turned his thin, pale face towards Warrant Officer Bill Mitchell, the lanky Canadian pilot of S-Sugar and mockingly asked: "Does he fuck and blind at the bombsight too? You really should do somethin' about his language."

A wry smile creased the lean face of Mitchell and his brown eyes twinkled. "Mac uses the finger and thumb method. It's very effective," he said.

"Yeah, your results look like it," Orly said brusquely. Then turning to Hopkins he asked: "You comin' down to the Flights with me then, Fred?" His mid-upper nodded. When they had gone Mitchell said: "What the hell do they want at the Flights?"

Mackay grunted. "They'll be joining our absent ones.

They usually play pontoon there at this time."

"You planning on going to the Swan tonight, if we're not on, Mac?"

The Scot nodded. "May's half expecting me and I wish to Christ they'd make up their bloody minds. The buggering around cocks up a man's love life."

Mitchell looked at the wall clock and saw it was just after noon.

"We should know in a couple of hours."

"Care for another?" Mitchell nodded and watched his bomb-aimer edge his way to the bar. His mind went back to the time they had first met at the operational training unit at Kinloss, in Morayshire. They had become close friends ever since. There had been something about the tall, dark-haired Scot that had instinctively attracted him. Mackay, he knew, had done a full pilots' course in the States, under the General Arnold scheme for training R.A.F. pilots and observers, before America had entered the war.

He had done his in Canada and was glad for he had been shocked at the stories that filtered through of the 'wash-out' rate in the States largely because there were not enough instructors, at the time, to handle the mounting stream of R.A.F. trainee aircrews. Rumour had it that the R.A.F., also puzzled, had sent a Battle of Britain pilot over as a cadet to find out the position but he was 'washed-out' half-way through his primary training. Mackay, he later learned, with only two weeks to go before getting his wings, had got into a brawl with an American instructor over a woman. Some said it was the instructor's wife but Mackay would never discuss it. He had heard the story from his brother who was with the Highlander in the States

The outcome was a court martial and Mackay never got the full brevet. Mitchell ruminated that he was not the only one who had come so close to graduating. His own brother had been one of three R.A.F. cadets who had lost out on their pilots wings ten days before they were due to receive them. They had 'beat-up' a little American town near their flying school and tossed out long streamers of toilet rolls they had tucked inside their flying jackets. They thought it a great joke but the U.S.A.A.F. thought otherwise. The verdict was that they were too irresponsible to fly an aircraft. Mitchell found himself smiling as he recalled how his brother had ended the story . . . "Gawd, wasn't that the spirit that won the Battle of Britain?" he had asked. His brother remustered as an observer, as Mackay had, and had gone down over the Ruhr just under a year ago.

Mitchell considered he was lucky having Mackay in his crew. He was not only a competent second pilot but had been trained, as bomb-aimers were, to take over from any other crew member in an emergency. All the gunners frankly admitted that in simulated turret firing he outclassed them.

Mackay had explained that it was mostly good eyesight and mastering the art of deflection shooting. Air-gunners were pushed through their course in six weeks, observers took two years and had more air-turret training than any air-gunner could ever get on their rush courses. The only damned thing he regretted about Mackay was that he had introduced him to Julie but then, he corrected himself, no one had forced him to marry the bitch. He thought of the telegram in his pocket and was about to take it out and show it to his bomb-aimer when his navigator, Flight Sergeant Jack Holton, came up to him. Holton had finely chiselled features, fair hair and a wisp of moustache on his upper lip. With him was Sergeant Ted Parke, their Manchester wireless operator. Parke had narrow, close-set eyes and a pimply face matched the the colour of his bright red hair.

Mackay returned with two half-pint tankards, handed one to Mitchell and turning to Holton and Parke said: "If you two think I'm going back to the bar again you've

11

another guess coming. Besides you two don't drink halves anymore, do you?"

Parke grinned. "You're a bloody mean Scot so we wouldn't expect it. Anyway, we could be on tonight."

"Butch Harris tell you that personally, then?" Mitchell asked.

Parke shrugged. "Cut the flannel. What's the diff'rence if we go tonight or tomorrow. We're gonners, the whole fuckin' lot of us. It's just that Jack has asked me twice since we left the Flights if I thought we'd be on and he's the flaming navigator. He must've another date with that bag Maggie."

Holton flushed and said sharply: "Don't call her that. She's a good kid who got a raw deal from . . . " He hesitated and Mackay interrupted: "What would you call her then?" There was a cold purr in his voice and before Holton could answer, the Scot spat out: "An easy lay?"

Holton fidgeted uneasily. "Just because she's an 'ex' of yours you don't have to malign her."

Mackay guffawed. "Jesus! You're not only funny but have an odd sense of language. Tell an ignorant peasant what malign means?"

Holton looked appealingly to Mitchell and said: "You married her sister, Julie, so why don't you tell him Maggie's a good kid?"

"Who told you that?" The snap in Mitchell's voice was whip-like. "Who in hell told you that?"

Holton paled. "Maggie, but I thought it was general knowledge and . . . "

Parke, sensing that what he had started as a light-hearted bantering was fast taking on a tense undertone, said quietly but firmly: "Belt up all of you. Are we going into town tonight if there's no 'ops' or do we drink in the village?"

Mitchell shrugged. "Let's get some food. By the time we finish it we should know."

He set off for the dining-room with Mackay. The other two hesitated for a moment and then followed.

When Sergeants Orly and Hopkins walked into the crew-room of Flight 'B' they saw it was empty apart from three of S-Sugar's crew, Chris Burrowes, the rear-gunner, Nobby Smythe, the Cockney engineer, and Sid Davis, the Welsh mid-upper gunner. They were seated round a tea stained and cigarette scarred table. Davis ran a hand through his thick black hair and contemplated the Queen and the seven of Clubs he held in his other hand. He winked to the two Sergeants from Q-Queenie and said: "Stick."

Smythe looked at Burrowes questioningly. "Stick," said his rear-gunner. Smythe turned the two cards in front of him face up.

"Christ, you jammy bastard! That's the second pontoon you've turned up in fifteen minutes," Burrowes said. Then looking up at the two newcomers he said: "You two wanna come in and break his flippin' luck?"

"Dunno," Hopkins said.

"Blimey, what in hell brought you down here then?" Davis demanded.

Orly placed a hand on Davis' shoulder and said: "You think you've got some exclusive club here, Taffy?"

"For Chri'sake are you coming in or not? You're holding up the bloody game," Smythe said fingering the pack.

"Okay, but it'll have to be a short one. We came down here to pick up a book from my locker," Orly said.

"Bet it's a dirty one," Burrowes said.

Smythe snorted. "Oh, Gawd, will you all belt up so we can restart this bloody game." He reshuffled the deck and deftly dealt them a card apiece. As they picked up the cards the station Tannoy crackled. "Attention! Attention! All pilots, navigators and bomb-aimers report navigation briefing room at 1500 hours . . . Attention! . . . All . . ."

"Blast it that's torn it," Hopkins said.

"Jesus! I'd a date tonight," Orly said.

"Could end in a bloody 'scrub'," Davis said.

Smythe threw down the pack and strode to the window. The clouds that had lain in dense banks over the airfield were slowly beginning to break up. He estimated the cloud ceiling to be around the six thousand mark. He walked back to the table, beckoned over his shoulder with his thumb and told them: "That shit's lifting. We could well be on."

Davis pushed back his chair and said: "It'll be the Big City then. There's no bloody let-up. I must've had a bone loose in my head to have joined this fuckin' mob."

Burrowes grinned at his mid-upper and quipped: "Don't you know Taffy there's a war on?"

"Bugger the war and if you say that again I'll thump you." The Welshman smiled. "But you all miss the point. What gets me is that our lot," and he nodded towards the others round the table, "have to bleeding wait before we know where we're going."

Hopkins laughed. "You're damned right Taff. They're treating us as second class fliers. You should form a trade union."

Davis scowled. "You wanta get some flying hours in. The point I'm making is that it's okay for our drivers, navs and shit-droppers to know in advance the target but it's not for us. That's not democratic when we're all in the same flaming, fuckin' coffin."

"Aw Christ, Taffy, don't panic," Burrowes said. "You know damned well it gives them time to work out the preliminary charts, bomb-settings and all that crap while we're pissin' around doing nothing."

Davis gave his rear-gunner a playful jab with his elbow. "We've argued before on this and never agreed. I'm going to get some grub."

They filed from the crew-room and their conversations

switched to the half-hour air tests they had made earlier that morning over the airfield in readiness for the operation that now seemed to be on. From the dispersal bays, off the main runway, came the deep throated growl of Hercules engines as ground-crew checked and re-checked on faults that had been reported.

Oberleutnant Werner Franz, Staffelkapitan of the 2nd Echelon at the Luftwaffe night-fighter airfield at Parchim, north-west of Berlin, swung his long legs from the bunk he had been resting on and reached for his tunic, draped over the chair at his bed-side. He strolled to the window and saw it was raining steadily. Huge banks of cumulo-nimbus cloud hung threateningly over the airfield. The wind that had howled all day, and the previous night, was gradually spending itself. He watched indifferently as it rolled the cloud base towards the east. The rain was becoming lighter.

Franz opened the door of his sleeping quarters and sniffed the cold, damp air that blew from the perimeter of the airfield, across a grass that had not been warmed by the sun for days. The German Meteorological Service had also been analysing the cold front of severe weather which had lain dormant over England the past few days. It was a more critical appraisal and was based on weather data unavailable to a solitary sky gazer. And the experts who had sifted through these more intricate reports concluded that the front had now moved towards Cherbourg and was gradually blowing itself out.

The wicked weather it brought had grounded and rested the bomber crews but it had also given a respite to the men who flew the night-fighters. So it came as no great surprise to the Luftwaffe ground controllers when their Freya radar detected a large bomber force assembling off the Wash. The

15

ever alert Freya sets, their radar ears continuously cocked towards the eastern English coast, were the first to trace the air tests of the bombers. They had long known that it was in Lincolnshire and Yorkshire that most of the Lancasters and Halifaxes of Bomber Command were based. The impulses from their radar navigation aids as they made their air tests, were easily picked up by the Freya to give early warning that a raid was likely.

Once the bombers penetrated German territory the more accurate Würzburg radar would take over and direct the fighters into the bomber stream. The Freya detections were flashed to the battle-opera-rooms, who in turn alerted the fighter staffels and the guns. The Oberleutnant lit a cigarette and slung his tunic loosely over his shoulders as the cold wind whipped his body. A pair of peewits protested mournfully as somewhere off the airfield's long runway the twin-engines of an Me. 110 shattered the stillness with a grating snarl.

The fighter's engines were pushed to maximum revs and gradually eased back. Franz had air tested his aircraft at noon and found it serviceable. A mechanic, he considered, was making a minor adjustment, more probably than not to the fuel feed system of some machine that had been reported faulty. What was needed, he thought, was more spare parts instead of tinkering with components that were past their scheduled operating life. He shrugged his shoulders. He was being posted to the night-fighter base at Mainz-Finthen, near Frankfurt, and there the aircraft might be better. He was about to slam the door of his hut when he saw two figures cycling towards him. As they came closer he recognised them as his radar operator, Oberfeldwebel Hans Petz and his gunner, Oberfeldwebel Heinz Kromer.

Petz, a twenty-four-year-old from Saxony, had been with him on eighty of the one-hundred-and-three missions he had flown against the bombers. He wore the ribbon of the

Iron Cross (1st class). He had taken the place of his previous radar man, who had been mortally wounded when a Mosquito intruder had attacked them while they were making an emergency landing at the night-fighter field at Loan-Athies some ten months ago. Petz had light brown hair, blue eyes and a bashed in nose from a crash-landing in his early training days.

The Saxon was very cool and very methodical. Franz noted that his stocky frame was bent almost double as he pedalled against the wind. He was a good radar man and had the added asset of being able to anticipate, through long experience, the likely movements of the bombers he picked up on his screen. He was not one to panic or get excited when a 'blip' slid onto his radar. All this, the Oberleutnant conceded, made him a top class operator although at times Petz was apt to think that he controlled the fighter and that the pilot was merely his driver to direct at will.

Petz huddled back-to-back of him in the Me. Behind him was Kromer, a tawny-haired, twenty-three-year-old from Bremen. Kromer had been assigned to them three weeks ago when their original gunner was sent as an instructor, after completing one hundred missions with some of the best night-fighter pilots in the 1st Gruppe of the 5th Nach-jagdgeschwader at Doberitz.

Kromer, the Oberleutnant mused, had the wide blue eyes that brought out the motherly instinct in women. And he showed the same naivety towards women as he did to the deadly business of night-fighting. The boy, he felt, had an almost child-like conviction that they would win the war within a few months and a pathetic hero worship for anyone with a Knight's Cross. Often he had caught him looking with open admiration at his Knight's ribbon. He recalled the time he had drank with them in one of the near-by village inns. Kromer, he found out later, knew by heart the grades of the various decorations but had made out he was not acquainted with them and had urged him to explain.

Perhaps it was the drink, but somehow he found himself relating the grades and Kromer had listened like a child to a bed-time story. He had got to the Eichenlaub with oak leaves when Kromer had interrupted: "I know, I know, it's . . . " Franz smiled as he recalled how he had snapped at his Sergeant for asking damned fool questions when he already knew the answers. He watched the two cyclists.

They dismounted, leaned their bicycles against the wall of the hut, and flung him a half salute. His hand came up in limpid acknowledgement. "Now don't tell me. Let me guess. Churchill has sued for peace?" He waggled a finger at them. "No, you want to know if we're going on posting leave at midnight, as scheduled?"

Kromer grinned sheepishly but Petz's face was impassive. "We're packed." Petz answered.

"Well, I've some bad news for you Oberfeldwebel Petz. You've missed out. You're to proceed independently to the Gruppe's advanced radar school for a crash course on the new SN2 airborne radar. Then you join us at Mainz-Finthen." The Oberleutnant smiled wickedly. "I'm sure that'll gladden your heart. You've always bitched for this new toy."

Petz frowned. "When did this come through Oberleutnant? They did not mention it to me when I was at the 'admin' office this morning."

"The order came through a couple of hours ago. Your instructions and travel vouchers are with the Adjutant."

Petz shrugged. "What does it matter. It's unlikely that anyone of us will be going on posting leave tonight. The weather is clearing and the bombers will come."

Franz stepped inside the hut and motioned them to follow. "Yes, we may well be 'scrambled' tonight. But we don't pick up our passes and ration cards until the morning, So it means we're up instead of in our beds, where I'd

18

much rather be. We lose some sleep but what is sleep with leave in the offing?" he asked, glancing at Kromer. Franz looked at his watch and noted it was nearly 1635 hours. The lowering sky was darkening. He closed the black-out shutters and switched on the light. He looked thoughtful and said: "Coastal radar has probably picked up heavy air activity off the English coast. Petz knows what that means. Being new here Kromer perhaps you don't. When the Tommis make their air tests they switch on their radar. They don't seem to realise that the impulses thrown out are detected by our Freya. Not that they have any option for the sets have to be turned on to be tested."

He paused: "That's invaluable warning to us. The English have no more fuel to waste than we have so their air tests invariably mean a coming night raid. Only last hour weather reports, showing that conditions would be unfavourable for landing afterwards, would 'scrub' such actions."

"So you think we'll be operating tonight?" Kromer asked.

"We're almost certain to be. The weather is clearing, although there's still a lot of heavy cumulo about, probably up to fifteen thousand, possibly higher. We'll have to go through it to reach them."

"It'll be Berlin again," Petz said.

The Oberleutnant nodded. "That's where they've been hitting this last while and there's no reason why they should suddenly switch. If it's not Berlin, it will be Hanover, Magdeburg, Brunswick or Leipzig." He broke off and added: "All within our range. Yes, I think they'll come tonight."

"How long can they take such losses?" Kromer said.

"A few more maulings and they'll be forced to go for shorter targets on the coast," Petz answered.

The Oberleutnant rubbed his ear-lobe. "We're fast getting the upper-hand. No bomber force can shrug off such losses. Lancasters and Halifaxes don't roll off the assembly lines like sewing machines. Their crews take a long time to train and with each raid they lose more and more." He again pulled his ear. "There's also the question of morale."

Petz said: "How long would you reckon was the average life-span of a Tommis bomber crew?"

Kromer said: "'Bout a week." Petz scowled. His question had been directed at his pilot and he was annoyed that an inexperienced gunner, like Kromer, should have had the audacity to answer it.

Franz said: "An exaggeration, but you may not be that far out. Personally, although night-fighting's a damned exhaustive and dangerous business, I'd rather be in my Me. or a Ju.88, for that matter, than in a Halifax or Lancaster."

There was a moment's silence and Franz added: "I've some things to pack so you'd better push off. I'd been hoping we could've slipped away later tonight but the Hauptmann had a feeling we'd be up tonight."

As they moved to leave he said: "My car's on the road again so I'll give you a lift to the rail centre in the morning." They thanked him and went out to their bicycles. He pulled a case from the top of his wardrobe and began to pack. The tank of his car had been filled that morning and he had managed to get a spare 'jerry-can' in the boot. He also had a good reserve of emergency petrol coupons in his wallet. Wolfgang had enclosed them in his letter asking him to collect the suitcases from his flat.

Franz considered that if there was not much heavy traffic on the roads he should do the journey to Berlin in a couple of hours. He would not normally spend his leave in the capital but had promised his brother to check his flat for bomb damage and collect the cases. Wolfgang was living in luxury in a Paris apartment and had promised to show him the sights if he ever came on furlough. Knowing Wolfgang, the sights would be brothels and night-clubs. He was not interested but why Wolfgang kept on his Berlin flat had

20

always puzzled him. Still it would be good to see Ilona again. It had been a long time since they met. Poor Ilona, she'd had it rough. Once leave was a magical thing for him but that was when his mother, Martha and baby Randal were alive. Now it was meaningless, except for the rest and the unwinding of taut nerves.

The long bar of the Afton Hotel was filling up and Ilona was conscious of the admiring glances that were coming her way from three Panzer Grenadier officers who had just come in with an SS Leutnant. She hoped the Feldwebel would come, otherwise one of them would make a move thinking she was a pick-up. She had met Munzberger by chance at lunch-time and although she had told him she was half expecting Werner to meet her in the Afton he insisted that he drop in for a farewell drink, especially when she told him she was being posted from Treuenbrietzen.

"It's not often I've the chance to meet night-fighter aces and I'd be grateful, Fraulein," he had said. Horst Munzberger, she reflected, was harmless enough and since she had made it clear to him months ago that there could be no affair between them he treated her in almost a fatherly fashion. There was the added safe-guard that she was an officer, while he was a senior N.C.O. Anyway, she had been glad of his company during the few times she was in Berlin.

Her thoughts centred on Werner. He had telephoned to say that he was being transferred and was coming to Berlin. He hoped to get away that day but if not would definitely be in the Afton the following day. She had packed all her belongings and sent them to her father's house in Nuremberg when the big raids on the city began. Only a few changes of clothing and toilet articles were now in her flat.

She had tendered the lease on it and this would be the

21

last night she would ever stay in it again. She would make the rail journey to Nuremberg the following afternoon. Werner, she knew, had married soon after her marriage to Johan. She was a girl he had met in Berlin and like hers it had been a short union. His wife and their three-months-old child had been killed, along with Werner's mother. They had gone to Brunswick to visit Werner's mother-in-law to show her the baby. Two nights after their arrival the Terrorfliegers hit the city and they died in the raid. She wondered if Werner had got over it. But in war-time, she knew, people had to adjust and adapt quickly. She was eighteen when her mother died and even after six years she could remember how she had cried and cried. Her father had never fully recovered from her death and had totally immersed himself in his newspaper column. His work and the long letters he wrote to her outlining life in Nuremberg was all he seemed to live for now.

She reached for the cigarette in the ash-tray and found it had smouldered to the butt. She lit another and her thoughts sped again to Werner and her love for him. He had planned to be at her wedding. He was then in France. There was, she remembered, a heavy R.A.F. raid on the Ruhr the night before her marriage and Werner was in ac-tion with his Staffel. It was better that he had not come. She knew now, for certain, that had he, she would have dashed to him and there would have been no wedding.

Werner and Johan, she reflected, were complete op-posites. Johan had been plump, pink-cheeked and rather immature. Although he was twenty-five, a year older than herself and Werner, he had been running to fat. But he was kind and had utterly adored her. Whereas Johan had red-dish hair, Werner's was almost blond. He was taller too than her husband, nearly five foot ten. He had a lean face which the winter sun of the Bavarian Alps had crisped to a light golden hue. She could never forget those bluish-grey eyes which had always fascinated her and the narrow lips

hat seemed to be so full of meaning, if one could just tip it
out of them.

He was so different from his older brother. Wolfgang was
devious and cunning, and had been so even at school. His
hair was darker than Werner's, his frame bull-like and his
watery blue eyes were seldom without a sardonic, contemp-
uous expression. Yet, she conceded, Wolfgang had done
well. He was now a Hauptmann, in the Gestapo Headquarters in Paris. She recalled the wedding gift of exquisitely cut crystal he had sent. The decanter alone, she thought,
must have been well beyond even a Hauptmann's pay and
he had it delivered by Wehrmacht transport. They said the
Gestapo could get away with anything and she was inclined
to believe it.

Ilona glanced in the long mirror and saw Munzberger
coming towards her. She swung round on her stool.

"I'm sorry Fraulein. I was kept checking some supplies.
Those thieving foreign workers will steal anything. But I see
your glass is nearly empty."

She smiled. "You're all out of breath. Sit down and relax,
Horst."

The Feldwebel settled heavily onto the stool beside her
and ordered fresh drinks. "Where is the Staffelkapitan? I
was much looking forward to meeting him."

"I too, but then he was not certain of getting away
today." She looked at her watch and saw it was just after
five. "I don't think there's any chance of him getting here
now until tomorrow."

Horst took off his peaked hat, laid it on the bar and
wiped his brow with his handkerchief. He was a short, tub-
by man in his middle fifties, with greying hair. His face was
streaked with splotches brought on by living outdoors in
rough weather. Most of the batteries and searchlight units
of the Berlin defences were manned by men too old for the
front line, but some of the guns were crewed by the
Flakhelfer, youths in their teens. Ilona admired them. They

23

had a tough and often unrewarding job to do.

Since the middle of November 1943 Bomber Command had been carrying out an almost ceaseless assault on the capital. It was now March 1944 and the massive raids were getting, if anything Ilona thought, heavier and more concentrated. Fortunately, she mused, the weather was nearly always unfavourable for visual bombing and the bombers attacked above cloud, unleashing their loads of high explosives and incendiaries on the 'sky-marker' flares of their Pathfinders.

Most of the havoc had been in the Eastern part of the city where her flat was, particularly in the Tiergarten area. Yes, she considered, the men on the guns and the searchlights had been having it rough. Munzberger raised his glass. "Good luck, Ilona. I wish I could get a posting to Nuremberg, even though I've a fat wife with a viper's tongue there." He chuckled into his beer.

Ilona arched an eye-brow. "I thought she was a Berliner?"

"Well, when the bombing got worse she went to live with her sister." He grunted and added: "Sometimes I think I prefer the bombs to living with her."

Ilona shook her head. "You shouldn't say such things. I'm sure she's a very nice person."

Munzberger gulped into his beer. "Enough of her Fraulein." He took another long draught from his glass. "So you go tomorrow?"

She nodded and he said: "You'll miss the battle-opera-room. You're at the hub of things there and know what's going on. We, on the other hand, are told very little, except to fire and keep firing." He ordered another drink and when she shook her head, he placed his hand on her arm.

"One more for the sake of the little chats we've had. Please, I shall miss you."

"Just one, then I must go."

24

He paid for the drinks, rose and said: "Excuse me a moment, I must go to the little boys' room." He smiled and added: "One of the draw-backs of middle-age."

She toyed with her glass. The Feldwebel was in many ways right. She would miss the battle-opera-room and her work with the Luftwaffenhelferinnen. The work of the girl communication auxiliaries was exacting, strenuous but seldom monotonous. As the grid numbers and references came through tracking the courses of the bombers, she and the other auxiliaries transferred them on to a huge glass map along with markers, representing the positions of the hunting night-fighters.

From all over German occupied Europe by teleprinter, radio and telephone the movements of the Terrorfliegers were plotted in the massive, concrete reinforced underground control centre. Linked to the supreme headquarters were the interception nerve centres of the Luftwaffe's other sectional divisions.

She had always been proud of her job and like the other women auxiliaries was a specialist. A month ago she had been promoted to Leutnant. The women auxiliaries made up seventy-five per cent of the aircraft plotting and reporting service of the Luftwaffe ground defences. Plotting that was done from curt, precise orders from experienced fighter controllers and radar experts, who had been carefully selected for their flair to visualise and anticipate the air battles that were waged, almost nightly now, in the skies above them.

More often than not, Ilona knew, the work was frustrating for they were seriously hampered by the radio jamming devices of the night bombers of the British Luftmarschall Harris and by the decoy feints they made. Recently, she was aware, they were carrying, in some bombers, fluent German-speaking radio operators, who impersonated the ground controllers and gave out false instructions. This had been counteracted by relaying orders

25

to the fighters through the women auxiliaries.

Munzberger came back and sat beside her. "I meant to mention it before but this is the first time I've seen you in civilian clothes. They suit you admirably."

She smiled. "It's been a long time since I've worn them."

He sipped his beer thoughtfully and said: "Well, are we to have a quiet night from the Terrorfliegers?" Before she could answer, he added: "There's heavy over-cast and a high wind coming up. Often they come on such nights."

"It's been bad this last while," she said.

"But think of their losses. How much longer can they go on losing at such a rate. Sixty-seven the other night. Fifty before that. No airforce can stand that for long."

"But still they come."

"Ach, it's madness. The guns took fifteen of them last time," he said."

"Ten," she corrected quietly and there was a hint of mischief in her eyes.

He shook his head. "Fifteen, I'm on the guns and should know," he said emphatically.

"Treuenbrietzen credited them with ten."

He pulled a face. "We were told fifteen, but then they'll tell us anything to keep the young ones eager."

Ilona finished her drink. "He'll not be coming now. I must go." He straightened up, rose from his stool, and said: "I shall miss you, Ilona. Good luck in your new posting."

She laid her arm gently on his. "Thank you Horst, and good luck." She slipped from the stool and he watched the tantalising swing of her buttocks as she walked to the door. He wished he was twenty-five years younger and a Staffelkapitan. He glanced at his watch and saw he had time for two more drinks before catching the transport back to his battery.

Chapter Two

An hour after the master teleprinter at Bomber Command Headquarters in High Wycombe stuttered out the first alert to Bomber Groups 1, 3, 4, 5 and 6 and to Pathfinder Group 8, the Group Commanders were informed by coded messages that the target for the night was again Berlin. The order was terse: "Maximum Effort . . . All aircraft to operate. Full instructions to follow."

On every station throughout Bomber Command there was the same intense activity. Everyone down to the cook-house erk had a job to do and all knew it was a Maximum Effort. The petrol load and the bomb-load was almost exactly the same as for previous raids on Berlin and although the ground crews were never told where the bombers were going it was quite easy to work out the approximate location of the target.

High loads and full tanks usually meant the Ruhr or some other target not too distant into Germany. Low loads, to conserve the bombers' petrol, indicated a deep penetration attack. A communications 'black-out' was put into force immediately. All outgoing telephone calls were blocked and all incoming calls intercepted. Virtually the stations were cut off from the outside world. The routine was the same throughout the bomber groups.

The pilots, navigators and bomb-aimers had at the preliminary riefing completed on their charts, tracks, courses and turning points, along with the estimated time of arrival at them. These in turn were jotted down by the pilots on their knee pads. Wing Commander John Brewis, D.S.O., D.F.C., who was flying with them that night, took the main briefing. Beside him, on the raised dais in front of the huge mercator wall map of Western Europe, was the Station Commander, Group Captain Ernest Havilland, D.F.C., A.F.C.

The clamour of voices in the main briefing hall faded as the Wing Commander jerked aside the curtains revealing the target and route on the wall map. He cleared his throat, surveyed the rows and rows of faces before him and said: "Tonight – it's Berlin!" His announcement triggered a wave of muttering and groaning. He waited a few moments, which seemed like hours, as the murmurs and curses died into electrifying silence. Brewis outlined the method of the attack, pausing now and then to let the full weight of his words sink in.

"Tonight, to get the maximum concentration of aircraft over the target and in the minimum of time, we've cut the intervals between each wave. So you must, I repeat must, keep to your allotted bombing heights to avoid collisions. They've been scaled to counter such risks."

The Wing Commander summed up: "Because we expect heavy cloud over Berlin the Wanganui marking method will be used. For the benefit of the new crews – and I gather there's quite a number of you – this is the least accurate of our bombing techniques but the only one possible when a target is obscured by cloud. The first sky-marker flares will be red and they'll go down at 0006 hours. Three minutes later – at 0009 – green target illuminators will be released by the Pathfinders. Zero hour on Berlin for the main force, who will attack in four waves, will be 0010.

"The duration of the entire attack is planned from 0010 to 0040. Pathfinder backer-up aircraft will continue throughout this time to drop fresh markers – they'll be again green. So the target should be well lit up."

Brewis looked keenly around the hall and went on: "Thirty-five minutes before you cross the enemy coast sixty aircraft from operational training units will make a dummy feint, ninety miles from your landfall. They'll be throwing out 'window' and this we hope will confuse the enemy controllers on where the main attack is to be."

At thirty-one, Brewis felt old . The majority of the crews that were coming on to the squadrons seemed to be getting younger with each replacement – most of them looked in their early twenties. He stepped aside for the bombing leader to say his piece. Then came the navigation leader, the gunnery leader and the wireless leader. They gave their specialised directions to their own particular section, called for questions and answered them the best they could.

The tension in the hall eased when the Met Officer, a soft spoken young man, with fair tousled hair and thick rimmed glasses unrolled his chart. Pilot Officer Ron Tresland, Q-Queenie's navigator, nudged his pilot, Flying Officer Reginald Cotton, a lanky, slow talking West Virginian whose mother had been born in Devon and said: "What a creep and what he knows 'bout Met I could scrawl on a 'lav' wall."

Cotton removed a hand-rolled cigarette from his lips and in a soft drawl said: "Yep. We've seldom got a correct Met forecast from him yet. It's patchy cloud here, patchy front there. Guess he should've been a grave-digger. But he's only relaying the crap that's come down to him."

The American had been sold on England since a child at his mother's knee. She had met his father when he had come over with the first contingent of Doughboys in the first world war. He had gone on his first leave to the Devon village she came from to visit relatives. It was instant love. Cotton had always looked on England as his country of origin and to the dismay of both his mother and father had slipped over the Canadian border and joined the R.C.A.F.

He showed a natural aptitude for flying and was soon commissioned.

When America entered the war he could have transferred to the U.S. Eighth Air Force with far higher pay and better allowances but had refused. He felt he had been too long with the R.C.A.F. and R.A.F. to switch loyalties.

Although his English born mother had never tried to influence him, one way or the other, he knew that she was proud that he had not made the switch. He had recently returned from a leave with his grand-parents in Devon and they too were immensely proud that he had stayed with the R.A.F. But his senior officers and crew mates never really understood why he had not transferred along with that small band of Americans who had joined the R.A.F. before their country had entered the war.

Tresland, a blunt New Zealander, had once told him: "You're flippin' bloody mad Yank. You could more than double your pay and live the life of a blinkin' Lord. Just don't understand it. But then some of you Yanks are bloody screwballs." He tried to tell them he was a Southerner but they didn't comprehend.

The Met Officer went on for a few minutes more. Mackay sitting behind Cotton, with the rest of the crew of S-Sugar fidgeted and said: "Christ! How long have we to go through this rubbish?" His remark triggered fresh mutterings among the fliers. Someone cheered mockingly. Others took it up. The Met Officer, his face flushed with embarrassment, glanced at the Wing Commander and thought he saw a trace of a smile on Brewis's face. Brewis signalled for silence.

"The weather," the Met Officer began . . . he coughed nervously and went on: "the weather is fair for this type of operation and . . ." A chorus of jeers and cheers greeted his words. Brewis again motioned for order. The Met Officer held up his chart, tapped it and said: "This cold front which has been hanging around for the past forty-eight hours or so has now moved up the Channel. Behind it is a lot of cloud but visibility should be fairly good. There'll be some breaks in the cloud and on the way out you should be able to see patches of land."

The Met Officer hesitated as another burst of ribaldry came from the back of the briefing hall. Hell, he thought, those jokers out there always made fun of him as if he was the briefing jester. What they didn't seem to understand was that accurate forecasting of weather was a chancy enough business in peacetime when meteorologists had at their disposal the latest reports from Atlantic weather ships, and Icelandic and eastern European stations. With shipping having to maintain strict radio silence and most of Europe occupied by the enemy, huge uncharted areas – vital to accurate forecasting – regularly appeared on their maps.

Mostly they had to depend on high flying Met flights but even these had, of necessity, to be restricted to specific areas. How in God's name, he told himself, did they expect anything more than calculated guess work on the limited data they had to work on? He petulantly rolled up his chart. Let them have their jokes. He'd be in a warm bed tonight when they . . . he shrugged and stepped aside.

Group Captain Havilland stepped briskly forward from where he had been standing beside Brewis. "That's it gentlemen. Good luck and good bombing." He was in two minds to give them a brisk pep-talk on hittin' 'em hard, Coventry and all that but he sensed the mood of the aircrew and decided against it. The last time he had done it, he recalled, had not gone down that well. They'd been having it rough for some months now and he didn't have to remember the squadron losses to know. At thirty-eight, he considered, he was, fortunate to be a station commander and banned from operational flying. It was bad enough earlier in the war when he won his D.F.C. on Wellingtons. Now it was not far short of plain suicide. He decided he would go down to the Flights later and watch them take-off. It was a ritual with him and the least he could do, he assured himself.

Perhaps his presence would show to them that he cared. So many faces swam before his eyes. Ghosts of others who had sat out there on the long wooden benches and, like many of them tonight, did not come back. More fleeting hosts to swell the ranks of the dead. The Wing Commander's order, dismissing the briefing, shattered his thoughts. He turned to Brewis and said: "It's going to be another sticky one. I can feel it in my bones."

A frown touched Brewis's lips. "They're all sticky." He raised an eyebrow and asked: "How long can this loss rate go on?"

The Group Captain said drily: "Until Command decides otherwise." He watched the crews stream from the briefing room into the drizzling rain. Dusk was falling and according to Met the drizzle would die out before they were due to take-off. They'd now go back to their quarters, some would write letters, others would be on the billiard tables or in card schools. Anything to break the nerve twisting waiting until they were airborne. This was the worst time, he knew, this and the standing around in the smoke filled atmosphere of the flight rooms until the canvas covered lorries took them to the dispersal bays and the waiting bombers. But that was still some hours away and soon they'd be sitting down to an operational meal of steak, egg and chips.

The Halifaxes of 187 Squadron lumbered from their bays in a long, snaky line towards runway 090. The take-off was to be into an easterly wind. The Group Captain parked his car off the runway and waited, as the first of the twenty-one Halifaxes taxied along the perimeter track to the start of the runway. Splashes of reddish-yellow flame from their exhausts, pierced the night. The great silhouettes moved slowly past and the sight of the powerful black shapes gripped and excited him as it always did.

A-Able led the crocodile line of black bombers with their coffin clipped wings. The Wing Commander crawled the bomber past the blue Dremlin perimeter lights and aligned it along the runway. He cleared his engines and the roar from the four Hercules engines, running at full throttle, battered the silent night air.

Brewis eased back the throttles, glanced at his bomb-aimer in the co-pilot's collapsible 'dickey' seat and nodded. Pilot Officer Green took a long look at the little group of Waafs, ground crew and others, who lined the top of the runway to wave the bombers on their way, and slammed shut the side window. From the control wagon, parked on the grass triangle to the port of runway 090, a green Aldis lamp flickered impatiently.

The Wing Commander, his left hand on the control column, pushed the four throttle levers firmly and smoothly through the gate with his right hand. Slowly, picking up speed with each second, the giant bomber loaded far in excess of normal safety limits, rolled down the runway. Brewis, his right hand hard against the throttles, curtly called, "Lock."

Green closed his left hand over that of his pilot while his right hand pulled back the locking lever. Brewis lifted the bomber and began the laborious climb into the cloud base. Flying Officer Stacey, his navigator, took a swift Gee fix over the airfield and from it worked out the course to their rendezvous with the rest of Bomber Command.

Group Captain Havilland nodded approvingly at Brewis's take-off. His Wing Commander had two tours behind him – sixty operations – against some of the heaviest defended targets in Germany. Such flying was expected of him. The Group Captain watched critically as the rest of the squadron followed, their navigational lights fading into needle points as they clawed for height.

In the dimly lit navigation compartment of S-Sugar, Flight Sergeant Holton adjusted the brilliance knob on his Gee Box, the radar navigation equipment operated from ground transmitters in England and was picked up by the receiving sets in the bombers. Holton knew that its effectiveness was limited as the Germans jammed it soon after they crossed the enemy coast. He would then rely on his dead-reckoning navigation and the constant readings Mackay would give him from the H2S set. The H2S was an invaluable aid to navigation but in early 1944 only the most experienced crews were equipped with it.

The H2S was a transmitting and receiving set which sent out radar impulses which bounced back from ground objects and indicated their bearing and distance. These were plotted on the Mercator chart. The device was also used to bomb a target 'blind'. When it was first used the R.A.F. believed that since its transmitter and receiver were both housed in the aircraft the impulses it threw out could not be picked up by the enemy. So the sets were switched on as soon as the bombers were airborne, the crews unaware that they had immediately alerted the Freya radar.

Mackay, like the other H2S operators, switched on his set as S-Sugar climbed to their assembly point with the rest of the stream. There was no purpose in having the H2S on over the sea but it provided him with an accurate landfall as the bomber crossed the English coast. He would not switch it on again until they neared the enemy coast.

Warrant Officer Mitchell had just banked the Halifax on to course for the assembly point when the intercom clicked: "Rear-gunner to Skipper. Okay to test guns?"

"Go ahead."

Hundreds of invisible hammers beat along the fuselage as

Burrowes thumbed out a half-second burst.

"Rear-gunner to Skipper, guns serviceable."

The intercom buzzed again. "Mid-upper to Skipper. Permission to fire?"

"Go ahead."

Four Brownings chattered angrily and the thick, sickly odour of cordite wafted into the cockpit.

"Mid-upper to Skipper. Guns working." Sergeant Davis reported.

Mitchell eased the control column back and watched the altimeter needle move down to 10,000. They had been on oxygen since 5,000 feet.

Holton laid down his dividers, rose from his bench and took a Gee reading. He studied the dancing saw-teeth of the blips, made an adjustment and plotted the reading. He glimpsed Mackay moving into the cockpit towards the blister of the astro-dome to take a star fix with his astro-compass. They had been insisting recently on bomb-aimers taking at least four astro fixes so as to keep them in practice in case the radar was unserviceable.

The Scot came back and handed him a slip of paper with the star fix. Holton plotted it against his Gee readings and his own dead reckoning. He nodded approvingly. They were dead on track. He snapped the intercom button on his oxygen mask.

"Nav, to Skipper. Four minutes to rendezvous and will you please watch your course. You're three degrees star'd off. And you're climbing too fast. Cut airspeed by ten knots."

"Sorry Nav, making corrections NOW," Mitchell said.

Holton and Mackay checked Mitchell's alterations on the duplicate instruments in the panel before them, their eyes on the compass repeater, the Air Speed Indicator and the Altimeter.

Mackay stabbed his intercom. "Read the other day Skip, in one of those technical mags, that they're working on an

35

automatically computed air position indicator. According to this bloke it computes air positions from the readings of the compass and ASI and it plots the actual course the aircraft flies and not the one the navigator gives to fly. It'll be a great fuckin' help when it comes along."

"It'll do you and Jack out of a job," Mitchell said.

"I'll cry," said Mackay.

They flew on in silence but in the vast isolation of his rear-turret Sergeant Burrowes was glad of the interchanges. The tail was a lonely place and at times he did not feel part of the aircraft. The calm voices of his pilot, navigator and bomb-aimer were reassuring. Mackay, he thought, was a real card. Mackay and Mitchell didn't care a damn for anything or anyone. Both had turned down commissions. He suspected the chief reason was their vanity. As Warrant Officers they were the 'King-pins' in the Sergeants' Mess and although as W.O.'s they would have gone straight to the rank of Flying Officer, skipping the Pilot Officer rank, they would not have the same seniority in an Officers Mess that they enjoyed in the N.C.O.s' Mess.

Burrowes broke off his thoughts and swung the turret, with its four Brownings, in a full sweep from port to starboard. The cold seeped through his electrically heated flying suit in swift, painful stabs. Always it was cold and draughty in the tail. He opened and shut his eyes, opened and shut them. Stare too long into the blackness and one could imagine things.

Lightly he felt for the knob controlling the light on his graticle sight and dimmed it slightly. Easier to focus on a fighter with minimum glare. But the fighter, he knew, usually saw them first. The thought chilled him even more than the cold. He thought of his next leave. It would be very soon. The bomber bucked and kicked in the slip-stream of those ahead. Nearly eight hundred bombers were on tonight's raid, they said. As if confirming his thoughts, Mitchell said over the intercom: "We're in the main stream now. Sharpen up everyone. It's a long way"

In the hooded glow of A-Able's cockpit, Flight Engineer Steve Turner checked the luminous dials on his panels, although the steady throb of the bomber's Hercules engines assured him they were performing perfectly. He moved into the astro-dome and peered out. In the astro-dome the illusion of flimsy protection offered by the fuselage was gone. He could see nothing but bank upon bank of cloud.

Here and there were fleeting, ghostly shadows some deeper than the rest. The cloud they had been flying through was breaking into layers. Now and then he caught a glimpse of a few stars, then they were gone. He stepped down from the transparent blister and looked over his pilot's shoulder at the altimeter, noting that it was creeping over the 18,000 notch. Wing Commander Brewis half turned towards him, winked reassuringly, and settled himself more comfortably into his armour plated seat. Turner felt very secure flying with the Squadron's most experienced pilot. "Navigator to Skipper. Enemy coast coming up in twelve minutes. Gee jamming started. Box so far readable. We'll take some H2S fixes as we cross," Flying Officer Pip Stacey said.

"Thank you Navigator."

Brewis stabbed his intercom and called up Flight Sergeant Wally Williams in the rear-turret. "You okay back there?"

A soft lilting voice with a heavy Welsh accent said: "Damned cold but otherwise fine, Sir."

"Mid-upper, you alright?"

The broad Geordie voice of Sergeant Len Groves said he was. Brewis had not just called them to enquire how they were but to check that their intercom plugs had not worked loose. Often they did and the un-plugged crewman seldom knew until someone clambered along the fuselage and thumped him on the back. Brewis checked on his wireless operator, Flight-Sergeant Nobby Sykes and his bomb-aimer, Pilot Officer Green.

Sykes, who for the last three-quarters-of-an-hour had been tuned into the late night Joe Loss dance programme, glanced at his watch and twiddled with the knobs until he found the wave length jotted on the pad in front of him. Carefully he re-tuned the set and listened out. Two minutes later the broadcast wind came through. This was the result of wind speeds and wind directions worked out by selected aircraft and transmitted to England. It was analysed and the mean average was re-broadcast to all the bombers ensuring that all would navigate on the same wind and so keep the concentration of the stream intact.

Sykes noted the new wind and found it had not differed very much from the one his navigator had earlier given him to broadcast. He scrawled it on his pad, tore it off and handed it to Stacey. The navigator discarded his own and worked out the new course they would be turning onto after they crossed the coast. The coastal batteries would shortly be opening up, and they, along with the new wind, the Gee readings, and H2S fixes on the coast, accurately pin-pointed their precise landfall.

Three minutes before their estimated time of arrival at the coast, Green, in the nose of the Halifax, reported: "Flak port bow." There was a pause and then: "Flak now coming star'd." Stacey smiled faintly. They were dead on course. Four minutes later he flicked his intercom. "Nav to Skipper. New course change 069 degrees magnetic. Speed 218. Turn now."

Brewis repeated the order and banked the Halifax on to the new course, levelled out and altered the aircraft's trim.

"What's that noise?" an unidentified voice said over the intercom.

"Ice breaking off the props. It's hitting the fuselage. I'm

going to get above it," Brewis answered.

Λ-Able climbed sluggishly, sheathed in ice. The 'thunk-thunk' came again, hollow sounding on the metal shell of the bomber. Brewis nursed the Halifax into the vast amphitheatre of a sky pierced with myriads of stars. Below them the cloud was breaking. The aircraft, he felt, was still sluggish in her cocoon of ice. In the turrets the gunners swallowed their pep pills.

Chapter Three

In the battle-opera-room at Treuenbrietzen the controllers watched critically as the readings from the Freya came in and were in turn transferred to the huge glass plotting map. Soon the enemy bombers would be within range of the Würzburg radar and would be tracked with greater accuracy.

Meantime, the controllers were concerned with reports that another enemy formation "windowing" heavily was approaching the Heligoland Bight. If they continued on the course they were flying they would cross the coast at Cuxhaven and if still on the same heading would stream between Hamburg and Bremen. Either city could be the target.

If the force continued without a change in course Magdeburg lay directly in their path. But before reaching Magdeburg they had Hanover and Brunswick on their starboard. It could be either a feint or a diversionary attack on one of those cities or it could be the real thing with the second force the diversion. The bombers could, of course, keep going towards Magdeburg then suddenly turn east towards Berlin. This was the constant and awesome dilemma the controllers faced every time the bombers were airborne.

The deputy controller wished to God his chief was there to take the decision, for it had to be taken fast. But his chief had been summoned to a top level air defence conference outside Berlin. He was in sole charge. He felt nervous and unsure. This was the first time, since his promotion two weeks ago, that he had been left in charge. He felt hot round the neck, the blasted tunic was too tight and it was too warm in the room. He found himself fidgeting with his collar. He would have to see about this damned air conditioning in the underground bunker. They never seemed to get the temperature right. It was either too cold or too hot. Conscious that he was twiddling with his collar he stopped embarrassed.

He strode over to the fighter dispositions board and studied it closely. Abruptly he turned to the aide at his side and snapped: "Parchim are on red alert. Scramble them to radio beacon "Bertrud" and flash early warning alerts to the Hamburg and Bremen areas."

In the anti-aircraft batteries in the pre-alert zones the tarpaulins covering the fresh stocks of heavy calibre shells for the big 8.8cm guns were pulled aside and the gunners laid neat stacks of them well clear of the breeches of the guns.

In the searchlight units, whose massive generators had enough power to light up a small sized town, final checks on the power units were made. Radar and range-finding gear were adjusted.

In the cities, sprawled on each side of the bombers' track, the early air raid sirens wailed. Air raid rescue workers, civil defence corps, police and fire fighters made their preliminary preparations. In the hospitals, doctors, surgical teams and nurses stood by. Blood plasma and oxygen equipment were set up in the emergency casualty wards. The routine was as near perfect as possible, devised and revised from the experience gained from countless night raids.

Oberleutnant Franz and his two crewmen lounged in the

well worn leather armchairs in the Alert hut at Parchim. Other crews sprawled in easychairs, their feet propped on the low tables spread throughout the hut. In their laps were their light leather flying helmets with their microphone and oxygen connectors. A thick haze of tobacco smoke, stale and pungent, hung over the room.

Franz had been patiently answering questions from his gunner on the defence tactics of the Lancasters and Halifaxes and was getting bored.

"Fortunately for us, Kromer," he said, "they've no belly-turrets like the American Fortresses. That's why they are so vulnerable to attacks from below. Why they've never realised this I don't know but they seem to think we come in from the rear to knock-off the tail gunner first." He was grinning at the eager Kromer.

"A few more sorties with Petz and me, and you'll see how successful our methods are. Briefly this is how we do it. Once the Würzburg controller has Petz within his radar range he takes over our 'twin' and brings us into the stream. Then we're more or less on our own. When Petz eventually picks up a Tommis and guides me to it I position myself beneath it, either to port or star'd, depending on our radar's sighting direction."

Werner used his hands to illustrate what he meant. "I then fire into the wings, where the petrol tanks are. I must then dive quickly to avoid the tremendous concussion that comes when the fire from the wings reaches the bomb-load. We never aim at the belly for that's where the 'cookie' is stacked and we'd go up with it. Besides, coming from below, the bomber is silhouetted against what starlight there is. On a dark night our range is about one hundred to one-hundred-and-fifty metres. On a bright night often more than two hundred."

Kromer thought for a moment and said: "But I've heard that the single-engined fighters make their attacks from astern."

"True," Franz said, "their guns are fixed ones so the pilot has to point his aircraft at the bomber. He hasn't the oblique-swivel guns we have. And making a pass from behind can be seen by an alert gunner who can warn his pilot to corkscrew into our fire and so cut our accuracy by drastically reducing our deflection angle. Dive away from the fire and the fighter pilot with a touch of rudder or stick can still follow him. No, the bulk of the bombers fall to us, the twin-engined fighters."

The Oberleutnant slapped his knee with the palm of his hand and his eyes held Kromer's. "I assure you it's a sinister feeling to hang only 35 to 50 metres under a bomber, always expecting them to see you and fire. So far it's not happened to me. Perhaps I've been lucky and the gunners were asleep."

Kromer looked puzzled. "It's a wonder the Tommis have never 'cottoned' on to this."

Franz pondered for a moment. "With the many foreign workers we have in our aircraft factories, and elsewhere, I too have often wondered why our tactics have never been passed back to England."

The Oberleutnant lit a cigarette and pulled on it slowly. "I used to attack from behind on very dark nights. On such nights you have to shoot from a very short distance – a hundred metres, sometimes less. But I hold this very dangerous position for only a few moments, just long enough to fire. As I've said, beneath and below is the best position. By the way Kromer, you don't smoke?"

"No sir, why?"

Franz smiled apologetically. "Well, as you must've observed I'm a rather heavy smoker. Find it calms my nerves. What would you spend in cigarettes for a kill?"

Kromer blinked and said swiftly, "Fifty."

"Have you that amount?"

"Yes, and a lot more, Sir. I save my ration."

"Perhaps you'll be fifty light tonight. That's if they come

43

and Petz finds one for me." The Oberleutnant looked up and saw his radar man approaching from the far end of the hut.

As he came up to them the loudspeaker, high in the corner of one wall blared: "Achtung! Achtung! 2nd Echelon to instant readiness."

The night-fighter crews scrambled from their chairs, zipping up their fur-lined flying suits which on very cold nights could be connected to the electrical supply of their aircraft.

The Me. 110s had already been warmed up by the ground crews and were ready to go. Franz lowered himself into the cockpit, plugged in his intercom leads and ran through the complicated take-off drill, his eyes expertly scanning the numerous panel lights that came alight. Petz settled himself in front of his radar sets and made his checks. Kromer, whose main job was to look out for long-range Mosquitos attacking from the rear, eased himself behind the rear guns. He was also responsible for changing the drums on the two oblique firing 2cm cannons. Each drum held 75 rounds and the cannons could shoot vertically and had an elevation of eighty-five degrees.

Franz had loaded one cannon with tracer, the other with armour piercing shells. Petz satisfied that his radar was functioning reported: "Radar in order, Herr Oberleutnant." Franz opened his throttles wide, watched the rev counter ratings and smoothly pulled them back until the engines were just ticking over. He waved to a mechanic, crouching under his port wing, and the chocks were pulled from the wheels. He taxied warily over the wet grass verge and swung on to the runway.

The order to 'scramble' had come through and control were broadcasting instructions to the other eight aircraft of his Staffel telling them which radio beacons to circle over until they were vectored onto the bombers. The Me.s from Parchim rose from the runway in fifteen second intervals. As they climbed to their allotted heights of 5,000 metres the runway lights below them were switched off.

At Treuenbrietzen, the deputy controller frowned as he read the signal handed to him. The Heligoland force had turned and were heading back to England. He swore. A damned diversion. The fighters from Parchim were circling their beacons wasting precious fuel. He was about to order them down when another signal was handed to him. The second force had now been identified as the striking one and if they held to the course they were flying Hanover could be their objective.

He sent orders to the Parchim Me.s to fly to Radio Beacon 'Marie', north-east of Hanover. There they could be effectively fed into the bomber stream and they would still have enough fuel for early interceptions. The 3rd Fighter Division from Twente and Quakenbrueck, flying twin-engined Ju 88's, had already been independently 'scrambled' by their divisional controllers who had rightly decided that Treuenbrietzen would have enough on their hands if the Heligoland forced turned out to be the main strikers. Aircraft from the other Jagd divisions were put on immediate readiness and would be sluiced into the bomber stream as the plotting position became clearer.

Franze in Me. 100 G had been circling beacon 'Marie' when the ground control station handling the Parchim echelon ordered him to make a 160 degree turn and fly at a height of 5,000 metres on his new course. The Oberleutnant had been flying his new heading for barely five minutes when control ordered him to climb to 5,500 metres and alter his course three degrees starboard. Control had obviously picked up a contact some distance away. Now it would be a cat and mouse game with the chess master - Radar.

He peered at his fuel gauges. The Me. had a flying range of three hours, two without spare tanks. But nearly all the Me.s had been fitted with spare tanks and Franz saw that he had two hours duration in hand. Allowing for the flying time to base it was ample enough. Petz watched his cathode ray screens knowing that his air-search radar wouldn't pick up the blip of a bomber until they were about 2,800 metres from it.

Control came through again. "Vossmeister to Gatz 4, climb 300 metres. Course change 2 degrees star'd."

Franz hauled back gently on the control column. At the same time he tapped on the rudder.

"Level out and increase speed by 20 knots," control ordered. Franz marvelled at the uncanny way the radar could plot not only his every move but that of the bomber they were vectoring him onto as well. It must still be some way off for Petz had not yet picked up any trace on his screens. Petz kept staring at his radar and wished the Me. had the new and vastly improved night-fighter search equipment, the Lichtenstein SN2. He cursed under his breath as he remembered that his leave was to be cut short so he could complete a course on it.

Still, he considered, it was an honour and an acknowledgement of his undoubted expertise, as a radar man, to be selected for such specialised training. He knew that unlike the set he now had the SN2 could penetrate the 'window' screens dropped by the bombers. Radar operators trained in the SN2 course had told him that its range corresponded with the height the fighter was flying. At an altitude of 5,000 metres it had a range of 5,000 metres but the lower the altitude the less its range. It was so accurate, they said, that it could measure the exact distance of the enemy aircraft. Moreover, it had a working angle of 180 degrees. Even in bad weather and thick cloud it could still seek out the bomber. His cut-back leave didn't seem to matter so much. He had always wanted to be an SN2 operator. Soon he'd be one and if his pilot was a bit more dashing they'd 'notch' up more and more kills, he reflected. Franz this last while, he thought, was getting a bit jittery. Not as enthusiastic as one would have expected of an ace.

The head-phones crackled and control said: "Vossmeister to Gatz 4. Steer 075 degrees and drop 100 metres. You should pick him up in two minutes." Franz banked on to the new course, throttled back and levelled out. Petz fiddled with the knobs on his two cathode screens, one of which gave the height and the other the bearing of the bomber.

He dimmed the brilliance. Almost immediately a clearly defined blip slipped on to the extreme end of his range circle. From its size it was unmistakably 'hostile'. He'd picked up too many to be confused. Fighters showed as smaller blips.

Petz called: "Target ahead . . . climb a bit . . . steady. Right . . . Right. A little higher. Steady . . . one thousand metres . . . eight hundred . . . six hundred." The radar man's voice, unhurried, was yet sheathed in excitement.

"I see him," the Oberleutnant said. Ahead of him, and about 300 metres above, Franz saw the reddish-yellow pinpoints of flame from the bomber's exhausts. Gradually he nursed the night-fighter under the bomber which he indentified as a Lancaster. It flew on unaware that it was minutes from oblivion. The crew of G-4 stared fascinated as the great bomber, laden with its high explosive and incendiary bombs, hung menacingly above them.

Franz worked the Me. closer. The cupola of the bomber's H2S radar bulged clearly from its belly. There was still no change in the Lancaster's course and again Franz was grateful that the British bombers had no belly turrets. He looked through the reflex sight, in the cockpit cover above his head, and ringed the port inner engine of the bomber. The sight was aligned to the two oblique 2cm cannons which protruded from the cockpit.

The Oberleutnant reflected that he could fly with the Lancaster on an almost parallel course and still shoot it down. The port wing of the bomber snaked across his sights. He thumbed the firing button on his control column.

47

The fuselage of G-4 shuddered from the recoil. Flames flickered from the Lancaster's port wing. Slivers of metal darted from its wing. Heavy smoke fluttered and then flames blossomed along the wing. Franz kicked the Me. into a diving turn to be well clear when the bomb-load erupted.

Kromer crouching over his double-barrelled MG 81 shivered. He was not sure whether it was from excitement, tension or fear. Perhaps, he thought, it was a mixture of all three. His eyes, wide and open in bewilderment, were glued to the flaming, windmilling mass in the part of the sky they had just plummeted from.

The death throes of the Lancaster lasted for barely two minutes. The flames roared towards the tail of the bomber. A few seconds later the crew of G-4 saw it disintegrate, throwing thousands of fiery debris into the blackness of the night. Kromer ripped his eyes from the scene, knowing that as long as he lived this first kill would be indelibly etched on his mind.

Petz logged the time and place of the shoot-down. It was just east of Wittengen. He settled down to watch the radar. The Pathfinder route flares, marking the dead-reckoning point at which the bombers were to abruptly wheel and head for Berlin, went down five minutes after G-4's interception. Set off by barometric fuses their parachute flares splashed in bright yellow stars. As they drifted in the wind, navigators were not expected to take them as accurate fixes of the course changes but only as a rough guide. Franz welcomed them as confirmation he was among the bomber stream.

The Treuenbrietzen controllers logged the bombers course change at Wittengen and the air-raid alert warning earlier flashed to Berlin was changed to Air Raid Imminent. The operation room's plotting map was showing a positive and accurate state of the attack. As reports of more interceptions and shoot-downs flowed in they were transferred to the map, along with the latest course change of Harris's heavies.

Treuenbrietzen, who had been holding back the bulk of the fighters assigned to the air defence of the capital, now gave the order to scramble them.

The Ju 88 Staffels, operating from the airfields in the Niedersachse and Prignitz areas, had already reported successful interceptions. The deputy controller looked at his watch, then at the master clock and saw it was exactly 2340 hours. Shoot-down reports, many of them unconfirmed, put the number of British bombers so far taken down as twenty-five. It was impossible for him to calculate the precise strength of the enemy force but he roughly estimated from the radar reports that it was between six hundred and eight hundred aircraft.

One of the girl plotters handed him a cup of steaming coffee. A flicker of a smile creased his taut, strained face as he muttered his thanks. He sipped it gratefully and found it was not the usual watery rubbish. He wondered where it had come from. It was the first break he had had for hours. He felt better for it.

The plot and the interceptions were going well. He worried at his lapse of judgement in sending the Parchim fighters to intercept what turned out to have been a feint but he comforted himself with the knowledge that it could have been the real thing. It was easy to look back with hindsight. No one could really blame him. Decisions had to be taken fast and furious, better a wrong decision than none at all.

Within fifteen minutes of G-4's first kill Petz got two fresh contacts on his screen. One was at a distance of 1,400 metres, the other on the outer range of his circle. He selected the near one and gave the range and bearing. Franz looked at the luminous dials of his fuel gauges and made some rapid calculations. He had about thirty-five minutes fuel left. If the next kill was as smooth as the last he

49

would get back to base with about fifteen minutes flying time in the tanks. It was cutting it a bit fine but not dangerously. Far ahead he saw a forest of searchlights, groping ceaselessly as they sought a contact. The next time he looked they had coned a bomber, a tiny silhouette which twisted and weaved to escape those bright harbingers of death.

Shells were hurtling into the cone of searchlights, exploding in vivid bursts of tangerine. A finger of flame spouted from a wing of the bomber and rapidly smeared its fuselage. Still the shells were lazily bursting around it. Franz reflected that it took about twelve seconds for a shell to reach 20,000 feet, the height he estimated the bomber to be. The fuselage of the aircraft was now well ablaze but it was too far away to identify it as a Halifax or Lancaster. Then the glowing fire-ball tumbled from the broad arms of the searchlights.

Petz called out: "900 metres . . . 800 . . . Port a little . . . stea-dy . . . 700 metres . . . "

"Got him!" Franz said and dropped the nose of the Messerschmidt, easing back the throttle levers. The enemy aircraft was weaving in a gentle crododile line. Perhaps they'd seen him. Franz thought it was highly unlikely, otherwise they'd have dived. More probably the enemy pilot was adopting this type of manoeuvre so as to give his gunners a wider search area. He brought the Messerschmidt closer and recognised a Halifax.

Franz juggled rudder and control column until he was underneath the bomber. The great black, clipped, port wing loomed above. He framed it in his reflex sight and was about to press his firing button when the bomber suddenly veered to starboard.

Franz followed the turn and coaxed the Me. to a new attack position. Again the bomber lurched, this time to port. The Oberleutnant swore. Unless he did something fast he would lose this one and would not have enough fuel to find it again. He decided the next time he got reasonably close he would give it a burst. He inched the Messerschmidt closer. The bomber made a gradual right-hand turn and its port wing angled above him at a distance of about one-hundred-and-fifty metres. He looked through his reflex sight and made out the identification letters NP on the fuselage.

He waited another few seconds and was about to correct his angle when the bomber snaked across his sights. He thumbed a long burst. The big oblique cannons deafened him with their roar. The gunfire lit the cockpit with a vivid greenish light. Flames fanned from the bomber's wing. He kept pumping his guns. Suddenly the cannons coughed and stopped. He cursed in disgust. The drums were empty. But the bomber was well on fire. He saw one engine breaking up with the white smoke of glycol streaming from it to mingle with the flame. Franz felt no elation. There was a dryness in his throat. The sweat from his face tasted salty as it trickled on his lips.

He threw the Messerschmidt into a diving, rolling turn. Levelling out, he banked the Me. and looked down at the bomber. He caught a glimpse of two men jumping from it and watched as their parachutes blossomed above them. Within seconds the Halifax broke into two flaming sections, the larger breaking again as it hit the ground. Kromer undid his safety straps. He crawled along the fuselage to change the seventy-five round cannon drums. When he had made the change he said over the head-phones: "Congratulations, Herr Oberleutnant. Two great kills."

Franz smiled and swung the Messerschmidt on course for base. "That's a hundred cigarettes you owe me, Kromer."

"Cheap at the price. It was a great experience, Herr Oberleutnant. I'll never forget it."

Franz was about to reply, decided not to and began his descent. He was tired and felt a little jumpy. The strain and the intense concentration of the combats had left him in no mood for idle chatter. His mind recorded that his two shoot-downs would bring his score of confirmed victories to fifteen. Ten more and he would get the coveted Ritterkreus. And where would that get him he thought? More strain, ragged nerves, the nightly brush with the bombers and a credit on death. Just one faulty, careless approach to a Lancaster or Halifax and their gunners would end it. And there were the Mosquitos, those fantastic night eagles of the devil, which could out-fly them and out-gun them. Franz was pleased he was low on fuel.

The bomber raids were getting heavier. With each raid more and more bombers were coming. The tiredness seeped through him. Would, he wondered, would this bloody war ever end. His eyes flicked again to the fuel gauges. They showed he'd still enough petrol for a quick interception. He fervently hoped Petz had switched off his radar. His radar man, he thought, was getting obsessed with his bloody sets, especially after kills. Any normal person would've been damned angry at having to forego posting leave, but not Petz. He was probably twiddling with the cursed gear.

Petz, he acknowledged, like all radar operators, shared to a large degree in the credit of shoot-downs. From past experience he knew he was bloody ambitious.

The height was slicing from the altimeter. Another night was almost over and soon he'd be with Ilona. It was so long ago.

"Achtung! . . . Target star'd . . . one thousand metres . . . Steer 280 degrees."

Franz cursed. It was as if Petz had read his thoughts. He instinctively hauled the Messerschmidt on to course, in a tight climbing turn, fully aware that the roughness of the manoeuvre could well lose Petz's contact.

"You've lost him," Petz shouted. There was no mistaking the exasperation in his voice.

"What do you mean, I've lost him," he snapped.

"You turned too fast, Herr Oberleutnant."

Franz's hands tightened on the control column. When he spoke there was ice in his voice. "Don't ever tell me again how I should fly this aircraft. I'm in command, Oberfeldwebel Petz, not you."

"Sorry Herr Oberleutnant, SIR. I was excited but I think I've got another contact."

"You're an experienced enough operator to know there's no place for excitement in a night-fighter. Whether you've another contact, or not, I've not an unlimited supply of fuel. We're returning to base."

"Very good, Herr Oberleutnant."

Franz thought he detected a veiled insolence in his operator's voice. He would have a talk with Petz when they landed. He glanced at his fuel gauges and decided not to push the matter. He still had enough fuel. It might be wiser to ignore the incident. But he knew, and the knowledge niggled him, that Petz was experienced enough to know he could have made the contact.

A strange feeling flashed to him that his nerves were playing up. He erased the thought. He felt like a cigarette. He remembered the hundred of Kromer's and pushed the Me. down through the cloud base. The luminous clock on his panel showed it was 2352 hours. At dawn he'd be on leave. Ilona's face screened before him. It couldn't come too soon. He felt like a tightly wound spring.

He shoved the control column forward and saw the airspeed needle rise. The Messerschmidt bucked as it hit the turbulent lower air currents. Franz tuned to the frequency of Parchim, gave his call sign, and found he was 98 degrees off course. He put that down to Petz and his damned contact. He swung the fighter on course for base and looked out of the cockpit canopy to the east.

The groping searchlights, their beams narrower and less brilliant with the distance, were sweeping a sky splashed with displays of pyrotechnics. Berlin was again under the bombs. He regretted promising his brother that he'd bring his things from his flat. Wolfgang was in a better position than himself and could have arranged for them to be collected. He slipped off more height. Somewhere to the south-east he glimpsed a glow of fire in the sky.

His thoughts came back to Wolfgang and the odd stories he'd heard about him. One, whispered in Feissendorf, was that he had been responsible for the arrest of Asaph, their old school-teacher. Wolfgang had never liked the old Jew and had taunted him many times after the first caning he'd got from him. Wolfgang, he considered, deserved every caning he'd ever got. He wasn't only devious but a damned rogue. He checked his fuel and eased his hold on the control column. He thought again of Ilona. God, she would have been under the bombs. He remembered she was to have been in the Afton tonight. Tonight, it was now tomorrow. Soon he'd know. He dismissed the worry from his mind. More reason than ever to go to Berlin. Maybe it was the strain of continuous night-fighting but he had an over-whelming desire to see her.

He remembered Feissendorf. They'd been happy there. He was now well clear of the cloud base. Ahead visibility was good. Ilona and the village had never been far from his thoughts. Ahead was Parchim's landing field. He lowered G-4's flaps and began the landing approach.

Chapter Four

Warrant Officer Mackay rose from his bench in the navigation hatch where he had been feeding Holton with fixes from the H2S and moved into the nose of the Halifax. He squinted to get his night vision back. For a minute or so he could see nothing. As his eyes became accustomed to the darkness he noted the grey wisps of cumulus cloud whip under him. The flight across the North Sea had been over heavy banks of cumulus. At their turning point at Wittengen the jagged tops wove into a dense layer of nearly eight-tenths. Above, the stars were big and bright in a moonless, inverted bowl of whirling, timeless darkness.

The monotonous syncopic beat from the bomber's four radial engines accentuated the eerie quietness in the nose. So used was he to their constant, seldom fluctuating, notes, he had to will himself to hear them. S-Sugar lurched as it hit the slip-stream of an aircraft ahead. Mackay's elbow bumped heavily against the butt of the free Vickers gun in the nose. He cursed into his oxygen mask. The gun would have to come out. It was more bloody trouble than it was worth. Once the spare drum for it had worked loose from its sprocket on the fuselage and had given him a painful glancing blow on the head.

It was supposed to be a scare gun. He'd long written it off as useless. The night-fighters never made head-on attacks. For one thing the speed of approach of such a tactic, combined with the darkness, made it impossible. He made a mental note to have it removed before their next operation. Command also realised the gun was superfluous and left it to the option of the bomb-aimer as to whether he wanted to retain it. He'd kept the bloody thing as it sometimes gave him a feeling of security. But that blow on the head and now the elbow decided him. There were enough people trying to kill him without aids that were supposed to help him stay alive.

He switched on his intercom. "That fuckin' Vickers nearly crippled me. I'll tell the armourer to get rid of it," addressing no one in particular.

Burrowes, in the rear-turret, chuckled into his oxygen mask, flicked the intercom button and said, "The Luftwaffe will be relieved to hear that. Anyway, 'cats eyes' here will look after you."

"Christ!" retorted Mackay, "I'd better keep it. I'd feel safer."

He knelt down beside the bombing computer box, and re-checked the pre-flight settings he had fed in at take-off. He set on the latest wind speed and its direction. The terminal velocity of the bombs and the target height set against the mean sea level of Berlin he left as he had first calculated. He slipped through the curtain which screened the nose from the navigation hatch and sat down beside Holton. The navigator rose and twiddled with the knobs of the dark green metal Gee box above his head. Lines of minute dog-teeth danced across the screen. He aligned the jagged points of light and plotted the latitude and longitude fixes on his Mercator chart. He cocked his thumb to Mackay. They were dead on course.

The buzz of a switched on intercom came over his head-phones.

"Flak bursts . . . star'd . . . three o'clock." He recognised the voice of Sergeant Davis in the mid-upper turret. The voice was cool, matter of fact, but then, Holton reflected, the Welshman never had much to say. Davis, a twenty-year-old from Cardiff, had wanted the rear-turret but the issue had been decided in a practice shoot-off in the gunnery training range twenty-eight operations before. It seemed a long, long time ago. Two more after this, Holton figured, they'd be finished and sent as instructors to some Operational Training Unit in the Group.

Mitchell banked the Halifax and looked over his starboard wing to the rear. He rocked the bomber back on level flight and said, "Okay, I see them." The bursts were rippling among the broken cloud layers in flashes of yellow light. Holton laid down his flight computer, adjusted the flexible arm of his table light, and marked the new course.

"Nav, to Skipper. New course 110 magnetic. Turn now!"

"Okay, 110 magnetic. Turning now!" Mitchell replied. Holton watched the duplicate panel of instruments in front of him and saw the Halifax steady on the new course. He logged the time.

Burrowes swung his electrically operated turret in a full sweep from port to starboard, straining his eyes as he searched down the black barrels of the four .303 Brownings. He felt easier that they no longer operated on moonlit nights. Bombers' moon they had once wrongly termed it. Fighters' delight it had turned out to be.

Depressing the Brownings he scanned the rear quarter, in quick, short glances. He didn't want to see things that weren't there. He turned the orange-coloured ring of light in his graticle sight a shade lower. He checked again that his firing button was on 'Fire'.

Mitchell called the wireless operator. There was no response and he said, "Navigator, for Chri'sake get the WOP to plug in his intercom . . . and if he's tuned into some dance music boot him." A few seconds later Parke came through. "Sorry Skip, my plug must've worked loose."

"You'd be a bloody sight sorrier if I'd said bale-out and you didn't hear. Christ! I've told you folk time and again to

57

keep checking on those plugs." Smythe the Flight Engineer, grinned as he searched the sky from the astro-dome. Mitchell was one of the best pilots on the squadron. For that matter, he considered, they were the best crew in the squadron. Mitchell was easy going whether in the air or on the ground. But this last while something seemed to have upset him. Like his close friend Mackay he didn't care a damn. The two were from the same mould. It was women, drink and flying. He thought he had the order right. He found himself wondering about Mitchell's wife. He knew they had a baby but Mitchell never talked about it and if he did it would only be to Mackay. They were pretty close those two. Both had done pilots courses and for some reason never fully explained, except for the banter between the two when they were in their cups, Mackay had got into some sort of trouble a week or so before wings graduation day and had been scrubbed from the pilots course.

Mackay, so rumour had it, was having it off with the landlady of the Swan. Before that he was said to have brought Maggie to the village and installed her in a rented flat. Maggie had a hot reputation. Parke seemed to know a bit about it but whenever he tried to quizz him he shut up. Now Holton was trying to make it with her. Smythe was glad he never had much time for girls. Not that he didn't like them. He just felt embarrassed in their company. He had never had a woman and it didn't really bother him. There was no great hurry. He was still some months away from his twentieth birthday.

Holton came on again and shattered his thoughts. "Course to target, Skipper. 075 magnetic T.O.T.-0009 hours. Get your airspeed to 180 or we'll be a bit late."

"Right cock! 075 it is. Air speed going up. Turning Now!"

Mackay went into the nose with a handkerchief wrapped round his torch. Kneeling beside the bombing computer he switched on the compressed air-cock and turned on the

58

electrical supply knob. After flicking on the graticle light on the Mark 14 bombsight he reset a new wind speed and wind direction on the computer box. He checked the bomb selector and fusing switches. Satisfied he looked through the transparent nose. Proper cat and mouse business this, he thought. He hoped the feint by the O.T.U. aircraft had been convincing enough to persuade the German controller to send the bulk of his night-fighters circling the Hanover-Brunswick-Magdeburg beacons. Outside he saw the vast black tops of the cumulo-nimbus. They were getting thicker. The Met boys, he mused, were right for once. There would be anything from eight to ten-tenths cloud over Berlin.

In an attempt to save Berlin from the bombs, the Germans had constructed a dummy city at Nauen, fifteen miles north-west of the capital, to decoy the bombers. Mackay remembered how once he had almost been fooled into dropping his bombs on it. The less experienced crews on that raid had been conned and he had watched pitifully as their high explosives and incendiaries rained down on the blazing decoy target, each load giving it more and more authenticity.

Bomber Command had retaliated by sending decoy bomber forces heading towards Berlin when, in fact, another city was their objective. The night-fighters went for the bombers heading for Berlin, while the main force slipped in, almost unscathed, to hammer their real target. It was nothing more than a massive but deadly game of chess with him as one of the very expendable pawns. There was little likelihood, he considered, with ten-tenths cloud the Germans would start fires in Nauen tonight. They would hardly be seen.

Parke tuned his transmitter to the kilocycle section of the German waveband he had been given to listen in to. It was a woman's voice and although he didn't understand German he reckoned by the intensity of her sharp messages she was relaying the orders of her ground controller to some fighters. In the port inner engine of S-Sugar, like most of the bombers, there was a carbon microphone connected to the transmitter. Gleefully he clamped down his morse key. The Fraulein would have her ear drums 'blitzed' from the powerful noise of the port engine.

Mackay, at his station in the nose, pondered on how long the Berlin defences were going to play 'possum'. Probably they were waiting until the Pathfinders positively identified the city and started to release their target indicators. They were in the first of the four waves of bombers detailed to attack and would take the full concentrated blast of the box barrage. By the time the last wave swept in the defences might well be saturated with 2,500 tons of high explosive and fire bombs dropped by the Lancasters and Halifaxes.

Stretching himself along the bombing mat he wondered again why it was not armour plated. Releasing the collimater handle on the sighting head of the bombsight, he squinted into the graticle sight. Leisurely, he watched the thick, oblong illuminated glass sway gently as the gyro took control. The outline of the sword sight glowed wickedly. Down the edge of the sword would come the sky-markers. When they reached the hilt intersection he would press the bomb-tit.

Theoretically the point on the ground covered by the cross intersection represented the point of impact of a bomb released at that exact moment. He extended the handle and picked up a billowing cloud top and watched it drift down the sight.

He liked the Mark 14 sight. It allowed the aircraft to bomb fairly accurately without the pilot having to fly dead straight and level. Even so its capabilities were limited. Exceed a climb of five degrees, a dive of twenty degrees, a bank of ten degrees, and the gyro toppled. Then it was useless for twenty-five minutes, the time it took the gyro to recover.

Suddenly the sky erupted in thousands of violent explosions. Then came the searchlights, countless broad avenues of light. Their naked dazzling whiteness dulled by the cloud layers they so ardently washed. The defences had decided not to wait for the target indicators. Berlin's concerto of murderous fire sprayed among the forest of searchlights. Down on his port, at eight o'clock, he saw long bursts of tracer criss-crossing above the cloud layers. There was a splash of deep orange. He caught the flaming outline of a Lancaster plunging from the sky, and a fleeting glimpse of a night-fighter pilot peeling from under it.

A bomber – too far distant to identify – blew up to his right. Another some hundreds of feet below slipped into a curving dive its port wing ablaze.

There was a blinding explosion to starboard as two bombers collided on their bomb-run. Flaming fragments from them scattered the night with giant matches.

"What in hell's keeping those fuckin' Pathfinders?" he demanded over the intercom.

"Their flares should go down in about ten seconds," Holton said quietly. He was glad he could not see what was going on around them. The last time he had looked out on a run-up to a target had almost put him off flying.

He computed a course out from the target and passed it to Mitchell. Once they had dropped their load they'd want to get away fast and this would save time.

Mackay eyed the inferno ahead, as the German ground gunners frantically raced to fill the massive sky box the bombers would have to fly through. He watched, almost mesmerised, the technicoloured arcs of the flak, the grotesque shapes the searchlights etched on the clouds, and the whole utter fantastic beauty of the massive pyrotechnic display.

He had seen it many times before but it always had a strange fascination for him. It was as if he were some timeless deity detachedly observing the creation of a miniature galaxy in the uttermost limits of the universe.

They had to go through it. This was the sky gateway to Berlin. There was no side door. Then he saw them. The vivid, unmistakable sky-markers of the pathfinding force, bursting and glowing in the clouds ahead. Breath-takingly lovely they looked, those splashes of brilliant emerald green. Cluster after cluster cascaded in fiery waterfalls of liquid colour. Suddenly from the centre of the green markers exploded equally dazzling clusters of red. The clouds looked as if they were on fire. The lead bombers droned towards the multi-coloured shroud which draped the doomed city.

"Master Switch on! Bomb switches selected and fused!" Mackay said.

"Right-Right – Steady!" Three globes of reds were floating steadily towards his sight.

"Bomb Doors Open!"

Mitchell repeated the order and saw the light appear on his panel as the belly of the Halifax yawned.

"Right a bit! Stea-dy . . . Stea-dy!"

Mitchell gently squeezed the starboard rudder. He caught clear glimpses of the black puffs of thousands of spent shells as camera flashes from the bombers ahead went off on their time fuses silhouetting the fuselage for fractions of a second.

They were now well and truly in the box. There could be no weaving on the bomb-run. Not that it would have done them any good, Mitchell reflected. They'd more likely weave into a burst. A faulty fuse setting could be just as effective as an accurately predicted shell. God, how he hated the steady run with the bomb doors wide open, revealing the unprotected bomb-racks. Strip teasing with the reaper, he thought grimly.

"Steady . . . Stea-dy . . . Hold it!" Mackay's voice was toneless. He was totally engrossed and completely hyp-notised by what he saw in his bomb-sight.

Mitchell's right leg tensed as he touched on the rudder.

His hands felt hot and sticky through his gloves. "Bombs Gone! Jettison bars across! Close bomb doors!" There was now a marked urgency in the bomb-aimer's voice.

Mitchell felt the Halifax buck madly as it leapt into the air, freed from its heavy load. He held S-Sugar straight for about half-a-minute so that their photo-flash would burst and record their theoretical aiming point. Not that there would be much trace, if any at all, through the thick cloud, he told himself.

He threw the bomber into a diving turn to starboard. He was going to dive, twist and dive again to give him maximum speed to clear the hell-fires they were in. The luminous needle of the A.S.I. shrugged against the time-lag and slowly lurched forward as the Halifax plunged through the flak.

Mitchell hauled it from the dive. He looked at his altimeter, saw they were at 12,000 feet. He had sliced 6,000 feet in the plunge and was well clear of Berlin. The added speed he had picked up in the dive would also cut the time of their homeward flight. Burrowes, in the rear-turret, saw far behind them, and thousands of feet above, batches of flares bursting. He studied them closely. There was little doubt they were being dropped by Beobacters – specially converted JU 88 observer aircraft – whose task was to follow and report on the behaviour of the bomber stream. Then to release flares over it to help the night-fighters in their interceptions. The high flying night-fighters, he knew, could see the vast gaggle of bombers silhouetted against the cloud layers and could pick them off visually. He was glad Mitchell had made the dive although it was contrary to the homeward flight orders.

Mitchell shoved the control column. The Halifax went into a steady gentle dive. He watched with satisfaction as the A.S.I. needle clocked the extra speed. To hell with the laid down heights they'd been given. He'd be a damned sight lower by the time they reached the coast. True, he told himself, it left him vulnerable to the deadly fire of the light coastal batteries, apart from making it easier for the radar to pick him up. But, he reflected, it was safer than being up there amid the night-fighters who would harry and hound the main force all the way to the coast until their fuel consumption forced them to break off. The cloud was thinning and he watched contentedly as the swirling vapour swept over the wings in fast flowing eddies.

Holton came through with a new course and reminded him that if he kept at the air speed he was doing they would cross the coast at the dangerously low level of 8,000 feet.

"Yeah, I realise that but I'm not going to lose this speed by climbing."

"I'll have to cook the plot again," Holton said. "It's all extra work. I wonder why they've never tumbled us before. They do check plots at base," he added plaintively.

"Balls to them," said Mackay. "We've been doing this since our seventh 'op' and it's paid dividends. So quit moaning, Jack."

"Jeez, it's this perpetual faking of the log. To think I was once a bank clerk," Holton said lightly.

"I'll give you a written testimonial that you're the best but most crooked navigator in Bomber Command," Mackay interrupted.

Holton shrugged, picked up his dividers, and with a rubber began to erase data he'd previously logged. He replaced it with the cooked figures. At first he had been reluctant to go along with this shedding of height in exchange for speed and the cutting of corners from the ordered flight plan. He had lectured Mitchell that, if every aircraft in the main force adopted the same flagrant disregard for meticulously balanced plans, there would be general chaos. It was not only cheating but bloody selfish and some of the crews had suspected them. He knew by their remarks when they landed, scanned the operation board, and found that S-Sugar was again the first back.

64

The Group Captain may have had a suspicion but the Wing Commander had long since tumbled it, of that he was certain. Brewis was too old a hand to be fooled. Holton shrugged and gave Mitchell the course for the coast.

The cloud layer held and it was still thick below them when S-Sugar hurtled over the enemy coast at 7,000 feet. Searchlights played on the cloud base and steady streams of light flak were coming up five hundred yards to their starboard. Mitchell saw a deep red glow where the arcs of the flak intersected. What seemed like a Halifax leisurely glided earthwards. He pushed the control column forward, tapped on port rudder. The Halifax went into a mild corkscrew. Hard on that bomber going down so near home but the ground guns were so occupied with it that they'd never now get on to him.

"Rear-gunner to Skipper. Bomber going down, star'd."

"Their tough luck. Just keep alert for following fighters."

Ten minutes after clearing the coast, Mitchell called on Mackay to take over the controls and squatted on the steps leading to the navigation hatch. He poured himself a coffee from his vacuum flask and began to munch his flying rations. This was always the best part of the trip, that and the hot meal on landing. Mackay leaned forward and indicated he wanted a sip. Mitchell hesitated for a moment. What the hell. Mac had known it for some time. He passed up the vacuum cup. Mackay took a sip, was about to take another, changed his mind and handed it back. The bomb--aimer's hand went to his intercom button, then fell away. Mackay beckoned him to lean forward and shouted something which seemed, above the noise of the engines, to be: "Strong coffee, huh!" Mitchell winked and poured some more from the flask.

The shell smashed through A-Able's rear-turret tearing

off the left leg of Flight-Sergeant Williams as Wing Commander Brewis closed the bomb-doors and swung her on course from the target.

There was no shattering explosion, just a jabbing blast in their ears and the Halifax swayed and reared crazily. Hundreds of razor sharp splinters of perspex from the transparent shell of the turret showered Williams. He felt another searing lance of pain, this time in his right eye. The over-powering smell of cordite and smoke seeped through his oxygen mask. Two of the port Brownings crashed on his thighs. Oil from a burst pipe sprayed over his helmet and shoulders. Icy blasts of air roared through the gaping hole in the turret. Panic, pain and horror froze his thinking. All he could hear was the cold scream of the wind as it buffeted through his shattered turret.

Amid the babble of voices over the intercom Brewis shouted: "Calm it. We've been hit in the tail. Bomb-aimer see what's damaged." Pilot Officer Green disconnected his oxygen from the main supply, clipped on a portable bottle, clambered from the nose and made his way aft. He plugged in his intercom to the spare socket, outside the shattered turret, and trembled at what he saw. Tongues of flame were licking the port side of the turret door. He glimpsed the huddled figure of Williams swaying backward and forward in the savage blasts of the wind.

"Bomb-aimer to Skipper. The rear-turret's a shambles. Don't know if Williams is alive. His intercom lead is severed. It couldn't have been a direct hit or the whole tail would've gone." He paused. "Maybe it was a direct one but didn't explode. Get the engineer back here with another fire-extinguisher. A small fire has started. Tell him to bring the axe as well."

Brewis called the engineer. As an after thought, he said, "Take the first aid kit with you."

Green unclipped the fire-extinguisher from the rack outside the turret and hose-piped the fire. He had got it out when Turner tapped him on the shoulder.

The gunner had swung the turret in a search sweep to port when they were hit and the turret would have to be turned to get the door back into the fuselage. He found the handle and began to turn the turret manually. Slowly the door came round. He was amazed it had not jammed. He jerked it open. The stench of oil, cordite and blood made him feel sick. Then a gust of icy air hammered his head.

Firmly, but gently, he tried to haul the gunner into the fuselage but stopped when he saw Williams' mouth gape open in a scream. Christ, his leg, or what was left of it, was trapped by the smashed port guns. Over the intercom he said to the engineer. "I'm going to try and free the leg. Then you pull him out, fast."

Turner, his eyes wide and anxious, nodded. It took them six minutes to get the gunner out, six minutes that seemed six hours and every now and then they had to stop and rest, as their lungs tightened with the exertion of gulping in and exhaling the oxygen. They carried, half dragged, Williams into the fuselage. Green ripped the tattered trouser from the gunner's leg. They were relieved that he'd lapsed into merciful unconsciousness. He fixed a tourniquet above the left knee. The rest of the leg was almost severed and the blood was pumping out. He took the tube of morphine from the firstaid box, unscrewed the cap, broke the seal of the hypodermic needle and jabbed it into the gunner's thigh. He squeezed half of it – about a quarter grain – double the normal dose. The rest they'd give to him if he came round.

"Bomb-aimer to Skipper. We've got the gunner into the fuselage. He's unconscious. His left leg is almost off. We've put a tourniquet on it and I've given him morphia. The Engineer is staying with him to check the tourniquet."

"Good work," Brewis said and added. "He's plugged in to the main oxygen supply?"

"They both are," said Green. He made his way back to the navigation compartment and collapsed exhausted on the bench beside his navigator. He watched, still breathing heavily, as Flying Officer Stacey computed a course for the coast. A few minutes later, Stacey said: "Skipper I don't think we should keep to the flight plan back, so the new course I'm about to give you is a dead straight one, aimed at getting us to base a bit faster. Okay?"

"Good, I was about to suggest that," Brewis said.

As he turned on to the new course he found the starboard fin and rudder floppy and sluggish. He adjusted the trim of the aircraft and considered, with careful handling and a lot of luck, he could bring it back, if they were not attacked again.

The Wing Commander put the nose of the Halifax down and pushed on throttle to increase their airspeed. The fuselage rattled alarmingly as eddies of air from the broken turret battered along the flimsy metal shell of the bomber.

He decided to come out of the dive. Slight as it was, there was a risk that the airstream, tearing over their damaged tail, might rip it off. The drag was such he could feel the rear of the Halifax slewing and bucketing. He again altered the trim and eased back on the throttles. He began to wonder why he'd volunteered for a third tour. The first two were bad enough.

He'd just graduated from the R.A.F.'s officer's college at Cranwell when war broke out. He had flown the old Fairey Battle towards the end in France, then gone to Whitleys and Wellingtons. Once before he had nursed a stricken bomber home. The last time was in a Wellington with a badly wounded wireless operator and observer on board. The wireless operator died of his wounds when they were a few miles from base and the observer, with half his left arm blown off, had somehow managed to navigate him to base.

He had got the D.S.O. for that, his observer the D.F.M. With a bit of luck, he corrected his thoughts, with skill and luck, he'd get A-Able back. Another four trips and he'd have a third tour under his belt. There were two other crews with about the same number of 'ops' to go to complete their tours. One was S-Sugar, the other Q-Queenie, but working on present odds he knew that only one of them would finish.

Ahead, and to their starboard, he saw spasmodic bursts of predicted flak. He called up the wireless operator and ordered him to start 'windowing' heavily. He had little faith in the 'windowing' of one aircraft in disrupting the enemy radar but it might help. He warned the navigator he was altering course three degrees to port and would fly it for four minutes. Their present course would track them straight into the flak. As it was the bursts seemed to be creeping nearer. Three shells exploded below and to starboard. Far enough below, Brewis considered, for them to miss the shrapnel they spewed. The flak ceased as suddenly as it erupted. For the next forty-five minutes they flew in silence, Brewis checking now and then on his gunner's condition.

"He's still unconscious. I'll give him the rest of the dope when he comes round," Turner said.

"Okay, Engineer, we should be over base by then," Brewis answered.

A few minutes later Stacey announced that the enemy coast would be coming up in six minutes.

They crossed the coast at fourteen thousand feet and Brewis began to slice off height. The starboard elevator was not responding as it should and he could not be sure what else had been shot through and wouldn't stand the strain.

They droned along the curving radar pulse. Stacey was bringing them home on Gee. Bridlington Bay was ahead with Flamborough Head on their starboard when Hilton said, "Skipper, Williams is coming round."

"You're sure?"

"Yes sir, his eyes are opening and he's groaning."

"Very well, give him the rest."

To the engineer Brewis said, "Change tanks for landing.

I'm calling base."

Warrant Officer Mitchell had just been given clearance to land and had swung S-Sugar on to the approach when he heard the Wing Commander's voice say, "A-Able calling Ponto-emergency. Seriously wounded gunner on board, request immediate landing and ambulance. Repeat, immediate landing."

Control swept into action. Two red Very cartridges burst over the runway and the R.T. set crackled in Mitchell's ears. "Ponto to Sugar. Do not land. Climb to two thousand and circuit."

"Roger – out." Mitchell opened his throttles and began the climb.

"Hear that?" he said to his crew. "The Wingco's gunner's copped it."

Brewis brought his Halifax on to the heading of the main runway when some fifteen miles from the aerodrome. With each mile he shed height. The runway lay ahead, a shaded match-box glimmering on both sides with ice-blue pinpoints of light.

He lowered his undercarriage and sighed with relief when it locked into position. He'd been worried that the hydraulics might have been damaged and that he would have to belly land the bomber. He doubted if his gunner would have survived a crash landing.

A thin smile creased his lips. S-Sugar was circling some 1,800 feet above him. He had flown a straight course for home and yet Mitchell was about to land when he had made his emergency call. S-Sugar was not only cutting corners but shedding height at a drastic speed to have got to base before them.

Other aircraft were now calling Ponto and were being given stepped up heights to circle. One of them, he noted, was Q-Queenie. The flare path was coming up gently towards them.

He lowered the flaps. His approach was good and his

70

rudder, although mushy, was correcting A-Able's slight drift. The blurred outline of the boundary hedge whipped under the Halifax's nose. The lights boxed him in.

"Cut!"

The bomb-aimer closed the throttles and the bomber touched the hard tarmac at just under eighty miles an hour. He tapped on the brakes and the Halifax lumbered to a stop.

He turned the aircraft and taxied it clear of the runway. The ambulance, its bells clanging, was racing towards them. Brewis released his harness, unstrapped his mask and pulled out the intercom plug. Then followed his bomb-aimer into the fuselage. He bent down and tenderly laid a hand on the gunner's brow. He was cold but alive. The fuselage door was thrown open. Gently they moved Williams onto the stretcher. A medical orderly was already undoing the wounded man's flying gear as they lifted him into the ambulance.

Chapter Five

The order to cease firing reached the 10.5cm heavy A.A. Battery Feldwebel Horst Munzberger was with as the last of the R.A.F.'s heavy bombers wheeled from Berlin on course for England. But it was not until 0130 that the battery got the order to stand-down.

Munzberger pulled off his steel helmet and ran a hand through his thinning hair. He was certain the continuous wearing of the heavy helmet had prematurely brought on his baldness. He hadn't smoked for over a week yet desperately craved a cigarette, although he derived some comfort from the knowledge that his meagre tobacco ration was mounting up and would net him a profit on the black market.

He estimated the battery must have sent thousands of shells into the air grid they were assigned to fill when the first of the Pathfinder flares fell. Four minutes before the first of the red sky-markers washed the clouds they had begun filling the air box. By the time the green target illuminators cascaded the empty shell cases were piling up faster than they could be cleared from the gun-pits.

The Feldwebel was sure the guns had taken down at least fifteen of the bombers. His thoughts flashed back to the red-headed girl he had met earlier in the Afton Hotel. When he had told her the guns had brought down fifteen in the raid she had the audacity to correct the figure to ten.

God, she was lovely, while he was lumbered with a fat wife who thought of nothing but her own comfort. He should never have allowed her to go to her sister's in Nuremberg. She was so fat she could never run to an air-raid shelter and with a bit of luck one of the R.A.F. bombs on Berlin would have freed him from her. But she insisted on moving out of the city.

Munzberger considered he got the short end of the stick every time. Nothing was fair in this stinking world. To be posted to the ground defence of Berlin was the last straw. Still, it could have been the Eastern Front.

He was pondering on what the red-head would be like in bed when a young gunner, clearing the empty shell cases, dropped one on his foot. He cursed the gunner, booted the case to one side and strode from the pit. The raid was one of the heaviest yet. They must have sent 800 to 900 bombers over. He looked towards Berlin. The city was burning. The flames from its blasted buildings and streets were reflected dispassionately on the cloud base. Dense black smoke hung heavy and ominously in the cold air over Berlin. The wind had veered and he sensed it through the stink of the cordite in the pits.

He was glad he was on the guns and not in that burning inferno. He thought again of the girl. The preliminary air-raid warning had been sounded in ample time for those in the city to have got to the shelters but bombs had before penetrated steel and concrete.

For that matter bombs jettisoned from a stricken bomber might fall on the battery and then the whole bloody lot of them would be blown sky high. It had happened to other A.A. crews. The thought chilled him more than the night air as he made his way to the canteen.

Ilona Stroheim lowered the volume of the radio in her flat, went over to her suitcase, hesitated and decided she

73

would not unpack. She would read for an hour and then turn in. She pulled out an old pair of slacks from the wardrobe and a thick sweater. She tossed them on the chair beside her bed. If there were a raid they'd be within easy reach.

She had begun to undress when the early warning sirens sounded. She stripped from the clothes she had been wearing and donned the slacks and sweater. Carefully she folded her skirt and blouse and placed them on top of the suitcase. Then she packed her overnight hold-all and lit a cigarette.

She took a couple of pulls, stubbed out the cigarette and switched off the radio. She reached the shelter as the tones of the sirens switched to Air Raid Imminent. She joined an orderly crowd mostly women who were filing down the entrance. Once in her allotted space she spread her blanket and propped a cushion behind her head. She tried to read but could not concentrate. Most of the people around her were middle-aged or elderly. Here and there were women with young children. Perhaps the children were too young to be evacuated on their own or their mothers had good reasons for staying.

There could be many reasons she thought. The faces around her were pale and drawn but they held a calmness from long adaptation to living such a troglodytic life underground.

Deep though they were they could hear the muffled roar of the guns from the city's outer defences and the 'thunk-thunk' from those in the inner defence ring. Someone began to play an accordion and gradually the player's melody was taken up. As the shock waves from the exploding 'block-busters' sent the ground overhead vibrating the tone of the accordion grew louder.

Above them the raid was rapidly reaching its climax. In the streets thousands of fires had taken hold engulfing entire blocks of buildings. The blast from the growing weight of bombs shook the city in violent, terrifying spasms.

Thick clouds of brick-dust floated like confetti above the fire-swept streets. Water mains were breached, power and telephone cables torn and twisted, gas mains ruptured and ablaze. The bombs of the Terrorfliegers fell with detached impartiality on railway stations, goods depots, industrial buildings, office blocks, hospitals, churches, water works, generating stations and abandoned homes.

It was carefully planned saturation to obliterate a city and those inhabitants who were brave enough, or foolish enough, to stay in it. The heavy H.E. 2,000 pounders and the light-case 4,000lb 'cookies' were exploding indiscriminately. Some of the armour-tipped 2,000 pounders penetrated the less deep shelters. Only those in the latest steel and reinforced concrete bunkers were safe from the pulverising bombardment.

As suddenly as it began it was over. The sirens wailed the all clear and those whose shelters had not been blasted, or whose air vents had not been scorched with fire, swarmed like bewildered moles from their holes. And they saw, as they had seen so often, another terse script of human tragedy and dramatic rescue. The heavy rescue squads of specialised troops, supported by gangs of foreign labourers, were already in action. The Civil Defence Corps and the fire-fighting forces had nearly been swamped by the fury and intensity of the raid but they too were now engaged in the mammoth, seemingly hopeless, task of clearing up the man-made mini-earthquake.

Ilona, as she made her way back to her flat wondering if the building was still standing, marvelled at the methodical and calm manner the rescue and demolition teams tackled the immensity of their tasks.

The dead, and most of them were either horribly mutilated or charred beyond recognition, were laid out in four foot high stacks, the wounded and half dead in neat lines to await the ambulances and the 'blood wagons'.

She crossed what was left of the street which led to the

square leading to her apartment block. The fires had their greatest hold on the centre and eastern parts of the city.

The western sections had not been ravaged so much as in earlier raids. As she reached the square near her flat she saw two men from one of the heavy rescue teams manhandling a telescopic ladder towards a man trapped on the fourth storey of a blazing block. He must be a fire watcher, she thought. Her body trembled as she watched the flames illuminate the outline of the figure against a window-less gash in the concrete.

Her eyes focussed on the man gesticulating from the fiery box of light framing the window. Fire was embracing fire in a devilish inferno, as if in a pagan ritual to some crazed god.

One of the rescue squad had almost reached him when part of the building toppled lazily, bringing down the overhead cables. Ladder and rescuer, grasped in its octopus arms, plunged to the street.

She had gone a hundred yards, which seemed like a mile, when she saw a six-strong section of the heavy rescue team clearing with grapples blocks of masonry and rubble from what she recognised as once a workers hostel.

They were using detectors to locate whatever was living under the debris. They had cleared part of the pavement and a row of bodies were laid out, covered by a tarpaulin. The sheeting did not entirely cover the limbs of the corpses. Some she saw had only mauled flesh for legs. Others were footless. The wind, hot from the heat of the fires, flung back part of the rough hempen cloth and two of the bodies, she glimpsed, had stumps where their heads had been.

A grey mongrel dashed from a corner of the wrecked building, almost colliding with her. Horrified she saw it had the severed hand of a child in its jaw. Her stomach turned over and she vomited.

She fumbled in her slacks, wiped her mouth with a handkerchief and found her hands were trembling. Another spasm of nausea swept over her as she stumbled across the square. Part of the street she had earlier left had been torn up by a bomb and although the fire-fighters had sealed off the gas mains, small fires from escaping gas smouldered. The windows of her block had been blown out but the stonework had only been partially damaged.

She groped her way up the stone staircase, pausing at each landing, until she reached her flat on the third floor. The heavy blackout curtains had prevented the broken glass from the windows scattering throughout the room. She picked up as many big pieces as she could find with the light of her torch and put them in a waste bucket beneath her writing table. She collapsed fully clothed on the bed, pulled the bedding over her head and tried to close from her mind the horror she had witnessed.

The starkness of the scenes had the strangeness of the transcendental, as if her eyes had not actually photographed them but merely glimpsed through someone else's mind the pitifulness of it all.

The thoughts quietened in her mind and she fell into an uneasy sleep.

The noise of lorries lumbering in the street, heavily laden with rubble, twisted cables, charred wood and masonry, awoke her. She went to the cooker and tried the switches. The electricity was still off. She went to the bathroom and tried the cold water tap. A trickle of water ran. She put a basin under it and waited patiently for it to fill.

She tried the cooker again. To her surprise the hot-plate began to glow. The pressure was low but at least it would be sufficient to make her a hot drink. The part of the city she was in had been spared the full fury of the saturation raid. It would be sometime, she knew, before heat, water and light would be restored to the areas that had borne the brunt of the attack.

As she waited for the kettle to boil, Ilona washed but decided not to change from her slacks and sweater. The coffee, weak and watery as it was, tasted good. She rum-

77

maged in her handbag and took out the last letter she had had from her father and re-read it:

My Dearest daughter,

As always I was delighted to get your letter and to learn that all is well with you. Thank you for the tobacco.

I am well and fine. On the whole this month has passed fairly peacefully. Now and then we have had air-raid alerts when single reconnaissance aircraft appeared over Nuremberg. But we had full raid warning, when the British dropped bombs on Stuttgart, Weissenburg and Rothenburg. Earlier this month they dropped some bombs on Klingenbruennein.

The people grumble because they are hungry. The old vegetable market is a sad sight. It has been laid down officially that 125 grammes of sweets and 125 grammes of dried vegetables for the children, and a third of a litre of spirits for adults, are now issued as special rations. Also each consumer is to get two eggs for a period yet to be decided. But here is the catch. Always providing, of course, there are enough eggs to meet the ration.

Two eggs . . . That's big news in these troubled times and it's the big talking point.

We have been told not to print anything about the order from the State Department for Iron and Metals which requires that all organ pipes must be dismantled and sent to the armaments industry. The pastors do not like it.

We have had another reduction in the ration of cooking gas, although already we could only prepare hot food once a day. It's good I'm not a big eater.

With the big raids on Berlin it seems that the British plan to reduce a number of our cities to rubble and ashes is in action. I know you are stationed not far from the capital but I hope you don't risk going to your flat. Why don't you give it up and move all your things here? I've got plenty of room. Things seem to be much worse in

Berlin than the authorities let out.

They're brave people the Berliners. They bury their dead, clear up the mess and go on with work as usual. I am afraid it's only to be expected that very soon Nuremberg will also be a target for the Terrorfliegers. Such a tragedy that our beautiful and historic cities are being destroyed – and what can the enemy gain by blowing up a church? Things are not so bad, I'm told in the villages, but then country folk can grow produce and no doubt keep some of it back.

Now and then old friends in Feissendorf send me a small parcel. Arnold still has the inn and is very good with the odd bottle of wine. But he must be nearing the end of his stocks. The times he and I and your old teacher talked and talked over his best bottles. He missed Asaph very much. Poor man he never hurt anyone and you were his favourite. Ah, but those were the happy days. As I grow older and look back I see you still, a little girl with pigtails and scarlet mittens trudging through the snow to the village school. Happiness, Ilona, is too often a fleeting moment, so grasp it while you can. Now, I must close my dear.

God bless you and write soon.

Your loving father.

She folded the letter carefully and placed it in her handbag. Her mind was made up. She would catch the first train tomorrow for Nuremberg.

Werner Franz dropped his two crew men, Petz and Kromer, at the railway station as he'd promised. Petz had looked at him oddly as they took their farewells. Neither of them mentioned the 'lost trace', although they had again congratulated him on his two 'kills'.

He had made the journey to Berlin without much trouble

although for the last few miles he was caught in a long crocodile line of heavy trucks and transport vehicles bringing emergency supplies to the bombed city.

It took him a full two hours to get to Wolfgang's flat in the south-west district, an area that had escaped most of the bombing. He found the two cases Wolfgang prized so much. They were locked and strapped. Fortunately, although heavy, they were not cumbersome and fitted into the boot along with his own case. As demolition gangs were still clearing the streets round the Afton Hotel he parked the car some blocks away and walked. Many of the buildings were smouldering and everywhere thousands of people were crowding the aid centres, many of them evacuated from the worst blitzed areas. All over the city the scene was basically the same.

Water mains in many areas were breached, power and telephone cables torn up, gas mains punctured and debris everywhere. It had been some time since he had been to Berlin and the damage appalled him. Whole blocks were reduced to rubble. Damage was particularly heavy in the industrial Tempelhof district. He remembered hearing it was estimated that thirty per cent of industrial establishments had ceased work as a direct result of the raids and a further ten per cent through lack of manpower and raw materials.

On top of that it was reckoned well over half of the commercial establishments, including retail firms and craftsmen, had been forced to close down. But despite the severity of the raids, industrial production in the city increased through the rationalization and standardization methods brought in by Albert Speer, the Reichminister for armaments and war production.

From what Franz saw he was inclined to agree that although the capital had taken severe punishment the general morale of the Berliners was stiffened rather than weakened. He knew from his own squadron experience the huge losses they were inflicting on Bomber Command. The strain on aircrew, machines and resources must sooner or later cause the British to call off their deep saturation raids.

The Luftwaffe High Command, he knew, did not grossly exaggerate the numbers of bombers brought down. The last figure he had seen put the British losses at over 1000 bombers shot down and nearly 2000 certainly damaged. That represented almost 10,000 R.A.F. aircrew lost since the winter. No airforce could take such losses for long.

It was not a question of boosting the morale of the night-fighters. It was high and would remain so for they were the front line defence against the Terrorfliegers. But looking at the damage everywhere he thought it would be hard to convince a Berliner that they were winning the Battle of Berlin and if they could hold out a bit longer it would be proved to them.

He felt a tinge of shame at losing Petz's trace but reassured himself that his fuel was low and there was nothing to be gained by taking a foolhardy chance and finding afterwards he had not enough fuel to land. What would they have said if he had taken that bomber and then had to order his crew to bale out because he'd not enough petrol to land? What sort of pilot would hazard not only a highly trained crew but a valuable and much needed aircraft?

His reasoning made him feel better, all the more so because he knew it was sound. He glanced at his watch and decided he could not reach Ilona's flat in time without risk of her arriving at the Afton and finding they had missed one another.

He'd be a bit early but it was better to wait for her at the hotel as arranged. If she did not turn up then he would go to the flat and, if it was not standing, would then check with the authorities if she had been one of the victims of the raid. He had been waiting for about half-an-hour and two beers later when he saw her reflection in the wall mirror.

It seemed a hundred thousand years ago if you believed in reincarnation. Perhaps it was a hundred or so. He couldn't say exactly when he first fell in love with her. Pigtails as red as fire, eyes of a melting greenish hue, scarlet mittens in the snow. He froze, as he had never done coming in under a Lancaster or Halifax. All other women, and he'd known a few, were wax figures in a puppet show compared to her. He tried hard to control his feelings and wipe out the memories of frozen lakes, ice-blue waterfalls and snow capped mountain peaks. He fumbled in his tunic, brought out a cigarette from one of the packs he'd won from Kromer.

Pretty little girl in a village school. He'd write a poem about her. He once did and she giggled as she read it. He'd blushed and walked away, ignoring her calls to come back. So very long ago. He'd loved only one girl in that village school — Ilona.

"Will the handsome Oberleutnant buy me a drink?" Her voice smooth as honey, her eyes quizzical and teasing, caused him to swallow hard.

He slid from the stool and took her hands gently in his. "I didn't think I'd ever see you again." She brushed his cheek with her lips, smiled a little wickedly and said, "I knew we would, somewhere, sometime, Liebling."

She took her hands from his and leaned forward and touched his cheek. "Do I get that drink Herr Oberleutnant?"

He beckoned to the barman. She took the cigarette from his fingers and lit it. She blew out the smoke she had not inhaled and placed it between his lips.

"You never used to smoke," he said.

"No and neither did you. But it's said to soothe the nerves."

He took her drink from the barman and handed it to her. "You were here during the raid?"

She nodded and took a sip from her drink. "It was horrible." She slowly put down her glass, lowered her head in her hands and sobs shook her body.

"I was very sick. I saw a . . ." She put her hand against her mouth. He led her to an upholstered bench at the end of the bar. The tears flowed from her eyes.

"Sit down and relax," he said gently. "I'll get you another drink, mein Liebchen." When he came back she was calm again.

"Are you spending your leave here, Werner?"

He shook his head and she said, "You're wise. You need a rest and there'll be no peace here."

"That's why I'm going to Feissendorf. It'll be . . .", he broke off and he saw the startled expression on her face.

"Feissendorf! Seriously?"

"Why so surprised?"

"Because I'm going to Nuremberg to see Papa. I'm being transferred there. There's a train at ten tomorrow."

He brought his hand up in a gay salute. "No, Ilona, you'll come with me. I've got a car and plenty of juice. Besides, it'll be more comfortable than a cold and crowded train. And I'll have you for company. Can I ask for more?"

Her eyes sparkled. "Wonderful, Papa will be delighted to see you. He always liked you." She sighed. "I'd love to see the village again."

"You shall. How long's your leave?"

"Enough, if I'm not recalled – and you?"

"Six," he laughed – "if I'm not recalled."

"When were you planning to leave?"

"Tonight, but I can always go back to Wolfgang's flat and collect you early in the morning."

She leaned over and he felt the warm pressure of her hand on his arm. "Let's go now. I don't want to stay here another night. I've little to pack."

"Splendid. I'll get the car. It's only a couple of blocks away." He downed his drink. "You'd better take a heavy coat and a blanket to wrap round your knees. I've coffee and some rations, so we won't go hungry."

"How far is it by road?"

Werner stroked his chin thoughtfully. "I've never done it by road. I should think about 400 kilometres. We'll be there before dawn, even if the traffic is heavy. We'll by-pass Leipzig, then make for Weissenfels. That's about 50 kilometres sou'west of Leipzig. Then it's straight through to Bayreuth. Another 70 kilometres and we're home."

She finished her drink and rose. "Home," she said, and her words were barely audible.

"Wait here Ilona. I'll get the car."

She smiled. "I'll come with you. You might change your mind and take some other girl."

He shook his head. "There was never really any other but you. Anyway, I don't pick up strange Frauleins."

"Am I not strange after so long?"

He rose, placed his hat at a jaunty angle. "You're my girl in pigtails."

She slipped her arm into his and they both laughed. Two hours later, after they had left the suburbs of the city behind them, he told her that he had come to Berlin to collect two suitcases his brother wanted from his flat and that it was only on the spur of the moment he had decided to go on to Feissendorf.

"I can't explain it Ilona, but I'd a strange compelling urge to go back there. I was all tense and taut. Somehow, the village seemed to hold the answer. Think I'm odd?"

"No, I'd a similar feeling. After the raid I re-read Papa's letter and just as suddenly as you decided to go." They drove in silence for a while and then he said: "I was sorry about Johan. We were very good friends."

"We all were. It was a shock but one I was expecting when I heard he was on the Eastern Front. It was as if . . ." She stopped abruptly and said, "I'd like a cigarette."

He passed her his pack.

He laughed and she thought it was a trifle forced. "Yes, I suppose I'll get it too one of these nights. The odds get narrower with each sortie."

"Does it bother you much?"

He changed down as they approached a steep incline in the road. "It does but there is little I can do about it. I don't take unnecessary risks but sometimes one has to take a calculated one and if one's calculation is wrong . . ." He shrugged his shoulders.

"How many have you brought down?"

"Fifteen, if they confirm the two last night."

"Your mother hated you flying but she would have been proud." She added softly "I too hate you flying, but I'm also proud of you."

"Shame on you to say that and you a 'battle-opera' plotter." He chuckled but there was no mirth in his laughter.

"Two is very good."

"There might have been three but . . ."

"But what?"

"I'd probably enough fuel to take another. I was not prepared to take the risk. I 'chickened'." His tone was low and serious.

He felt the pressure of her hand on his thigh. "No, you were right. You're not the man to 'chicken'."

"Uh, uh-I wish I was so sure. It's been bothering me. You, and all those people under their bombs and all I think of is whether I've enough fuel to take on a third. Hardly the image of a Luftwaffe ace." There was a long silence. "My radar operator was not impressed."

"Then he's a stupid man."

"No, he's a good and experienced operator." He handed her the pack of cigarettes and said, "Light one for me, please."

He took a thoughtful drag on it, saw the road ahead was clear and changed gear.

"Do you like night-flying? It's so dangerous."

When he answered his voice was far away. "It's a bitter experience and it's broken many nerves. There's always the tension and anxiety. Not so much in the actual combats, where we've a much better chance than the bombers. It's in having to fly in atrocious weather conditions. No man in his sane senses would set foot in an aircraft in such conditions."

"Do you hate them?"

"It's war." He glanced at her, "Do you?"

"Yes, after last night . . . I hate them." He was surprised at the venom in her voice.

"Night-fighting in anger, inspired by hate or because a comrade has been killed or someone close to you in a bombing raid, is not possible. To do your job and stay alive it's essential that experience and concentration should be uppermost in your mind." He paused and added, "It should be clinical."

"You sound like an instructor."

"You raised it. I'm sorry. I've been boring you." He pushed his foot down hard on the accelerator. The Mercedes leapt like a hound from a taut leash.

Her hand stretched out and he felt the light pressure again on his thigh. "I'm sorry. I shouldn't have said that I'm all mixed up. I wish I were dead."

"We all feel like that sometimes. Try and sleep, leibling." His voice was low and gentle.

"I want to talk."

" 'bout what?"

"You're angry with me."

"Shut up or I'll pull your pigtails."

She laughed and the irritableness fell from him and he found himself laughing with her.

"Remember how we fought?"

"I slapped you when you pulled them."

"I rubbed your face in the snow when you did," he said

86

"Ah, they were happy days. Why can't they always be like that?"

"Like the pigtails you once had, they are a thing of the past. Now go to sleep. There is still a long way to go."

"I want to talk."

"Light me a cigarette, please."

"You're smoking too heavily."

"I got a hundred in a present last night."

"From whom?"

"Marshall Goring."

"Seriously?"

"Look at the monogram on them."

She struck a match and in the driving mirror he could see her examining the tip. "Liar."

"Any more of that and you'll get out and walk."

"Achtung . . . Achtung . . . Lancaster . . . 200 metres . . . steer 085 . . . Call sign . . . Bitch."

She laughed and looked at him quizzically.

"I've heard worse over my ear-phones. Perhaps one night I'll be helping to vector you on to a Tommis . . . and I'd hate it. Sometimes it's the night-fighter that goes down," she said and there was deep apprehension in her voice. "I've heard some go down."

"Try to sleep, liebling." He reached with his arm and pulled a thick driving rug from the back-seat. He draped it over her shoulders. "Tuck this around you."

"Um, um, that's cosy but I still want to talk."

"Well, go on then."

There was a long pause and her voice which was light and happy became grave: "Why do they always get through?" Before he could answer she said, "An old greybeard of a Merchant Navy Captain I work with told me he admires the excellence of the Terrorfliegers navigation. He said it was something to do with the seamanship of the British, a question of getting accurate fixes and expert dead-reckoning."

"They're good, that's true. What else did he say?"

She had sunk deeper into her seat and from the depths of the thick rug her voice was drowsy. "That their radar aids are better than ours and can jam every electronic device we use to counter-act them."

"That's because their reconnaisance aircraft monitor our wave lengths. Our Air Staff, for some inexplicable reason, refuse to assign aircraft to do the same over England. They also . . ."

Glancing in the driving mirror he saw that her head had slumped against the back of the seat rest. She was fast asleep.

His partially blacked out headlights flashed as they bounced off bumps in the road. He slowed down. It began to snow, gently at first, then fell in thick flakes over his windscreen. He flicked the wipers and hoped that they would not freeze as the snowflakes built up into hard wedges of ice. Outside the whole world was white but here and there he could make out a faint pencil line where the trees marked the edges of the highway.

Chapter Six

Bomber Commander Headquarters were housed in an old country mansion, screened by dense wood, on the outskirts of High Wycombe in Buckinghamshire. Only those with the special but little known buff coloured passes were allowed on its precincts and then they were thoroughly checked before being escorted down a long dimly-lit passage, down dark stone steps, which led deeper and deeper into the earth.

A massive steel door blocked the entrance to the Command's Operations and Planning room. Shortly before noon on the day following the night attack on Berlin the steel doors swung open and the two tough-looking armed sentries of the R.A.F.'s Special Police snapped rigidly to attention, their steel heeled boots ringing on the cold stone.

The bulky figure of a stern faced man in the uniform of an Air Chief Marshal strode briskly from the Operations room. His grey eyes stared coldly ahead. The Air Marshal at his side said something and got an expressive grunt in answer. There was a metallic crash as the great doors slammed closed. Even if the two sentries had dared to risk a glance at the forceful figure that had passed them, they would have gleaned no inkling whatsoever from his poker face of what was going through his mind.

Tension in the great room eased as the doors opened and then closed. A buzz of conversation followed as senior officers, from the nagivation leader at Group to the flak and intelligence experts, discussed what their chief had said.

Their tones were grave and there was no lightness in them. There was little to be elated over. Forty bombers had been lost in the raid while four more severely damaged aircraft had crashed while attempting to land in England with the loss of their crews. Two more were known to have 'ditched' in the sea and little hope was held out that the Air Sea Rescue would come back with any survivors.

Many in that room were convinced that the Command's assault on Berlin would have to be called off and the bombers switched to other targets not so costly in men and machines. For the past months tens of thousands of tons of high explosives and incendiaries had been dropped on the German capital every week. In their wake they spread rumours, fear and despondency throughout the Third Reich but there was no evidence that the morale of the Berliners had been broken.

These experts recalled that in the four major attacks on the city carried out in November 1943, when the assault on Berlin began in earnest, the 'missing' rate for the bombers reached the surprisingly low proportion of four per cent; and in all of the major attacks on German targets, including the capital, it was no more than 3.6 per cent. But they were chilled by the knowledge that by the following month, despite the bad weather, the German night-fighter force had dramatically increased its efficiency.

In most of the big raids, which included four more on Berlin, it succeeded in intercepting the bomber force while it was still on its way. As a consequence, bomber losses were appreciably higher and the loss rate in the Berlin operations rose sharply to over 7 per cent. The scales, they knew, had tipped decisively in favour of the night-fighters, supported by A.A. fire which was becoming more and more effective.

The men at High Wycombe had gone carefully and

meticulously into the causes and there was little doubt in their minds that the night-fighters were the main cause of the losses. The Northern route the bombers were taking to Berlin was fast becoming a vast graveyard for Harris's heavies. But Berlin too had suffered — one-and-a-half-million Berliners were homeless through the raids. The Command had shrugged off the appalling and crippling losses inflicted on them by the night-fighters as of almost no consequence but those who assessed the results of the bombing were faced with the cold and uncomfortable fact that the German air industry was still producing.

The steel doors swung open and the plotters, planners, specialists and experts filed in little groups from the underground block house, knowing there would be no operations that night and none probably for a few nights. The stand-down to the Groups was on the teleprinters within the hour.

It reached 187 Squadron shortly after lunch, when the bars in the Officers' and Sergeants' Messes were still open.

Group Captain Havilland, anxious faced and solemn eyed, stroked his narrow face with his index finger and said in an empty voice to his Wing Commander, "Four last night and you could've been the fifth, John."

Brewis sippped his gin and vermouth. "A half second or so and that shell would've been well behind us. As it was we got the shrapnel from it."

The Group Captain frowned. "A half second or so earlier and it would've blown off the nose and you with it." He paused and added, "The Senior Medical Officer tells me they've amputated your gunner's leg. It was done in the local hospital. Seems they got him in time. What's his name, again?"

"Williams."

"Married?"

"Don't think so. He'd more sense that I had."

"That was no reason why you should've gone back on operations." The Group Captain savoured his drink. "The days when men joined the Foreign Legion because a marriage or a romance had broken up are long since gone. You shouldn't have taken it so seriously John. There are others."

Brewis shook his head. "I've no death wish, if that's what you're thinking. It was just one that didn't work out." He knocked back his drink, glanced at his watch and said, "I've some paper work to do. You'll excuse me?"

The Group Captain nodded and watched detachedly as his Wing Commander walked from the mess. He idly scanned the big room and saw Flying Officer Cotton come in with his navigator. He beckoned them over. He had briefly chatted with them when they had landed but an informal chat in the mess, he considered, helped morale. Cotton was an American he recalled, and his navigator he thought was an Aussie, or was he a New Zealander? Such places had different outlooks on formalities.

"What are you drinking, gentlemen?" It was more an order than a question.

"A half pint." The voice was unmistakably New Zealand. "And you Cotton?"

"I'll have the same, Sir."

He waited until their drinks were poured and said, "It was bad last night."

"There've been worse ones," Cotton drawled.

The Group Captain had asked the same question many times before and invariably got the same answer. He considered he would've been surprised if he'd got any other. He had to admire them. They always erred on the side of under-estimation. "Not that bad." It was bloody hell, they knew it and he knew it. It was pointless asking such questions, but if he didn't they might think him callous and indifferent.

He was as glad as them of the stand-down. There would be none of the torture of waiting in the crew rooms before the wagons took them out to the aircraft, none of the tension waiting for the Aldis lamps to flicker, sending them on their way. Once they were airborne it was not so bad. Too many things to do, hosts of dials and switches to watch. And they had the fighting man's illusion of invulnerability. It was always the other who 'bought' it – never themselves . . . to be precise never yourself. The Group Captain knew that the more this happened – even though it was to their closest comrades – the stronger the illusion grew. If they didn't have this they could never go out night after night.

Murderers, villains and terror-flyers, killers of women and babies, according to the Germans. It all depended which end you were on. Rotterdam, Coventry, London, Glasgow, Manchester and other bomb-scarred cities had been on the receiving end of the German bombers. Now the boot was at the other head.

The two men before him, like the countless others who had gone before them, epitomised to his mind Britain's only effective way of bringing the war home to Germany until the second front could be launched. And for long years they had borne the brunt of the war. Churchill, he recalled, had said in 1940 that the Navy could lose the war but only the Air Force could win it.

"Tell you one thing though. I'm bloody glad we're not on tonight." The nasal twang of the New Zealander's voice jolted him from his thoughts.

He smiled and said, "Don't go too wild in town tonight. They look on you as their own personal brood and we don't want to spoil that, do we now?"

"There's never been any real trouble," Cotton replied.

"There was when Mackay and his friends smashed up the Red Lion," the Group Captain said tersely.

Cotton smiled. "They were goaded by some Yank interlopers."

The Group Captain stuttered awkwardly. "But you're a . . . an American?"

"I'm a Southerner but those guys were still wet behind the ears. I know so. I had to bounce one myself."

The Group Captain studied Cotton with unblinking eyes. "You've almost finished your tour, if I recall correctly. Do you intend to transfer then? You'd automatically get a higher rank in the U.S.A.A.F. Certainly more pay."

Cotton took a swig of his beer. "Reckon I'll decide that one when we finish."

"We'll finish alright, Reg," Tresland said. He fingered the green Maori charm attached to the whistle on his battledress collar and added: " 'Tiki' here will see to it."

The Group Captain nodded. "I'm sure you will. Now excuse me, I've to get back to my desk."

When he had gone Tresland said, "Not a bad bloke for a limey station-master. Toffee nosed but not a bad cobber."

"Yep, he's okay," Cotton said.

"Well, are we going to make Mitchell's birthday party?"

"Hell, I nearly forgot about it."

"Then let's get out of these togs," Tresland said.

In the back-room of the Swan, Mackay and Mitchell were manhandling a long table against one of the walls when Mitchell said, "You know Mac, I'd forgotten about this being my birthday until you mentioned you'd fixed up a party and May was looking after the food side." He paused and added: "May's a sweetie. She's plainly gone for you." He looked thoughtful. "What's going to happen when her husband comes back? He's in Burma isn't he?"

Mackay nodded and Mitchell said, "When he gets back he's going to be looking for you with a specially sharpened kukri."

Mackay arched an eyebrow. "You assume we'll both be around by then?"

94

When Mitchell didn't answer Mackay said, "This is going to be a long war and he could cop it in Burma as easily as we might." He reflected for a moment. "I know a few think I'm laying her."

Mitchel snorted. "There's a lot more who know. Why, we seldom see you nights we aren't operating."

"Maybe so and maybe no, but you're the only one who knows for sure."

"Like hell," Mitchell said. "What about Fulton, the village bobby? He looks at times as if he'd like to strangle you. Why?"

Mackay pushed the table hard against the wall. "Fulton tries anything with me and he'll wake up in his own cell with the key thrown away." He lit a cigarette and inhaled deeply. "This is a small village. May's mother held the licence for this pub, like her grandmother before her. Her old man died when she was a baby. There wasn't much man choice in a place like this before the war. May married the local mechanic. She went to school with him. Along comes the war and he joined the county regiment. They got married on his embarkation leave like a lot of other idiots."

"That was before we got here," Mitchell interrupted, "and from what I gather she was faithful until you appeared on the scene."

Mackay shrugged. "So she's told me and oddly enough I believe her. She's not a lying cow like Maggie."

Mackay cast a critical eye over the room. "Guess that's it. Maybe we'll need a couple more chairs over there. Otherwise everything's drink-shape. It'll be a good party, Bill."

Mitchell smiled a trifle uneasy and Mackay said, "What's up?"

"Just thinkin' ".

" 'Bout what?"

"That I wish to hell you'd never introduced me to Maggie's sister."

"Christ! Haven't we gone through all that before? And haven't I told you time and again I regret it. But how in hell could I've known then that Julie was a bag like Maggie?"

Mitchell brought out his cigarettes, lit two and handed one to his bomb-aimer. "But you knew Maggie before. You fixed her up with a room when we were at the Conversion Unit and then with a place when we moved here."

Mackay looked intently at his pilot. "Look Bill, I've told you most of it so you might as well know the lot. She was on the game when I met her during a leave in London. She'd been in the nick too for dipping into the wallets of those she picked up. The only good thing you could say about Maggie was that she wasn't too bad a screw. Not great, but not bad."

Mitchell looked long and hard at the Scot. "You are not making this up, Mac? She doesn't talk like one."

Mackay grunted. "You don't have to speak with a rough accent to be a whore. All I've told you is true. She told me all about herself. She got some kind of kick from telling me about her past when we were in bed. Her folks were decent enough but she broke their hearts. They separated and neither Maggie nor sister Julie knows where they are."

Mackay fingered his chin. "It was her idea to follow me here. Any affection I had for her has long since gone. She was just a plaything for bed. She'd some crazy idea I might marry her." Mackay grinned. "She used to spend hours writing poems. God! but they were awful. Utter rot."

He drew heavily on his cigarette and his voice softened. "She's a schizophrenic. Was in a 'funny-farm' once and will probably end her days in one. A normal healthy mind can cope with the great mass of impressions that come to us all the time and make sense out of them. She's so mixed up that it's impossible for her to hold down any relationships or jobs.

"As I said, once in a moment of drunken madness I thought of marrying her. When I sobered up I decided nothing could be worse. She became hysterical when I told her it wasn't on and tried to slash her wrists."

Mackay shook his head slowly like a confessional priest disdainful of what he was hearing. "Maggie's not only the most selfish piece I've ever come across but a self-confessed nympho. She'll jump into bed with almost anyone. That's why I ended it, made it clear that I could never contemplate marrying her. The crunch came when I found she was sleeping around when I was operating. The last time was with a coloured Yank. Then she began to get hooked on 'spades'."

The Scot broke off and laid a hand heavily on his pilot's shoulder. "I've told you all this so it might give you a different outlook towards Julie. There's little, if any, difference between them so don't take it to heart anymore, now that she's skipped with your kid. They are both rubbish." He paused. "Holton doesn't understand but Maggie's whoring around so much she's bound to pick up a packet, if she hasn't already. I don't want her passing it to Jack."

There was a long silence. Mitchell stroked the lobe of his left ear and then rubbed his chin.

"I'm sorry Mac, I just didn't know. But I'm glad you've got tied up with May. She's a decent sort. Pity she's married."

"Forget it Bill. Things will sort themselves out. Anyway, what's a ring between friends? Now, let's get a 'booster' before the party starts." Mackay stubbed out the butt of his cigarette and added, "Now you know why I despise the cow."

Mitchell noted there was no venom in his bomb-aimer's voice. It was as if a judge was clinically announcing his verdict after studied consideration of all the evidence. He knew there was no bitterness now, just contempt. Mac, he reflected, had hidden resources of recovery.

"Let's get a drink. Two pints and two whiskies, right?"

As Mitchell made a move into the other bar the Scot looked at his brown, almost blond hair, his open face and gentle blue eyes. He again cursed the day he introduced him to Julie Gregor. It all flooded back to him in fast flashes. Julie had come to stay with her sister for a weekend which turned into a six weeks stay. Both had managed to avoid the women's services by getting themselves classed as factory workers. They'd done about three weeks in a factory making sparking plugs for trainer aircraft. Mackay shuddered at the thought of some poor bastard, somewhere, flying on an engine that might have been fitted with their plugs. He was comforted by the knowledge they had once told him that their work was always checked and most of their plugs rejected. They had thought it a huge joke. Within ten days of meeting Julie, Mitchell had married her. The irony of it was he was the best man and Maggie the bridesmaid. He even remembered the wedding lunch – curry and rice. Mitchell and himself had hated the stuff but Maggie had a passion for curry. Looking back he now wondered if the child was Mitchell's. He had a feeling at the time that she was about six weeks gone. Just a hunch, nothing more, born perhaps of her eagerness to marry Mitchell. He'd never mentioned it to his pilot and there was no point now, although it still niggled in his mind.

Mitchell came back with the drinks. "The Scotch is on May. She's fixing the food and will be through shortly," he said.

They knocked back the Scotch and Mitchell said, "There's something I want to tell you about Julie and the kid. I meant to tell you before but somehow couldn't get round to it. Now, after our talk I find it easier . . ." Before he could finish the taproom door opened and in came the rest of their crew.

"Looks like the party's started," Parke said, eyeing the pints in Mitchell and Mackay's hands.

Mackay held up his free hand. "Hear this . . . hear this!

It's Bill's birthday. He's a bloody good bloke as well as a damned fine pilot, so we're gonna give him a party."

There was a loud cheer and Parke shouted: "We've heard Mac, so quit the yap and let's get down to the booze."

"Okay," the Scot said, "just one thing more. I've reserved this back-room for our exclusive use and . . . ." He broke off as a tall, slim girl, with warm brown silky hair over her shoulders and a smiling sensual mouth, swept into the room with a huge tray of sandwiches.

There were shouts , "Hi-ya May," as she laid the tray on the table beside Mackay. He leaned over and grasped her waist. She kissed him swiftly on the mouth amid a roar of laughter from the crew of S-Sugar.

She waved to them to be quiet and said, "There's more on the way." Again Mackay held up his hand. "She's the best inn-keeper in Bomber Command."

"Why limit it?" Mitchell said.

"For Chri'-sake can we get some bloody drink?" Parke said wearily.

"Right!" Mackay said. "It's a quid for the room and the grub. And I want a quid from each of you for the booze . . . so start coughing up. One thing more, Q-Queenie and A-Able will be coming along . . . not for free, though."

"What about gate-crashers?" Smythe, their engineer shouted.

Mackay looked at him as an exasperated father eyes a backward child. "We throw them out laddie, as we did in the Red Lion." He turned and patted May on the bottom. "Okay, get your peasants weaving."

A buxom, fresh faced girl, with bright yellow hair, slid a tray of pints through the hatch and placed two bottles of Scotch beside it, along with a big pitcher of water.

"The Scotch is part gift from the Mess so they'll have to be a small cover charge for it," Mackay shouted.

"You fuckin' well fiddled it, Mac," Burrowes, the

rear-gunner bawled.

Mackay poured three fingers of the whisky into a glass, did the same with another, and handed one to Mitchell.

"Is this a private session or can anyone join in?"

Mitchell stretched an arm affectionately round his mid-upper gunner's shoulder. "Have a Scotch, Taffy. I know you only drink beer but it's my birthday."

"Well, just a small one."

Mackay moved to the fire-place and slung a couple of logs onto the fire from the tub beside the grate. Smythe sat down at the cigarette-scarred piano with its yellow keys, and thumbed out the opening bars of Lili Marlene.

Mackay felt the pressure of soft fingers on the nape of his neck. He turned and looked into the warm grey eyes of May. She was wearing that suggestion of a smile which made the regulars of the Swan think it was reserved solely for the man she was serving. She looked, Mackay thought, as if she had dark secrets to share with someone she really loved. He scanned her trim figure with fast, searching glances, as a navigator fixes the stars. It was untrammelled by constricting underwear. She was twenty-five, he knew, a year older than himself, but many of the women he'd known, and there'd been many, had taken him for twenty-eight. Flying, with its perpetual promise of death, had added the years.

He thought there was about a hair's breadth between the two. Ruth, in Florida, whom he'd been court-martialled over, with the subsequent loss of his pilot's wings; Shirley, in Detroit, who'd cost him his Flight Sergeant's crown, through a long over stayed furlough; Monica in Toronto . . . he slammed a shutter on the memories. It was March 1944 and he was in Yorkshire with a Halifax squadron and the bomber war was at its height. And like the rest of the crews the odds were high that he'd be on the way to cremation before the week was out.

His eyes swept back to May. Her figure was as firm as a

nineteen-year-old and that was not so long ago, he reflected. He thought she looked beautiful with her hair lying carelessly over her shoulders. He noted, almost with detachment, the taut breasts that seemed to start their firm swell almost from her collarbone. It was though he had never seen her in all her loveliness. He hadn't had her for over a week and he wanted her now. As if reading his thoughts, she whispered: "Darling, you'll be staying tonight?"

"Try and throw me out."

She ruffled his hair and said, "I must go. I've the main bar to look after and with the stand-down we'll be busy." He watched with approval the sway of her buttocks as she moved towards the main bar.

Mitchell, who had been munching a sandwich, moved over. "I envy you, Mac." Mackay was about to answer when there was a loud hammering on the back-door. Holton, a few feet from them, put down his glass. He strode briskly to the door and pulled back the bolt. Mackay thought he seemed disappointed when Cotton and the crew of Q-Queenie came in. With them were Stacey, the navigator of A-Able, Green the bomb-aimer, and Sykes their wireless operator. Cotton had his arm round a strikingly attractive WAAF Corporal, with neat blonde hair carefully pinned, in regulation fashion, under her service hat.

Cotton affectionately pressed the WAAF's shoulder as they approached Mackay and Mitchell. "Let me introduce you to Sue – Corporal Sue Hart. She was posted here three days ago."

The Scot looked over the girl with appraising eyes. "We could do with a few more postings like you," he said. She smiled and he saw her eyes were a deep blue and her teeth perfectly shaped. Sue, he decided, had a beautifully sculptured face and lips that teased.

"What department?" Mitchell asked.

"Parachute packing." Her voice was low, serious and almost musical.

"Christ!" Mackay said, "we'd better not muck around with you. You could take a terrible vengeance."

Cotton squeezed the WAAF's shoulder. "We're going to get engaged." He bent down and brushed his lips on her cheek. "She hit me between the eyes when I walked into the para shed." Seeing the enquiring look in Mitchell's eyes he added: "She was playing with a ping-pong ball, took a swipe and it hit me there . . ." He tapped the centre of his forehead with his fingers.

"Hell, I thought you people were there to pack 'chutes," Mackay said with a trace of irony.

The Waaf flushed. "We weren't actually playing. Just trying to get a dent out of the celluloid."

"I'm greatly relieved," Mackay said.

She flushed and Mitchell said, "What would you like to drink?"

Mackay coughed. "Pardon the crudeness. But the cover fee's a quid a head. I hate to mention it but I'm the treasurer." The newcomers chipped in and Mackay added, "Thanks. The club's now closed. We want elbow room."

There was a loud thump on the door. Mackay frowned and moved aggressively towards it. He pulled back the bolt and they heard him say, "Screw off – this is a private party."

"Who was that?" Holton asked anxiously.

"Some creeps from K-King," Mackay said.

"They are no trouble," Holton said.

"No, but we're overcrowded," Mackay told him. There was another knock on the door; almost a gentle tap.

"For Chri'sake this is getting like Paddington Station. See who it is Nobby – and tell them to fuck off," Mackay said. As Smythe put down his glass Holton moved hurriedly to the door and opened it. A girl with dyed yellow hair, bobbed close to her head came in. She had a plumpish

102

figure but fairly attractive legs. Her eyes were a watery blue. They had a wide, near frightened look in them as if she'd been on drugs.

Holton waved an arm airly round the room. "I think you've met most of them at the last Mess party. But first, what d'you want to drink?"

She asked for a gin and Mackay said brusquely: "We've no gin Maggie. If I recall aright anything does equally as well with you." Her eyes mocked him as she squeezed Holton's arm. She drew her lips back in a slow tight smile to reveal nicotine stained teeth. Vicious little teeth they could be, he recalled.

"I didn't know it was a stag party so I'll . . ."

"It's not," Holton interrupted angrily. "Ted and Sid's girls are coming along with a few more. The kitty's big enough to stand gin or anything else you want, Maggie."

He moved over to the hatch and they heard him call for a bottle of gin. He'd hardly begun pouring from the bottle when there was another rap on the door. Two brunettes and a red-head came in. Fifteen minutes later four more girls arrived.

Mackay nudged Mitchell. "Same again?"

Mitchell nodded and watched his bomb-aimer push his way to a table laden with bottles. He considered he was lucky having Mackay in his crew. He was not only a competent second pilot, but like most bomb-aimers had been trained to take over from any crewman in an emergency. And the gunners admitted that in simulated turret training he out-classed them. He himself had been surprised at Mackay's accuracy.

Cotton came over with his arm round Sue. "Helluva good party, Bill. But where's your drink?" Mitchell nodded towards Mackay who was coming back with two tumblers.

"I think I'll get smashed," Mitchell said as Mackay handed him one of the glasses. He surveyed the room. Some were dancing, others were draped round the piano singing lustily, while a few couples were in tight clinches on the big, old fashioned settee along one wall. Smythe was still thumping it out on the piano, a cigarette dangling from his lips like some Western 'one-eyed' jack.

Mackay splashed some water in Mitchell's Scotch. Nodding towards the girls he said, "Why don't you pull one of 'em, Bill?"

"I've just said to Reg here, and the lovely Sue, that I'm going to get smashed."

"Why not? It's your birthday," Mackay said, wincing visibly as he saw Holton moving towards them with his arm round Maggie.

Mitchell also noticed them and turning to his bombaimer asked mischieviously, "Who was it that wrote a verse about a whore? I think it came from Omar Khayyam . . . it went something like this, 'She's not a whore, she who lies abed making love with him and them and thee and me . . .' "

Mackay looked at him sharply and a smile creased his lips. "You're pissed Bill. That didn't come from Khayyam, you ignorant bastard. He wrote about getting drunk under a tree."

Cotton laughed and kissed Sue lightly on the lips. "Let's dance, honey. We're in bad company."

Holton, his arm tight round Maggie came up. "She wants to wish you a Happy Birthday, Bill." Maggie eased herself from Holton's arm and handed him her glass. "Be a darling, and get me another drink. I don't think there's any more tonic left. Try the main bar, luv." As Holton dutifully elbowed his way towards the other room she looked directly at Mitchell and her voice was strangely soft.

"I wondered if you'd heard from Julie? The last letter I got from her was about six weeks ago. There was no address on it. I'm a bit worried."

Mackay thought he detected more than a tremor in Mitchell's hand as he took a long sip from his glass.

"Why? What's so different about that?"

"It was postmarked Southampton . . . it was bombed shortly after I received it."

"Did she say if the baby was with her?" Mackay asked.

"She didn't mention it."

Mackay grunted. "The bitch probably dumped it in some home."

Mitchell was about to speak when Maggie swiftly reached out and took his whisky from his hand. Whirling round she shot it into Mackay's face. The Scot's hand came up snake-fast, stopped abruptly and dropped to wipe the drink from his tunic.

Turning to Mitchell, he said icily. "There was water in it so it won't stain."

Then he swung round to Maggie. "Now piss off W-H-O-R-E." His words were cold and emphatic.

Mitchell thought he saw tears in her eyes as she pushed through the crowded bar.

A little later Holton came back with a gin and tonic.

"Where's Maggie?"

"She's pissed off, and if I know her she's heading for the Yank base at Saston. She's an eye for colour. She thought it dull here," Mackay said.

Holton put down the drink and rushed to the door. A little later he came back.

"There's no sign of her at the bus stop." Then glancing at Mackay, he said accusingly, "You bloody well upset her, didn't you?"

"Ask her when you see here," Mackay said curtly.

He turned from Holton and said to Mitchell: "It'll be closing time shortly. May will fix you up in the spare room if you like."

"I'd like that Mac. I don't feel like going back to the base."

Then turning to his navigator Mitchell said gently, "She upset herself, Jack. Looked like she was half cut before she came in. We'll tell you about it sometime. Meanwhile Mac and I are staying here the night. See yuh."

It took them a good half hour, after closing time, before they cleared the aircrews from the back-room and another full hour helping May to clear up the mess, wash the glasses and sweep up the broken glass.

They followed May into the little lounge, off the main bar, where she fed logs to the dying embers of the fire.

"There's still thirty-bob of the kitty left," she said."

"I'll get us another bottle," Mitchell said.

She shook her head. "I can't. My quotas nearly finished and there's one or two regulars who like a drop of Scotch now and then, you know."

"Bring it out, I'll take another from the Mess," Mackay said.

She looked at him and there was warmth in her eyes. 'They're going to catch you out on that fiddle, one of these days, Mac."

Mackay smiled. "They won't. The S.W.O.'s up to his neck in it as well."

Her eyes mocked them. "Oh well! Now sit down both of you," she ordered. "No more drink until you eat something. I've plenty of eggs and bacon. One of the advantages of living in the country." She laughed and went into the kitchen.

A little later she came back with a platter of eggs and bacon, plates, knives and forks and laid them on the coffee table.

"I dunno about you two but I'm damned hungry," she said.

"You're a great girl and a great cook," Mackay said as he finished his meal.

"She sure is," said Mitchell.

"That's why I love her so much," Mackay said.

"Someday I'll get you to put that in writing," May said.

"Evidence for the divorce court?" Mitchell said.

She flushed, collected the plates, and went into the kitchen. She came back with a bottle of Scotch and a jug of water.

Outside the wind blew steadily out of the nor'-nor'-east. A strong bitter wind, it howled through the cobbled village street, furiously rattling the drain-pipes and sending loose shutters clanging. A wind full of jagged knives, it carried with it a lashing, icy sleet which battered at the blacked out leaded windows of the inn.

May lifted an interrogatory eyebrow at Mitchell and Mackay. "Better take it easy on the Scotch. You don't want hang-overs tomorrow." Her tone was motherly, tinged with anxiousness.

Mackay seemed genuinely amused. "Not to worry darling, there'll be no 'ops' tomorrow if this keeps up and from what Met reckoned before we left, this front will be with us for a couple of days."

Mitchell guffawed. "Tha's waas thay tol' yuh but tha's bastards are more often wrong than right," there was a distinct slur in his voice.

Mackay nodded solemnly. "Agreed, oh fearless aviator! But if anyone goes out in this shit it will be the Mossie boys. 'Butch' will want to stoke the fires we started."

"You wanna put a quid on that?"

"You're on," Mackay said. May moved towards him, slipped on to his lap and began to stroke his hair. She glanced towards Mitchell and said, "No hurry Bill, but I've made a bed for you in the spare room."

Mitchell didn't answer and they saw that his eyes were closed.

"You flaked out, Bill?" Mackay shouted.

He opened his eyes. "Jus' thinkin', jus' thinkin'."

"Bout that quid you're going to lose," Mackay said.

When Mitchell answered there was a strange soberness in his voice. "No, just about the incident in the pub with Maggie." The slur was going from his voice.

The Scot's lips tightened. "For Chri'sake ignore that bitch. She's a bloody trouble maker, always was and always will be."

Mitchell looked past him, silent and expressionless. His face was set, stonily impassive, the face of a man with a deep sorrow.

"They're both dead." His voice was toneless.

Mackay said quietly. "You're pissed Bill. Bloody well pissed."

Mitchell leaned forward in his chair. "They were both killed in the raid. I got the telegram about a week ago. They had to be identified and it took some·time. Eventually they found some old letters from me and the kid's birth certificate. There was also a letter she'd written to me sometime ago but never posted. That's what I was going to tell you before the crew came in."

Mitchell poured himself some more Scotch. "I suppose I should've told Maggie. I was going to tell her when she flung the drink at you. Somehow it seemed hardly the time."

May slipped from Mackay's lap and poured some water into Mitchell's whisky. She knew both of them well enough not to interrupt. She'd get the whole story from their exchanges.

But she decided to ask one question. "Do her parents know?"

Mitchell shook his head. "I don't think so May. They broke up some years ago. Neither Julie nor Maggie knew where they're living. They couldn't have cared, anyway."

"I didn't know you were married, Bill."

Mackay reached out and pulled May back on his lap. "There was no reason for him to tell you May." He studied Mitchell for a moment and said. "I'm sorry about the kid. But she was no good. Rotten like her sister. It's probably better this way, as I told you earlier."

May jerked forward in Mackay's lap. "Good God!" she

ejaculated. "How can you say such a thing."

Mitchell's shoulders sagged but his words were becoming less and less slurred. "He's right, May. She was a tramp. Mac knows the whole story. He started the first chapter."

He downed the remnants of his Scotch and rose wearily from his chair. It was as if a hundred years had passed since he'd met Julie.

"Room's through the kitchen, right?"

"Door on the left. Have a good sleep, Bill," May said.

"Go'night, Mac."

"Goodnight, Bill."

When he'd gone, May looked quizzically at Mackay. "What did he mean when he said you'd started the first chapter?"

He slipped his arm round her and gently propelled her towards the stairs and the bedroom he knew so well. "I'll tell you in bed."

Chapter Seven

The village of Feissendorf lay heart shaped on the west
bank of a broad, shallow stream that crept indolently, like a
snake, in the watery winter sunshine. Its thatched barns
and sturdy wooden houses, with their sloping chalet roofs,
formed an illuminated picture against the snow capped
mountains and deep, dark forests.

Some of the houses had yellow and blue painted window
frames. A few had little porches with rough hewn seats. A
windmill stood where the stream curved in a gentle bend,
its great arms spinning furiously in the rising wind. A white
painted stone church with a slatted belfry rested on the
hillock overlooking the village's main street.

A little to the west of the church was the village school
half hidden by birch trees. In front of the school was a stone
playground with two sets of swings and a large wooden
see-saw. At the rear the grass playground had been ploughed in long furrows to grow potatoes and other vegetables.
East of the valley, which housed the village, the mountains
stretched as far as the eye could see.

Dusk had fallen when Werner and Ilona drove up to
Arnold Raufft's inn. Stringy stalks of goose-foot, willow
herb and thistle tipped with dead tufts, sprouted alongside
the timbered walls. Lit from ground level by the setting sun,
they rose in ghostly shapes, like mute sentinels keeping
motionless watch on the inn. Werner parked the car at the

rear of the inn. Taking Ilona's hand he went round to the front, climbed the wooden steps and thumped on the cast-iron knocker.

There was a shuffling of feet and the sound of a heavy bolt being drawn back and they looked into the startled face of Raufft. His usual ruddy face had a sallow unhealthy look about it. His grey close-cropped hair was thinning to baldness at the crown but his grey eyes were alert and bright.

He wore an old pair of creased black trousers and a heavy woollen grey cardigan. The first flash of perplexity had gone from his eyes and he looked thoughtfully at them. He stroked his iron-grey moustache and snapped a finger. Recognition set his eyes twinkling.

"Pon my soul. Ilona and Werner." They laughed and saw his eyes were now misty.

"Never did I think I'd see you again. Come in, come in." He fluttered around them as he ushered them into the back living room. He kicked the remains of smouldering logs and threw fresh ones on the bed of dull embers.

They took off their coats and sat down on the cushioned bench in front of the open fireplace. He shuffled back to the porch. They heard the bolt being shot across and the turn of a key. When he came back there were two bottles of wine in his hands. The pine and birch logs kissed by the reviving embers of the fire, crackled, spluttered and flamed. Raufft placed the bottles on the hearth, mumbled and shuffled over to a wall cupboard. He brought out three stemmed glasses and a corkscrew.

Outside the wind screamed through the pine trees to the rear of the inn, sending the branches moaning in a strange concerto of wild abandoned music. Raufft pulled the corks from the bottles, laid one down and filled the glasses from the other.

"To the old times that'll never come again," he said, and there was warmth in his voice.

111

They rose, touched glasses and Werner thought it was the best hock he had had for years.

Raufft looked long and searchingly at them. "How good it is to see you. But what brings you here?"

Ilona, her eyes looking at Werner, said laughingly, "I don't really know where to begin. We're both stationed not far from Berlin and arranged to meet. It was the night after the air-raid." Her eyes widened as she recalled the horror of that night.

Raufft interrupted softly. "It must've been very bad."

"It was terrible,." she said.

She took another sip from her glass. "I was on leave and decided to visit Papa. Werner had already decided to come here for a rest and offered to drive me."

"Have you seen your father?"

"Yes, we saw him as we passed through Nuremberg. He's very busy with the newspaper and hadn't a lot of time but he was delighted to see us. When he heard we were coming here he made us promise we'd look you up. You're a very dear friend of his and he's told me how very kind you are to him in the things you send."

Raufft waved his hand. "Hush, it's nothing. But I hope you'd have looked me up without your father making you promise?"

Ilona leaned forward. "Of course Arnold."

She placed an arm lightly on his elbow. "You know Johan is dead?"

"Yes," he said slowly. "Your father told me. I'm sorry, he was a good boy."

Raufft fumbled in his cardigan pocket, took out a battered pipe, lit what remained of the burnt tobacco, and puffed thoughtfully. After a moment, he said, "You're not going back to Nuremberg tonight in this weather?"

"We thought if it wasn't too much trouble we would stay as paying guests for a few days," Werner said.

"Of course, of course, but not as paying guests."

Ilona shook her head commandingly. "Arnold you're a darling but we . . ."

"No, no, I'll be glad of your company but the rooms haven't been used and they'll be cold. I'll light fires," Raufft said.

"No," Ilona said emphatically. "I'll do that. You sit and talk to Werner."

Raufft applied another light to his pipe. "You'd better use the two rooms on the first landing. There's logs, sticks and paraffin rags in the grate. The bedding's in the cupboards."

Ilona got to her feet. "Good, then I'll make supper. Werner has some rations in the car and a bottle of brandy. You'd better bring them in liebling."

She flushed a little as the endearment slipped out but the inn-keeper seemed not to have noticed.

Werner rose. He brought the luggage from the car. Opening the largest of the travelling bags, he brought out two bottles of brandy.

Seeing the look of surprise in Raufft's eyes he said, "They're Wolfgang's. I had to bring some things from his flat in Berlin and it would be a shame to have these smashed by the Tommis."

The old inn-keeper picked up one of the bottles and examined it carefully. "Good stuff. You don't get it easily nowadays." As an after-thought he added, "How's Wolfgang?" There was little warmth in his question.

"Same as ever. He's in Paris."

"Still with the Gestapo?" Werner was not sure whether he detected a touch of hardness in the old man's voice.

"Yes. He's now a Hauptmann."

Raufft filled the glasses and looking into the fire said in an almost inaudible voice: "We had some words you know, after Asaph was arrested."

Werner lit a cigarette and handed his pack to the inn-keeper.

"I didn't know that," he said quietly.

Raufft took the cigarettes, glanced at the brand and said: "I don't usually smoke them, but the pipe tobacco is hard to get." He paused and added: "You didn't know?"

Werner shifted in his seat and took a deep inhale from his cigarette. "No, but I'd heard rumours, Arnold."

"They were more than rumours, Werner. Most of us here know that it was Wolfgang who had Asaph arrested." There was a short silence and the inn-keeper said, "He was an old friend of mine and of Ilona's father. There was no harm in him."

"I too was sorry. I liked Asaph. He was a good teacher and a good man."

Raufft gazed thoughtfully at his drink as if undecided whether to pursue the matter. He eyed the Oberleutnant speculatively and said: "Did you know Wolfgang has now . . . er . . . inherited his property here?"

Werner jerked forward. "Are you sure of that?"

"Why should I lie, especially to you?"

"I didn't mean that, but what you've said is a grave charge."

A thin, sardonic smile creased Raufft's lips. "Against whom? A Gestapo major. They are very powerful, much more important than Luftwaffe Oberleutnants . . . no matter how brave."

Werner flushed and took a pull at his cigarette. Raufft saw his embarrassment and said: "I'm sorry. I shouldn't have said that." His eyes searched the night-fighter pilot's face, as a photographer evaluates his subject. "Asaph often remarked as we played chess here at the difference between you and your brother."

Werner tossed the end of his cigarette into the fire. " Did he suffer much?"

Raufft shrugged. "There was no way of knowing. How could there be? I understand he died within weeks of being taken." He tapped out the remnants of his pipe and said,

"Asaph's property is worth quite a bit." He stood up and his eyes focussed on the Knight's ribbon on the Oberleutnant's tunic. "My eyes are not what they were. Congratulations. How many?"

"Fifteen," Werner said quietly.

A troubled looked crossed the inn-keeper's eyes. "Ilona's Papa told me in a letter that Nuremberg's high on their list?"

"I don't know but it's possible," Werner said, in a flat voice. They smoked in silence for a moment, then the old man looked up.

"I don't envy your job. You must have good radar to find them."

"There's better coming along. Stuff they can't jam. Some Staffels have already been equipped with it. I expect to have it at my new station."

They heard Ilona's footsteps on the stairs and they turned round as she entered the room.

"The fires are lit and the beds made. I've put those old warming pans into them to air the sheets."

Werner made a mock bow from the waist. "Fraulein, you are not only beautiful but magnificent."

"Now I shall make the supper," she said lightly. "What's the Oberleutnant got in his ration sack?"

He handed her the bag. "There's good coffee in there. I took it from Wolfgang's flat."

"Good coffee is something I haven't tasted in years," said Raufft. He glanced at the clock above the fireplace.

"Opening time?" Ilona queried.

The old inn-keeper smiled. "I don't expect any on a night like this. They'll bang on the door if they want me."

After a supper of cold ham from Werner's rations, and potatoes from Raufft's larder, they sat round the fire drinking and talking of the old times.

As the drink flowed the old man became mellow. Before they retired for the night he looked long and hard into the embers of the fire and said, "You'll marry again Ilona and I think I know who it'll be." He raised his eyes and saw the flush on their cheeks. It could have been from the heat of the fire but somehow he thought otherwise.

He rose and said, "Well, I'm going to bed. The excitement of seeing you both has made me tired and the brandy – what splendid brandy – has made me drowsy."

They rose with him and Werner stiffled a yawn. Ilona noticed it and said, "You must be dead tired after that long drive."

"Oh, I've recovered from that but, like Arnold, the brandy's made me sleepy."

On the landing she kissed him lightly on the cheek and slipped into her room.

He heard her gently close it. He listened for a moment but there was no sound of a key being turned in the lock. Outside the wind moved through the pines. His head hardly touched the pillow and he was asleep.

Dawn broke with a lukewarm sun that was just strong enough to charm the breeze that blew from the snow-capped peaks. Werner opened the chalet window and looked towards the mountain. The rarefied air embraced him with the headiness of vintage champagne. It mingled with the sweet smell from the log fragments smouldering in the grate at the end of his bedroom. He felt peaceful, content and utterly at ease. The sun was coming up stronger and its light, washing the mountain tops, was unbearably delicate.

He took his shaving gear and went down stairs. Raufft was already preparing breakfast. He took some hot water from the stove and went into the bathroom.

"Ilona's tired. I'll take up her breakfast later. She was caught in the Berlin raid and is still very shaken," he said.

The inn-keeper poured him coffee and said, "I've been extravagent with it. I've made it strong."

Raufft set out a breakfast tray. Werner took it and made his way up the stairs. Balancing the tray in one hand, he opened her door with the other. He smiled as he found it still unlocked. Laying the tray on the dressing table he looked at the peaceful face of the woman asleep in the big double bed. Her dark chestnut coloured hair flowed over the pillow case in soft waves. God, he thought, she was more beautiful in sleep than awake.

He reached into the pocket of his trousers and brought out a pack of cigarettes. He hesitated, put them back, and crossed over to the bed. Gently, he shook her.

"Ilona, breakfast. We've had ours."

She stirred and opened her eyes. A sleepy smile formed on her lips. She raised herself in the bed, wrinkled her nose. "Um-m-m, that smells like real coffee."

He went over to the dressing table and placed the tray on her lap. Then he drew the heavy curtains and slightly opened the window.

"Smell that air. It's heady," he said.

At the door he turned and said, "We're trying to run a bath for you. There's not much hot water. Don't let it get cold."

As he was about to close the door, she said softly, "Werner. I'm so glad I came."

Raufft packed them a light luncheon when they told him they were off to walk in the mountains. It had stopped snowing during the night but even so they found it hard going as they trudged along the footpath to the lower slopes of the mountains. Here and there where the sun played on clearances in the forest glades the snow was melting. Water tumbled from half frozen streams and sang loudly as it gushed down the rocks filling every pool to over-flowing. It gurgled and foamed through the woods, now and then sinking into snow which hindered its path.

Ancient pine trees, perched on dizzy heights, sagged under their blankets of snow. The sky, cold blue, was splotched with heavy white clouds. They watched entranced as the great billowing clouds kissed the tops of the mountains drenching them with moisture. Ilona was filled with an obscure happiness so strong that she found her eyes were wet. She turned to Werner and pointed to where the path widened into a boulder strewn copse.

Excitement heightened her voice. "We used to play here and gather the white mountain flowers, remember?" He nodded and smiled. "And there were two great waterfalls. The top one fell from the big lake further up and tumbled ito the deep pool where our waterfall was."

"Yes, yes," she said eagerly. "It's not to be forgotten. That's why I wanted to come here. Our waterfall can't be far. Let's find it and wish beside it as we used to do. I wonder if the flowers will be out? They used to begin flowering about now."

She stretched out her hand. He took it in his and felt the pressure of her squeeze through her gloves. She pulled, half dragged him up the twisting path. Suddenly, she stopped and cocked her head. She put a finger to her lips. "Listen and you can just hear it." Her eyes sparkled and the mountain air brought a flush to her cheeks. They climbed higher and the incessant noise of falling water dominated each step they took until every sound was blotted out by the thunder of cascading water. On each side of the falls giant icicles hung mutely, dripping tears into the dark pool below. Tall pines, crusted with snow, formed dense sentinels of the falls. Splotches of white spread in patches from the moss layers proudly protruding above the thawing snow.

"Look Liebling, the flowers are in bud and some are in bloom. How utterly beautiful!" Ilona exclaimed, with emotion. "How magical this place is. The very sound of the water creates an illusion of some ecstatic refuge. It's strange that something so powerful should become so soothing, so very, very peaceful."

She looked at him enquiringly and he saw that her eyes

were moist. "Why can't things always be like this? Oh, God! When will this terrible war end?" There was deep sadness and anguish in her voice. An icy coldness stabbed Werner. It pricked the soft skin round his eyes and triggered in spasms through his body. He found himself trembling. Ilona, her eyes still on him, saw his face grow ashen.

"What is it?" she asked anxiously. He shook his head. "Nothing, just a strange feeling."

He broke off and she prompted, "Of what, Werner?"

"I don't know. It came when I looked at that ledge where the waterfall flows from the pool." He stamped his feet on the snow. "It's the damp I think."

She looked searchingly at the ledge. "Remember what old Heinrich the surveyor used to say?" He looked at her enquiringly. "What was that?"

"He said the ledge was not sound and neither was the bigger one where the water cascades from the lake into the upper pool. They'd been eroded by the millions and millions of tons of water that has swept over them since time began. He said if these natural sluices collapsed the upper lake would flood down and the village would be submerged in a tumbling maelstrom of water."

Werner looked thoughtful. Then he laughed. "There's no risk of that. They've been there for thousands and thousands of years and will still be there thousands of years from now."

His eyes glanced from the ledge and rested on the white spray as it tinted into hues of blue, green and yellow.

"Liebling, what are you thinking?"

He said without looking at her, "That your eyes are more beautiful than the colours the waterfall is throwing out."

He felt her arm on his as she turned him gently towards her. She opened her eyes in mock surprise and said, "Werner, you were never much good at poetry but I like that."

Their eyes held for a moment and he said quietly, "I love you Ilona, I always have. I shouldn't have brought you here and I'd no right to say that but –"

She interrupted him softly. "I'm glad you said it, because I love you. Have always loved you. It was a stupid quarrel and I did a stupid thing."

He took her in his arms and was astounded by the eagerness and passion with which she responded, smothering him with warm kisses. She broke away, buried her head in his shoulder and he felt the cold fur of her hat brush his cheek.

She raised her head, put her arms tight round his neck and whispered: "My darling, my darling. I'm so happy I' crying."

He cupped her face softly in his hands, caught a teardrop on the knuckle of his finger and pressed it to his lips. They turned still in each others arms and looked for long moments at the waterfall. A waning sun had turned the falls to a metallic blue.

"We'd better be getting back. It'll soon be twilight," he murmured.

As they made their way back the long shadows of the stirring trees formed intricate patterns on the snow draped slopes. It was as if winter, with its grinding frosts, was reluctant to be ousted by a sun that as yet had little warmth in it. It hung like a massive orange globe over the peaks, its amber rays weaving a fairy tale picture of a forest aflame.

They stopped for a moment and in silence gazed at the splendour of the fast approaching sunset. Ilona's grip on his arm tightened and she said, "I always said this was a magic place. I know for sure, now." The sun slid between two towering peaks showering bursts of fiery life onto the lower mountain tops. Its darting arrows pierced every gap, fissure and chasm as it raced towards the valley cradling the village.

A light wind, strong and pure, rustled the pines. The

120

path widened into a cart track. From childhood days they knew the path and the gulley. From where they were the village looked toylike. A little to the left of the school they picked out the inn. Thin wafts of smoke curled from Raufft's chimneys and they felt they could almost smell the burning pine logs with their sweet odour of resin.

The sun sank lower and lower. Its light was of an almost unbearable delicacy and tenderness, as if it were reaching out to soothe the bleeding heart of a war torn world, terrified of the coming of night.

"God! If there's a God do not let them come here tonight, or any other night, to destroy the simple beauty of this place," Ilona said the words to herself with the earnestness of a prayer.

Werner tugged on her hand and she found herself running like a child towards the little stone hump-backed bridge that spanned the village stream. They were half way across when they saw two little girls of about eight, with long flaxen pigtails coming towards them. Ilona stopped them and asked if they had come from the school. They nodded shyly and she told them that they too had gone to the village school long years ago.

"You're twins, aren't you?" Werner asked.

Ilona laughed. "Isn't that obvious?"

Werner fumbled in his greatcoat pocket, took out a large bar of chocolate and splitting it in two handed a half to each of them.

"What beautiful children," she said. Then looking mischieviously at Werner, she added. "Perhaps someday they too will make a tryst at the waterfall."

One of them hearing what Ilona had whispered asked shyly, "Were you at the waterfall? We often go there to collect the white flowers." Ilona smiled and bending down to the twins said, "Yes, mein liebchens. The flowers are coming out and we are to be married before they wither."

They clapped their hands happily and the less shy of the

two asked: "Can we come to your wedding? We'll bring posies of the white flowers."

"Of course you can come. It'll be in the village very soon." She patted their heads and added, "It's getting dark. Better run home now or your mother will worry."

They thumped the snow from their boots on the steps of the inn's veranda and Werner said, "I'm going to tell Arnold to bring wine and do what he can in the way of a celebration dinner. I'd like us to be married here at once."

Raufft took both their hands in his when they told him. Although he was genuinely happy there was no surprise in his eyes. He grinned at them. "I always knew you two were for each other. The only surprise was when you married Johan. He was a good boy but not the one for you, Ilona."

A slow, sad smile crossed her face at the mention of Johan. "I think he knew too that I'd always loved Werner." Ilona had barely cleared up the supper dishes when there was a knock on the door. They heard Raufft welcoming four of the villagers as he ushered them into the taproom. The four had known Werner and Ilona since they were children. One of them they found was the uncle of the twins.

Raufft explained that they were on leave. Ilona had been posted from the 'battle-opera' room near Berlin to take up controller duties in a unit not far from Nuremberg. Werner, on the other hand, he told them, had been transferred to the crack fighter station at Mainz-Finthen, south west of Frankfurt.

The inn-keeper raised a clenched fist and said laughingly, "So if the Terrorfliegers attack this area they'll have to reckon with these two."

Two of the villagers persuaded Raufft to take out his accordion and although he protested he had not played it for years they sang and drank till near midnight. Before Werner and Ilona retired, they insisted on drinking one more toast . . ."To a gallant night-fighter ace and his

122

beautiful bride to be," the uncle of the twins said and raised his glass. They stayed for yet another drink before Ilona slipped her arm through Werner's and made their good-nights.

On the landing leading to their rooms, Werner hesitated. As if sensing his unsureness, Ilona took him gently by the arm and led him into her room. He lit one of the tall candles. Her big, velvety green eyes were star-bright under the sweep of her lashes. She leaned toward him and he caught a handful of her wonderful hair and wound it tenderly round her throat. Then with a stifled gasp her arms went round him and they fell on the bed. His lips crushed on hers. With feverish fingers they raced to undress each other.

It was with a lover's hands that he drew her yielding body into his arms. Her arms tightened around him and he felt her nails deep in his back. Perhaps it was the drink but lights spun before his eyes and the room was turning over and over. He could feel her taut, well formed body thrusting against his. He closed his eyes. It had never been like this with his wife. Never. This was for him. This was his life force.

Her tongue darted snake-like in his mouth and her hands swept down in urgent caressing movements. The world and the stars were exploding inside him.

"Mein liebling! How very much I love you," she whispered. The wood fire in the grate burned to a pale hot ash. The candle dripped wax and spluttered. She lay quietly in the bed and with a great joy watched him sleep.

It was the third time they had made love that night and now the grey light of the morning filtered through the drawn blinds. A stray shaft of sunlight fell across his face. He seemed to be smiling. She raised herself on the pillow and kissed him lightly on the mouth. He had fallen into a deep sleep, with one hand imprisoning her waist with unconscious possessiveness.

She lowered her head into the pillow and felt infinitely content for the first time since she left **Nuremberg**. Flakes of snow whirled against the rimmed window-panes and from a snow-covered byre in the distance there came the lowing of cold and hungry cattle.

Chapter Eight

Mosquitos of the R.A.F.'s Light Night Striking Force, each carrying a 4,000lb "block-buster" bomb in their bellies, roared high over Berlin in what Supreme Headquarters at Treuenbrietzen classed as "nuisance" raids and which Harris called "stoking the fires". The Mosquito, made almost entirely of wood, was undoubtedly the finest aircraft in operational service at the time with any air-force. It had a ceiling of nearly 40,000 feet and a maximum speed of over 400 m.p.h. It could out-fly and out-speed any German night-fighter.

Yet few realised that this remarkable aircraft, with its two man crew, could take 500lbs more of bombs to Berlin than the American B17, Flying Fortress. The B 17s lower load was largely accounted for by the routing they had to take in daylight to Berlin and the need to carry large amounts of ammunition to keep the German fighters at bay.

FOOTNOTE. Air Vice-Marshal D.C.T. Bennett, in his book *Pathfinder*, says "The argument, which subsequently became current, was that one Mosquito was worth seven Lancasters. A Mosquito carried a little over half the bomb-load of a Lancaster to Berlin. Its casualty rate was about 1/10th of that of a Lancaster. Its cost was 1/3rd of the Lancaster, and it carried two people instead of seven . . . value for war effort was certainly well on the side of the Mosquito compared with any other aircraft ever produced in the history of flying."

It was a forlorn hope of the men who flew the Halifaxes and Lancasters that someday enough Mosquitos would flow from the aircraft assembly lines to make their aircraft obsolete.

The Mosquito force – ironically termed the "light strikers" – bombed Berlin with their four thousand pounders on sixteen nights when the main force bombers were grounded and their loss rate was around one per cent. As Treuenbrietzen knew well, in one raid on the capital a hundred Mosquitos unleased 400,000lbs of high explosives on the city. Treuenbrietzen marvelled that once the British Air Staff had turned down this astonishing aircraft. Working on the number of British heavy bombers shot down on the Berlin raids and the number of aircraft that the B.B.C. disclosed took part in them, German Supreme Headquarters calculated that on average R.A.F. Bomber Command had lost about seven to eight per cent of their attacking force.

Yet for home propaganda consumption they underplayed the role of the Mosquitos. But as Berlin reeled under the devastating impact of the Mosquitos' four-thousand-pound bombs it would be a foolhardy person who would have written them off as mere "nuisance" raiders. Certainly, Feldwebel Munzberger and his heavy 10.5cm battery had no illusions. Their predictors had long since told the guns that the attacking force consisted of fast flying Mosquitos and the guns had accordingly responded to the data fed to them.

The first wave of Mosquitos struck Berlin at exactly fourteen-and-a-half minutes to midnight and they bombed with unerring accuracy on the red and green target indicators dropped by their Pathfinders. The light case four-thousand-pounders screamed and screeched down on the city, battered a few nights earlier by the full might of the heavies of Bomber Command.

They blasted whole city blocks into shattered shells and

flattened buildings already badly damaged in earlier attacks. Gas mains, hurriedly repaired in recent raids, erupted like coffined dead who refused to lie buried.

The raid was fast and furious. But unlike the saturation attack by Harris' four engined bombers the sky was conspicuously clear of exploding bombers and the technicoloured patchwork of tracer. Fifteen minutes after the first target markers left the bomb-bays of the Pathfinders the raid was over. Thirty minutes later the all clear sounded. The stand-down came through to Munzberger's battery sixteen minutes later. He dug in his tunic and took out a crumpled packet of cigarettes. He had decided his nerves were more important than the money he got from selling his tobacco ration on the black market.

In the "battle-opera" room at Treuenbrietzen the controller sifted through the clipped teleprinter sheets handed to him by the dark haired woman auxilliary. Last time her hair was red. He remembered the red-head had gone on posting leave to a station near Nuremberg. The cryptic messages informed him that another force of Mosquitos was approaching Grid EA where the radio assembly beacon Marie was situated. Ju 88s, from the airfield at Quakenbrück, and Me 110s, from the sister night-fighter field at Vechta, were ordered to fly to beacon Marie and await instructions.

The controller relaxed for a moment and reached for the coffee that had been handed to him earlier. It was stone cold. The new Mosquito force if they continued on their heading would come over Magdeburg or they could fly further south and hit Leipzig. The telephone at his elbow buzzed. He picked it up and glanced at the grid map as he listened. He replaced the receiver.

"Verflucht nochmal," he cursed. Turning to his aide he

snapped: "The bastards have turned off . . . they're in Grid FC heading for Berlin."

His aide shrugged his shoulder. "They're too fast and too high. The fighters will never reach them."

The controller cursed. "Get Parchim airborne. They might intercept some on the way back."

He reached for his coffee, hesitated, and recalled that it was cold. Another teleprinter flash was handed to him.

"Verdammt nochmal," he swore. Another force of Mosquitos was approaching Keil and because they were "windowing" heavily there was no way of telling how strong the formation was.

He did not have to consult his list of top strategic targets to know that Keil was the most important canal in Germany, connecting the Baltic with all the North Sea ports. It was also, he knew, of vital importance for the movement of heavy submarine parts and other U-boat equipment from the Baltic to Wilhelmshaven, Bremen and Hamburg, apart from being a well used U-boat waterway. He snapped out an order which would send the night-fighter Staffels from Oldenburg and Neumünster into Grids AA and AU where he considered they would have a fair chance of intercepting the mine-laying force.

He realised that if a mine-laying operation was to be successful from the air the Mosquitos would have to descend from a considerable height, from a point about five miles back, and then cross the canal at not more than 50 to 60 feet and at an angle of around 20 degrees to it. Then they would be at their most vulnerable – sitting ducks for his fighters if they got there in time.

He looked at his watch. It would be desperately tight. Most likely the Mosquitos would have dropped their mines and would be on course for England before his fighters reached them.

The woman auxiliary listened intently as the urgent voices of the night-fighter pilots came over her head-phones. She knew by their anxious tones that among the Light Night Striking Force were Mosquito intruders whose job it was to search out the hunting night-fighters and destroy them.

She immediately alerted her superior who passed the warning to the controller's aide. There was no point in passing it on. The night-fighters must already know that they the hunters were now the hunted.

The pilot of a Messerschmidt 110, whose identification call she could not pick up was shouting to another 110: "Achtung Heinz! Du hast ein Mozquito hinter dir!"

But his warning came too late. She could not hear the burst of fire which the Mosquito on his tail hosed into the night-fighter. Her ears caught only the last gasps of the stricken night-fighter pilot and she knew they would be indelibly etched on her mind for all time, jumbled and contorted as they were . . .

"Hilfe! Hilfe! I've been hit . . . I'm finished . . . I'm crashing . . . "

Grating coughs all but drowned the rushing noise on his microphone. There was a nervous twisting scream of utter agony and then silence.

"Adler One from Adler Three! That was Heinz. Did you see it? He'd no chance . . . Achtung . . . "

"Adler Three from Adler One! Yes, I saw it. But watch out. He's still behind us."

"Damn and blast it. My God, where are you? Shit! My red lights are flashing. Fuel's at danger level . . . breaking off . . . "

"Achtung! Adler One to Adler Three. Where are you? Reply if you're there . . . Adler One to Adler Three . . . if receiving me . . . Back to base . . . Nach Hause fliegen.".

The girl auxiliary knew the night-fighter pilots conversations were monitored and recorded. She wished those who dismissed the attacks by the British Light Night Striking Force as "nuisance" raids could have heard what she had just listened to. They would then think otherwise.

Feldwebel Munzberger cursed vehemently as his battery was put on Stand-To again. This was one of the heaviest raids he had yet experienced from the Light Night Striking Force. The second wave of Mosquitos hit Berlin one-and-a-half hours later, their timing fixed so that their 4,000lb bombs fell on the fire-fighters and rescue teams which had gone into action immediately the first all clear sounded.

Munzberger's battery was on predicted radar fire but so far they had not seen one aircraft explode in the shell splashed sky they were firing into. The Mosquitos were difficult to hit, unlike the slow vulnerable Halifaxes and Lancasters, he considered ruefully. In the distance he could see the fires of Berlin. He was due to go there on a 48 hour pass. He wondered now if it was worth the risk. Perhaps there was a chance he'd again meet the red-headed girl in the Afton. Maybe what she said about being posted wasn't true. Strange, he thought, how he couldn't get her out of his mind.

Mosquito Z-Zebra began the bomb-run on Berlin at 26,000 feet. Its bomb-doors opened smoothly but when the navigator pressed the bomb-tit there was no welcoming rearing from the aircraft, as was normally the case, when the four thousand pounder parted from its racks.

"Christ! We've got a hang-up," Zebra's navigator shouted.

"Jesus!" his pilot answered, knowing the hazards of trying to land with a light case 'cookie' in his bomb-bay.

"I'm going back to see if I can prise the bloody thing off."

There was a grunt from his pilot. "I'm not stooging around Berlin while you're trying. I'm turning off. We can drop the bloody thing anywhere and hope it hits something — even if its only a bloody cow."

"Expensive way of slaughtering live-stock, ol' cock," his navigator said lightly, his voice back under control, and added: "I'll see what I can do."

He checked his oxygen and crawled towards the panel above the bomb-bay, a heavy torch in his hand. A little later he was back. He tapped his pilot on the shoulder, "Okay, cock. I think it's cleared. Shoot across the jettison bars when I say Now and keep your fingers crossed."

"What was wrong?"

"Don't rightly know. I'm a navigator not a bloody mechanic. I think it was a faulty circuit and icing."

Z-Zebra reared like a frisky bronco as the 'cookie' she had nursed spewed from her belly.

"Where'd you think it landed?"

"Dunno," said his navigator, "but with a bit of luck it might've hit something." He laughed and added: "Course for coast coming up . . . try and steer it accurately this time."

"Balls to you, navigator," Z-Zebra's pilot said, as he banked the Mosquito on course for home.

The final stand-down order of the night came to Munzberger's battery some seconds before Z-Zebra's hang-up screeched into his gun-pit. His thoughts were still on the red-haired girl when the light-case 'cookie' exploded in a searing flash of orange light. A couple of micro-seconds later there was an even more colossal explosion as the rows of neatly stacked heavy calibre shells detonated.

Gun battery and searchlight unit erupted like a small world colliding with a gigantic meteorite somewhere in another galaxy. The concussion from the violence of the explosion roared through the camouflaged wooden huts on the perimeter of the pit with the fury of a tornado, showering the emplacement with thousands of razor sharp fragments and jagged pieces of shrapnel that once were highly costly and sensitive predictors, range-finders, computer boxes, searchlights and mobile electric power units.

Those in Munzberger's pit went to eternity in assorted chunks of flesh and bone. The tremendous explosion heated the air to fantastic temperatures and caused a raging fire storm which cremated those in the other gunpits. Gunners who had been trudging back to their sleeping quarters were engulfed by the ferocity of the holocaust. Their frenzied screams were still hanging on the night air long after Z-Zebra's hang-up primed the inferno.

The B.B.C.'s news bulletin led off with the Mosquito raid on Berlin. The aircrews of 187 Squadron who had bothered to go to their mess for breakfast, heard it with more than detached interest. Every single one of them would have transferred long ago to a Mosquito of the Night Striking Force if they had been given the chance.

It was like switching from a cart-horse to a sleek, fast thoroughbred. Their survival odds would have lengthened beyond their wildest dreams, but they had long since stopped dreaming or living in the realms of fantasy. They were in the mass killing business and the great majority of them lived with the certain knowledge they would one night be in a flaming coffin, seven seconds away from cremation. If they were not too badly wounded they might just be able to bale out in that time, provided their parachutes were intact and the exits hadn't been damaged or jammed.

There was hardly a comment when the announcer disclosed that two Mosquitos were missing from the operation. They were used to three, four and sometimes five never get-

132

ting back from the twenty or so bombers that went out from the Squadron almost every other night weather permitting. Two . . . it made them think. But they must not think. Their contract was signed. There was nothing they could do about it unless, of course, they went L.M.F. Some who were near breaking point preferred to go to their deaths with the fear locked in their hearts, rather than face the shame and the stigma of being labelled with such humiliating letters.

Mackay and his pilot were having their third cigarette, after they had breakfasted, when the tannoy system blared summoning the crews of S-Sugar, Q-Queenie and A-Able to the briefing room in thirty minutes time. Mitchell stubbed out his half smoked cigarette, let loose a yawn and looking at his bomb-aimer through bleary eyes said, "That, Mac is the bloody air test we've to do on Fishpond. Why can't they do their radar practice on the ground? It'll be as bloody boring as the technical crap they pumped at us yesterday."

Mackay shrugged his shoulders. "Well, that's. the W.O.P's department. All the same if he picks up four 'blips' all the same size it's a four engined job. But if a fifth slides on to the screen and its smaller and moving in on us then it's a fighter for sure. Christ! that's something we want to know, isn't it?"

Mitchell rose and brushed some crumbs from his tunic. "Sure. Sure. Anyway, it'll give you the chance of getting in more time at the controls. Fly her after take-off but follow me through on it. Maybe one day you'll have to land it."

Mackay drew on his cigarette and replied through a cloud of smoke "I doubt it."

They left the mess and made for the briefing room. An hour later they were airborne on a Fishpond cross-country familiarisation exercise.

The station transport made its first stop at the Swan

before going into town. Mitchell and Mackay were the only ones to get out. The stand-down had come shortly after they had landed from the cross-country. Fog which had kept the bombers grounded the previous night was slowly creeping in again. The hang-over they had from the previous night's party had long since gone. Well before they were due to take off on their Fishpond flight the crew of S-Sugar went out to their aircraft. Slipping on their oxygen masks, they turned on the main supply and swallowed long draughts. Mackay's sworn cure — oxygen — had cleared their heads once again.

Mitchell and Mackay were surprised when they went into the back bar to find Cotton already there. With him was the Corporal Waaf. "Christ! You must've taken off quick," Mackay said. Then glancing towards Sue, he added: "You on a day off or just taking it off?"

The American laughed. "We got a lift in Stacey's old banger. He's in the other bar, with your navigator." He paused. "Sue's on a day off. Any more questions, Mac?"

Mitchell fidgetted uneasily. "You say Holton's through there?"

"Yeah, why?"

Mackay frowned. "Jee-sus! He's meeting that cow, Maggie."

Cotton looked puzzled. "What's wrong? She seems a nice enough girl."

"Seems is the operative word," said Mackay. "Forget it. What di'ya want to drink?"

"Nope, this one's on me. Sue and I are on the way into town to see a movie. So what'll it be?"

"A pint," the Scot said.

"Make it two," added Mitchell.

While they were waiting for their drinks, Mackay nudged his pilot. "You owe me a quid or were you too pissed to remember?"

Reluctantly Mitchell dug in his pocket and handed over

two ten shilling notes. Mackay winked at Cotton. "He was stupid enough to bet that the Mossie boys wouldn't be stoking up our fires."

The American looked thoughtful. "I dropped into the Intelligence room after our Fishpond lark and they said the Mossies slammed Berlin hard."

Mitchell shrugged. "And they only lost two. Christ! They can do it every bloody night for my money."

"We'd be out of a job, then," Cotton answered.

"Suit me fine," Mitchell said. "What are you after a bloody V.C.?"

"Nope, just to finish this war and get back home."

Mitchell was about to reply when Stacey pushed his head round the door. "You two love-birds ready? I'm going."

They had barely left when May popped her head through the serving hatch. "I saw you get out of the transport. Come into the other bar. There's a fire through there and I'm not lighting one here until the evening." Tauntingly she added, "Don't you two know there's a war on."

Mitchell breathed carefully. "So that's why there's so many aircraft flying around here?" He slipped a half-crown on the hatch counter. "Set us up two pints through there, luv."

Mackay grimaced. "We're alright here, Bill. Jack's through there and that means he's meeting Curry."

Mitchell's eye-brows puckered. "Curry?"

His bomb-aimer nailed his eyes on Mitchell. "That's a pet name I had for Maggie, when I found she was being screwed by a coloured." He chuckled again. "It gets her real mad." Then wickedly he added, "I must use it in front of Jack and watch his reaction."

Mitchell nodded towards the other bar. "I'll have to tell Maggie sooner or later. If she's meeting Jack then this is the time and place."

As they moved to the main bar, he added: "I don't want

to dwell on this and I won't mention it again. For what it's worth Julie once said that Maggie loved you deeply. Was insanely jealous of losing you. Maybe that's why she went off the rails."

Mackay snorted. "That's balls. She was too long whoring to love anyone and she went off the rails – as you put it – long ago. Now forget it."

Mitchell rolled a look at his bomb-aimer and said, "One thing more. Did you tell May about Julie?"

Mackay nodded. "Also about my affair with Curry."

"What did she say?"

"She was bloody angry that I should've got tied up with a slut."

When they went into the other bar they saw Holton leaning on the counter, dee: in thought. He turned when he saw them and nodding :o the two pints beside him said, "May said you'd ordere. them. She's gone upstairs for a moment."

The bar was empty except for three farm workers, who were playing darts, and a burly thick-set man they recognised as Fulton, the village bobby.

"You want one?" Mackay asked Holton.

"No, I've enough here."

Mitchell eyed his navigator critically. " Something needling you Jack. You look as if you'd buried someone."

Before Holton could answer Mackay quipped. "Curry stood you up then?"

Holton turned slowly towards him and there was open puzzlement in his face. "Curry?"

"Mag-gie." Mackay spelled out the name with marked emphasis on the last syllable.

Holton slammed down his pint. "For Chri'sake lay off Mac. I know she once went with you." Then as an after thought, "I don't get the 'Curry'."

The Scot took a long pull from his pint. "Listen Reg and try and believe me. Both Bill and I know a helluva sight more about her than you do. She's a whore and that's why we're trying to wise you up. She's trying to get at me through you but it's not on, never will be. She's got 'spade' lovers from the Yankee base at Saston. That's why she's called Curry. Ask her if you doubt me."

Holton was about to interrupt when Mitchell interjected. "It's true Reg. We've seen her with them in town."

Mackay laid his hand firmly on his navigator's arm. "We don't want you to get a dose. We've all but finished this tour. If you catch a packet from her and go for treatment they'll give us a new navigator. We don't want that. Besides you might have to start your tour again and that would mean with a 'sprog' crew."

Holton was about to speak when the door creaked and Maggie came in. She hesitated when she saw Mackay, then as if changing her mind brashly walked up to them.

She kissed Holton lightly on the cheek. "Sorry I'm late luv, but so was the bus."

Holton was about to ask her what she wanted to drink when Mitchell said quietly, "You'd better have a large Scotch, Maggie. I've some bad news for you."

Her eyes widened in fright. She looked anxiously at Mitchell. "Julie?" she asked in a distant voice.

Mitchell nodded. "She's dead and so is the baby. Killed in the raid. I suppose I should've told you sooner."

She swayed on her feet. Mackay watched stoically, undecided on whether it was an act. Holton caught her as she collapsed. The Scot went round the bar, bent down, and lifted a half empty bottle of whisky from a shelf and poured a stiff one. He took a sip of it and replaced the bottle. The farm workers had stopped playing on the board and Fulton was about to move towards them when Mackay shot him a frozen look and waved him away with the glass in his hand.

He handed the glass to Holton. "Give her this when she comes round. If it's a bloody act I'll charge her for it."

Holton said nothing but began gently to pat the girl's

137

face. Slowly her eyelids flickered. Mackay thought it was like some third rate actress in a church pantomime. Holton helped her to her feet and ushered her over to a chair and slowly fed her the whisky.

She sat up, took the whisky from Holton and deliberately drained the glass. Her eyes seemed to swim a little before focussing on Mitchell, who had bent over her.

"Tell me what you know about it," she said in an almost inaudible voice.

"Not much. I got the telegram about a week ago. They were both killed in the raid." He paused. "It took a little time for them to be identified. They were buried in a communal grave."

She got unsteadily to her feet and looked appealingly at Holton. "Please take me home."

When they had gone Mitchell said, "I'm pushing into town. There's some shopping I want to do." Glancing at his watch, he added, "The bus will be along in five minutes. Wanna come?"

"No. I'll stay put."

"See yuh."

After May had closed the bar and locked the outer doors they both had a sandwich lunch in the little sitting-room.

Mackay eyed the empty glass in his hand. "I'd like a strong Scotch."

She rose from her chair. "Well, just one." She sloshed some whisky into a glass. He drank it without removing it from his lips. He felt the fire burn his throat.

"Mac, darling Mac, please don't drink like that. It worries me." She came to him, enveloping him with her warmth.

"You've not been operating for two nights. It's the reaction. This is about the longest break you've had for a while. I listen each night you go out."

She waved a hand loosely round the room. "The whole place vibrates when the squadron goes over and I cry and cry." She looked up and he saw her eyes were wet. "You think I'm silly, Mac, but I love you, love you so very much. I don't know what I'll do if some night you . . . "

He stroked her lovingly and placed a finger over her lips. She took his finger in her hand and gazed intently into his eyes. Dark brown eyes that had suddenly lost their gaiety, she thought.

"You've the two to do?"

He nodded. She turned her head sideways and stared into the glowing fire. "You know the old lady who sometimes sits on the high chair in the taproom?" He chuckled. "The original Gypsy Rose."

"You mustn't mock her, Mac. She's really a gypsy and she can see into the future. When I was a schoolgirl she told me I'd marry a man from the village but it wouldn't be my true love. She also said I'd be widowed young and that I'd meet my real love when the great black ravens came to Farmer Tufton's fields. I've often thought about what she said. Tufton's fields are now your bomber airfield and the ravens must be the Halifaxes. She said this long before the war, long before there was an airfield here."

"Others will come when I am gone," he said tonelessly.

She turned her head slowly and he saw tears in her long eyelashes. "There'll never be another like you. I've never known anyone like you. I don't think I ever will."

"Nonsense, you're getting morbid. I'll get you a drink."

She shook her head. "When you finish where will you go, London?"

"I won't spend my leave in London."

"Where then?"

"With whom, you mean?"

Her eyes sparkled through the tears. He pulled her head towards him and kissed her tenderly on the mouth. "With you, my darling – with you. But far away so we won't have our sleep shattered by bombers going over."

"And where on this island would that be?"

"A tiny, out of the way hamlet in the Highlands."

"Where you were born?"

"Where my grandmother was born. Where the pines sweep down from the mountain slopes to white sandy shores. I used to play there as a child." He laughed. "There's one snag – the midges."

She laughed too and went over to the window. As he watched her draw the curtains his thoughts swept back to a little cemetery in those mountains where a recently dead mother lay. A loving hard working mother who learned from elsewhere that he was flying and died of a heart attack one night listening to the news of the Command's losses on some target long since forgotten – a raid he wasn't on as he learned at her funeral. But that was yesterday, many yesterdays. She was gone, as he would be gone, but he'd never lie beside her in that Highland grave. His, he reflected, would be ashes in the sky.

When May came over to him she thought there was mist in his eyes and a strange look in his face as if he'd glimpsed the future or it could have been the past. There was no way of knowing, she thought, with Mackay.

She kissed him and whispered. "I want you to love me."

"Don't I always?"

"I want you to love me NOW. Then we'll sleep before opening time."

In the upstairs bedroom where they'd slept so often May kicked off her shoes, unzipped her tight skirt, unbuttoned and removed her blouse. Mac eyed her approvingly. She was wearing a very tiny bottle-green suspender belt and shiny black-seamed stockings that showed off her long slim legs. Her firm up-tilted breasts thrust out proudly from a half bra of bottle-green satin.

She stood and watched him as he leisurely stripped. Her lips parted, showing her white moist teeth and there was an inviting challenge in her smile.

He walked over to her and kissed her passionately – her

140

mouth, shoulders, breasts – his tongue exploring wantonly every place he could reach. Deftly he undid her bra. His firm fingers pressed down and pushed her panties over her hips until they dropped to her ankles.

She raised a foot and with the other flicked them off. Their bodies entwined as they fell on the big bed. Mac felt her breasts become harder as he raked them with his tongue. In turn he felt her caress his back with her nails as she squirmed beneath him.

His fingers ran lightly up and down her firm, strong thighs as his lips switched from her throbbing nipples to her wide open mouth.

Their playful tongues and hungry bodies writhed in genuine and blissful ecstacy as they twisted and tossed in uninhibited love play. His tongue darted between her parted lips while his fingers played delicately with the flesh at the apex of her thighs.

His hands moved swiftly from her thighs and grasped her firm buttocks. Her arms pulled hard down on his neck as she rolled her body from side to side while her head, with its long hair hanging loose, hung over the edge of the bed.

"Oh, darling . . . now . . . NOW!" He slid into her and she quivered with pleasure as he thrust deeper and deeper into her. Suddenly, like riding a giant surfer the wave of their sensuality crashed over them, in splashes of passion and pleasure.

For a long spell they lay exhausted in each other's arms. They were still asleep, their arms lightly round one another, when the alarm clock rang. May lazily stretched out an arm and turned it off. With her head resting on one hand she stroked his thick black hair with the other. When he awoke she brushed and brushed her tongue on his mouth.

"What a joy you are in bed. What a marvellous lover you are. God! how I love you. Don't die on me, darling. Don't die on me – promise?"

He pulled her to him and kissed her hard on the lips. "I love you as much as I've ever loved anyone."

She slid from the bed and he said "We'll make even wilder love tonight, my love."

As she slipped into her clothes, she looked at him inquiringly. "Was Maggie good in bed?"

He raised himself from the pillow and pulled his teeth across his lips in a sinister smile. "Maggie was a whore. You see May there was no love. You're a beautiful, sensitive woman and there's love between us. I never had any for her." A coldness came into his voice. "Forget her. In my book she's dead."

Chapter Nine

The weather cleared. May saw the breaks in the heavy cloud which lay over Merton Wold as she slipped from the bed shortly after dawn, to make the sleeping figure some tea. She knew from long experience of living on the doorstep of a bomber base that the bombers would be out that night.

An hour later the tears swelled in her eyes as she watched the lanky figure of Warrant Officer Mackay stride from the inn to catch the early morning transport to the airfield.

She decided she would telephone him at lunch time. If no in-coming calls were accepted she'd know they were ON. She found her hands trembling. Two he had to do. They said you couldn't beat the odds. Too, too many battle weary aircrews with only a few trips to do had drank in the Swan the night before and had never come back.

Pellets of rain spattered against the window pane. The fire in the bedroom grate was going out leaving dim embers smothered by splinters of charcoaled chips of wood. She prodded the glowing remnants of the logs and they responded with darting tongues of fire. She hoped the bus would burst a tyre, swing off the road and injure Mac. Not badly, just enough to put him in hospital. But that she knew would accomplish nothing, merely postpone it. The contract said thirty . . . he had two to go.

Her thoughts flashed to Harry out in the sweating hell of Burma – The Forgotten Army – the Press called it. He was

143

a sweet person but she had no love for him, only for this dark-haired bomb-aimer with the smiling lips and the wicked eyes. She sat down and poured herself a Scotch. She started as a knot exploded in the fireplace logs and spewed a shower of sparks onto the hearth. A clouded look came over her face as she emptied the glass.

The target was again Berlin and one hundred and forty lips making up the crews of the twenty Halifaxes of 187 who were to take part in the action parted in loud groans, as the curtain covering the wall map was drawn aside.

The pilots, navigators and bomb-aimers had already been given the target at the navigational briefing and now the entire crews assembled for the main briefing were equally shocked.

Sergeant Hartley, Q-Queenie's bomb-aimer, sorrowfully shook his head. "Je-sus Christ! 'Butch' is determined to kill us."

Sergeant "Dusty" Miller, his wireless-operator, grunted. "There'll be a bloody high "chop" rate tonight. You see."

"Aw shuttup! You're a bloody prophet of gloom," snapped their engineer, Sergeant Phil Batten.

A target is seldom received with elation and the nervous reaction which followed Wing Commander Brewis's disclosure triggered more than a few nervous titters at the forced jokes which greeted it.

Once in the air that nervousness would vanish for each man had a precise job to do. But for the moment it was apprehension. Most of them had struck at Berlin a few nights earlier, and many nights before. They had no illusions about what lay ahead.

Brewis outlined the mode of attack and the general tactics to be used. The Lancasters would be carrying a bomb-load of 10,000lbs. a 4,000lb "Cookie" H.E. and 6,000lbs. of incendiaries. The Halifaxes, because of the higher petrol consumption of their radial engines, about 3,000lbs. less. Weather conditions, they were told, would be bad, as they invariably had been during the entire Battle of Britain. "Skymarking" techniques would be used – the bombers releasing their loads on floating flares dropped by the Pathfinders above the cloud.

At 1900 hours the canvas topped lorries took them to the flight bays. As Mitchell's crew got out at the S-Bay, Holton said to Mackay, "You look a bit tired Mac. Looks as if you didn't get any sleep last night.

The Scot scowled and said laconically. "I'll have a nap over the target, Jack. You can drop them on H2S."

Holton snorted. "My, we're getting touchy."

Group Captain Havilland, as was his custom, drove down the main runway, parked and watched the Squadron take-off. The big black Halifaxes roared down the runway in half-minute intervals. There had been no last minute hitches and he'd be able to confirm a Maximum Effort.

Dusk and the drizzling rain quickly hid Merton Wold from the climbing bombers. One by one their navigation lights were switched off as they made course for their rendezvous far out to sea with the rest of Harris's heavies.

As S-Sugar wheeled over the village Mackay thought for a fleeting moment, of the fire-side calm and bar-room warmth of the Swan and the brown haired girl whose bed he had slept in the previous night. He remembered the look in her pale, beautiful face when he'd reminded her he had more to do. He found his hand trembling slightly. He turned to the H2S set and switched it on, unaware that the impulses he had just released were immediately picked up by the powerful German Freya along with the impulses from the other radar bombers.

Police Constable Fulton, lounging beside the log-fire in

the taproom of the Swan, sipped the first of his evening's pints as the muffled sound of the bombers came to him. Swiftly it rode on the air currents and rose to a thundering crescendo of ear-shattering noise.

He watched the girl behind the bar frantically polishing a thin pint glass. It slipped from her fingers and smashed on the stone floor. May, he thought, was unusually nervous tonight.

The supreme command control at Treuenbrietzen had decided when the bombers made their third course change, north west of Magdeburg, that their ultimate target must again be Berlin. The night-fighter Staffels from Oldenburg, Twente, Quakenbrück, Langensalza and Vechta were already airborne with orders to circle radio beacons Marie, south east of Bremen, radio beacon Philipp, south west of Hanover, and radio beacon Ludwig, near Osnabruck.

Now he snapped the order for the five Gruppes' of the crack 1st Jagddivision at Doberitz to take off. These squadrons stationed at Stendal, Parchim, Brandis, Erfurt and Powunden were the back-bone of the Berlin night-fighter defences. They screamed down the runways in ten second intervals their radio frequencies tuned to the beacons they'd been allocated to circle.

A few miles north of Magdeburg A-Able's mid-upper gunner, Sergeant Groves, reported "Flak star'd-bow level!"

"Flak port-bow high," bomb-aimer Green in the nose reported.

"Then we're dead on E.T.A.," navigator Stacey said.

Brewis rolled the Halifax in a gentle weave from port to starboard to give his gunners maximum vision.

"Course for target coming up," said Stacey. "Course 075

compass. Reduce speed to 180 Indicated."

"Is that early or a bit late?" Brewis asked.

"Bang on time," Stacey answered.

Ahead of them the sky erupted as the heavy 8cm ground guns belched their shells into the aerial box the bombers would have to fly through.

Flashes of light scattered death in thousands of lethal splinters of white-hot bolts. Here and there they burst in threes – triangles of terror – for each cluster represented predicted radar controlled fire.

A fiery cross blossomed ahead of them outlining the Halifax that formed it. To port, and below them, another bomber exploded in a dazzling cascade of technicoloured light.

Brewis watched the flak drifting all around him with detachment for there was nothing he could do about it. He'd bombed Berlin many times but each time he thought the flak got heavier, more intense and more deadly. A streamer of flame curled lazily some hundreds of feet to his port. This time, he noted, it was a Lancaster. Then in a brilliant explosion of light it disintegrated as its bomb load erupted. The concussion rocked the Halifax and he fought the controls to keep her on an even keel.

They were still nine minutes from the city when the fighter flares floated down in dazzling waterfalls of light. More and more of them were being released, stripping the bombers of their fickle shield of darkness.

The sky was now criss-crossed with red, white and green tracer fire. The fighters were among them and Berlin seemed centuries away. The thick cloud below glowed in a dull whitish hue as powerful searchlights sought to pierce the thick cloud.

"Rear-gunner to skipper. Fighter! Star'd quarter up."

"Identify it?"

"Think it's a Ju 88 . . . 'bout five hundred yards on parallel course. Don't think he's seen us."

147

A-Able shuddered and her nose bucked as the first of the 20mm cannon shells hammered into her port wing. The rest of the cannon stream-high explosive mingled with armour piercing and incendiary shells ripped through the cockpit and the navigator's hatch.

Brewis felt a searing pain in his left side and stomach as two of the shells ripped his inards apart. In the heart-beats of time, before he collapsed over the controls, he realised the fighter the rear-gunner had seen on their starboard had purposely positioned itself so they'd be a sitting duck for its twin coming up on their port. God! with his operational experience he should have known. A great heat enveloped him soothing the intense agony wracking the lower part of his body. As he dropped into unconsciousness he had a glimpse of flames roaring along his port wing.

Seven seconds later the high octane petrol tanks blew up setting off the Halifaxes bomb-load and blowing A-Able, and its seven man crew, into eternity. The radar men in the two Ju 88s logged the kill as some fifteen miles west of Berlin.

Warrant Officer Mackay saw the Pathfinder skymarkers float down on their parachute flares to hang in the thick cloud over Berlin, two minutes before they were due to bomb.

All around him aircraft were exploding, cartwheeling in balls of fire into the night. More and more fighter flares were bursting above and on each side of the bomber stream. He'd experienced it before and knew they were being dropped by specially converted Ju 88s to make it easier for the 'free-lance' fighters to select their targets. They had a chance to see these fighters. It was the radar controlled and directed ones he worried about.

The flares were terrifying for they threw the black

floating pockmarks left by the spent A.A. shells into sharp, frightening relief – grim reminders of what they had flown through and had still to fly through.

He saw the dark shape of a Halifax, below his starboard quarter, suck in long streams of tracer before bursting into a reddish-yellow glow. A few seconds later the bomber exploded and illuminated a Lancaster on its port bow. He idly wondered if it was one of Merton Wold's. He thumbed forward the drift handle on the Mark 14. bomb-sight head and aligned the green sky-marker in his graticle sight, just a few more seconds to go.

"Bomb-doors open."

"Bomb-doors open," Mitchell repeated.

"Bombs fused and selected."

"Left! Left . . . Steady! . . . Stea–dy . . . Hold it!"

Mackay stabbed the bomb-tit as the marker touched the cross-hilt of the sword sight and S-Sugar reared as the bombs left her racks.

"Jettison Bars across!"

"Jettison toggle pulled!" Mitchell reported as he closed the bomb doors.

Tracer shells zipped under their starboard wing.

"Corkscrew star'd, Go!" The voice of Burrowes in the rear-turret was sharp, imperative.

Mitchell slammed the control column forward, jammed on right rudder and dropped the starboard wing. The Halifax twisted into a fast sickening screw to starboard. Mitchell neutralised the controls and flung her into another corkscrew – this time to port.

"Up star'd!" Burrowed ordered at the same time stabbing his firing button. The hammering of four Brownings vibrated along the fuselage. The thick cordite fumes from the .303s' seeped into the nose and penetrated their oxygen masks.

"Dive port!" Burrowes shouted.

Mitchell sent the Halifax plunging down chasing its

wingtip. Burrowes took his thumb from the firing button. "Think he's pissed off, Skip."

"Did'ja hit him?"

"Naw, but reckon I scared him a bit. They don't fuck around with alert gunners . . . only the sleepy ones and there seems to be plenty of them around tonight judging by the shoot-downs."

"Okay Chris, Good work!"

"Course for the coast coming up," Holton said.

"Thank Christ for that," an unidentified voice said over the intercom.

Flying Officer Cotton, at the controls of Q-Queenie, had just closed his bomb-doors after Hartley, his bomb-aimer, had bombed on the green 'skymarkers' when two flak bursts exploded below their port tail. The concussion flung the Halifax's fins in the air and Cotton had to wrestle with the controls as she careered in her dive. There was another flak burst, this time to starboard. Again Q-Queenie ploughed in a dive. Bombs were raining down all around them. The cloud cover over Berlin was alight with massed searchlights and murderous flak.

Cotton saw a series of violent explosions through the clouds, and thought they were the flashes of bursting 4,000lb 'cookies'. Occasionally when the cloud shifted, he saw huge red fires. On the run up he had recorded temperatures as low as minus forty-one degrees and the spreading vapour trails from aircraft ahead of him made visibility still more difficult. If only the trails were not such deadly tell-tale markers for the fighters to home on.

He fought the controls and brought the Halifax level. Q-Queenie's starboard outer had taken some shrapnel for he found that it rattled in uneven revolutions. He was not anxious to 'feather' it until they were clear of the city.

Feathering would stop the motor driving it and turn the propeller-blades so they'd cause the minimum wind-resistance but it would lose him power and that he needed now above all.

Cotton banked the Halifax in a steep diving turn away from Berlin and the galaxy of light that was a living nightmare. Below he could see 'cookies' exploding one after another in slow vivid crimson flashes. Photo-flashes were bursting at all heights as bomber cameras clicked on their theoretical aiming point. The flak was thinning out and he knew it could mean only one thing. The night-fighter staffels were among the bomber stream and the ground guns had lessened off for fear of hitting their own aircraft.

Tresland, his New Zealander navigator, computed their next course and wrote it on a slip of paper, which he gave to the wireless operator to hand to him.

All around them were air-to-air combats with some of the bomber gunners, he suspected, firing on anything that was near them, whether bomber or fighter. Now and then Q-Queenie leapt alarmingly as it bounced on slipstreams of aircraft ahead. Flashes and explosions continued to surround them and they could smell flak in the smoke-saturated clouds they were in.

"Hell!" Cotton swore softly. There was a danger of icing in the cloud. He pulled up the Halifax's nose, pushed forward the throttles and started to climb clear of it. He was out of the cloud but back in a sky that was liquid lightning pock marked with spent A.A. shells.

"Corkscrew port! For Chri'sake Go!" Orly in the rear-turret screamed.

In the split second it took Cotton to throw the Halifax into the dive his eyes flicked upwards and he saw the air space they'd just fallen from criss-crossed with cannon trace.

"Up port!"

The sickly throat tickling cordite filled the fuselage as

Orly thumbed his turret in a three second burst.

"Dive starb'd!"

Cotton dropped the Halifax's nose and stood her on its starboard wing-tip before falling in a stomach twisting screw. His tactics made it difficult for either fighter or bomber gunner alike to align their sights.

As he brought the bomber out of the dive, Cotton called the wireless operator. "What in hell have we got Fishpond for? Have you forgotten it'll pick up fighters or aren't you working the bloody set?"

The sharp tone of his voice lanced through Miller. In the excitement and tension of the bombing run he must have switched the set off. He flushed under his oxygen mask and hurriedly twiddled with the 'radar-eye' knobs. As the set came on he dimmed down the brilliance.

"No trace, so far, skipper . . . hold it! There's a blip coming in fast on the port quarter . . . by its speed it must be a fighter . . . WOP to rear-gunner . . . align your guns seven o'clock port."

Orly dextrously swung the turret to the angle he had been given, his thumbs resting lightly on the firing buttons. The wavy lines of the contact he had picked up embraced both sides of Miller's screen, indicating that a confrontation was imminent. One mistake by him, or by the rear-gunner now, and they'd be fiery splinters in the night sky. Miller began to sweat profusely. He felt it run from his brow in icy trickles into his mask and on to his lips.

"I see it . . . I see it . . ." Simultaneously with Orly's shout came the rattle of his Brownings as he directed a long point-blank stream of fire at the fighter.

"He's on fire! Going down to port!" Orly shouted.

Cotton banked the bomber to port and Hopkins in the mid-upper turret shouted. "I see it . . . he's in flames."

"Good work," Cotton said. "But keep alert. I don't like the sound coming from the starb'd outer. I'm going to feather it."

The starboard outer spluttered, coughed and gradually the airscrew stopped turning.

"Navigator?"

"Yes, Skip.?"

"I'm going to dive a bit to off-set the power we've lost. Then give me a course for the coast. We're going to cut some corners. It'll mean crossing a bit lower than the flight plan but we'll make it with any luck . . . and we've had it with us so far."

They flew on in silence. Then Hartley in the nose announced. "Flak ahead . . . mostly light stuff."

"Yeah, I see it." Cotton said.

"That's the coast," Tresland said. "Swing three degrees starb'd. That should take us clear. Fair dinkum?"

"Roger-out!"

The flak from the light, more manoeuvrable, coastal guns – effective up to twelve thousand feet – curled towards them in lazy streams then flashed past them with the speed of light. It was well to their port. Cotton shoved the control column forward. The Halifax hurtled over the coast . . . while the gunners watched the vivid pyrotechnic display of streaking lights now well behind them.

Their elation was short lived. Orly in the rear-turret saw the cones of light flak converge in a fiery triangle. There was a vivid explosion that could only mean a homeward bound bomber.

"Some poor bastard's copped it right on the coast," he said.

There were barely a half-dozen people in the Swan when May opened for the lunch-time session and by 12.30 p.m. they had dwindled to three. They were all locals – not a blue uniform in sight. Fulton came in fifteen minutes later and ordered his usual pint.

He took a long draught from it, brushed his thick lips

with the back of his hand. "Hear they took a real pasting last night."

"It's not been on the news yet. How do you know?" May said anxiously.

"I dunno 'bout the over-all losses but four from the squadron are missing. Transport driver from station tol' me when he stopped at the general stores. Anyway the hospital ambulances were called out."

May glanced at the clock and saw it was three minutes to one. She turned on the radio on the shelf behind the bar. Usually she didn't drink at lunchtime, except perhaps for the odd shandy. She felt she badly needed a drink to brace herself for the one o'clock B.B.C. News bulletin. But she didn't want Fulton to see it. To hell with him, she decided, and poured herself a Scotch.

Fulton frowned. "Bit early for that ain't it."

"Mr. Fulton, I don't comment on what you drink. So do you mind?" Her tone was icy.

The one o'clock pips came over and then the detached, unemotional, stereotyped voice of the announcer: "Last night Bomber Command were out in force. In a heavy raid on Berlin, the second so far this week, Lancasters and Halifaxes dropped over 2,500 tons of bombs on the German capital's vital war factories. Big fires were seen raging and crews reported a number of huge explosions. The railway marshalling yard was badly damaged . . . Seventy-three of our bombers are missing."

May slowly drained what was left in her glass and went into the kitchen. She found herself shaking and sat down in a chair with her head in her hands. When she got herself together she'd force herself to telephone the station . . . that is if they were accepting calls. God! with a loss like that they couldn't go out again tonight. She remembered it was only five short of the losses the Command had when they attacked Leipzig, towards the end of February. But 73 Halifaxes and Lancasters – 511 highly skilled aircrew for the delivery of 2,500 bombs. Her shoulders shook . . . it was too costly . . . not worth it . . . it couldn't ever be worth it.

Unknown to the landlady of the Swan, in her remote Yorkshire hamlet, the Chiefs of R.A.F. Bomber Command were at that moment carrying out their own analysis and agonising appraisal of the previous night's losses. They found that like the equally disastrous Leipzig operation night-fighters had accounted for nearly all the bombers lost. It was also not lost on Air Chief Marshal Harris that the extent to which the fighters were committed to the defence of Northern Germany was clearly indicated by the interception plot which showed little activity on the southern route which was followed by part of the surviving force on the way back.

Before the top brass of Bomber Command H.Q. in High Wycombe that day was also a memorandum from the Director of Science at the Air Ministry. This stressed the difficulty of evading the German night fighter forces when routes over Northern Germany were followed by Bomber Command. These factors were considered, weighed and the decision made. Bomber Command was not only to change its tactics but also its strategy – the attacks on Berlin must be broken off.

Now the Command was to concentrate the greater proportion of its effort against cities and towns in the Southern part of Germany. High Wycombe decided also to reduce severely the number of route markers dropped. For they found they not only served as a course guide to the bombers but to the German night-fighters as well.

One plan put forward was for the attacks to be divided into two waves which would approach the target by different routes and strike at different times. And a much greater effort was to be thrown into diversionary operations to fox the enemy controllers as to the main attack.

But to the Bomber Groups, and thence down to the Squadrons, the teleprinter message that day was . . ."Stand Down."

Chapter Ten

The snow was falling steadily on the village of Feissendorf when Arnold tuned his radio to the news. Beside him relaxed and happy in front of the log fire, drinking mulled wine, sat Ilona and Werner.

The German news gave a longer and more detailed account of the raid on the capital and claimed that over eighty-five of the Terrorfliegers had been shot down – but they had included known 'ditchings' in the sea which were never disclosed in the Air Ministry bulletins. The R.A.F. contended they knew where these bombers had gone down and were therefore technically 'not missing'. They were influenced also by the forlorn hope that these crews might yet be picked up by the Air Sea Rescue launches.

Ilona smiled at Werner. "Mein Liebling! How happy I am that you were not flying."

He leaned forward and kissed her. "And I'm happy you're out of Berlin and won't have to go back. It'll be quieter here. You'll be bored to death."

"Nein, nein, never when you're with me, liebling." she said.

Arnold tuned into some music. "So, you're getting married by special licence this afternoon?"

Ilona nodded. "All the papers are in order. We could've been this morning if we liked but . . ."

Werner laughed. "But she wanted time to think it over."

She teasingly pulled his hair. "I wanted you to come along as one of the witnesses. Better than strangers from the bureau office. Besides the twins are coming."

Her eyes became serious. "There's one sorrow. When you were out Werner telephoned Mainz-Finthen — his new station — to see if he could have his posting leave extended by a few days." She wrinkled her nose. "Schwein! They told him that with the intensity of the British air attacks he was lucky in getting any time at all off . . . they want him back by Monday at the latest. That gives us just a three day honey-moon."

"Two days, Mein Liebchen!"

She looked up startled and he said, "I'll never make it in time by road. The old car is likely to break down anytime. We're lucky it took us this far. There's a military aircraft leaving Nuremberg for Paris on Sunday and then on to the air-field. It's half empty. I've got a place on it."

Ilona sipped her drink. "Yes," she mused, "I'd forgotten it was so far and it would be so tiring with many of the roads snow blocked."

She was silent for a moment. "If you're going to Paris you can take Wolfgang's precious cases."

"No," he said. "I asked them but the aircraft is taking only half its passenger capacity. The rest is loaded with urgent freight. I'm only allowed an overnight bag. The rest of my things I'll send by rail. I'll freight them when we go into town later."

"With Wolfgang's?"

"No, I'll leave his cases with Arnold. Wolfgang can make his own arrangements for collecting them." He pulled on his cigarette. "I shouldn't think with the fuss he's made about them that he'd risk sending them by rail. Foreign workers on the railways are pilfering anything they can get away with. For that matter I don't think I'll chance sending my gear by rail either. I'll take it with me to the aerodrome and see if I can persuade them to load it. After all its only two cases. If not they can send them some other time."

"What are in the cases that Wolfgang values so highly?" Arnold asked.

Ilona laughed. "Knowing Wolfgang, I'd say it was loot."

Arnold shrugged. "I'll store them in the cellar."

The wedding of Werner and Ilona was austere and simple as registry weddings were in Germany or, for that matter, anywhere else in time of war. They were in and out of the civic hall in under five minutes. The twins – they found their names were Heidi and Heiti – were demurely dressed in their best frocks of white starched linen, frilled with lace. They carried little posies of white flowers in their hands. They had pleaded with their uncle earlier in the day to pick them from around the waterfall.

After the brief ceremony they handed one posy to Ilona, the other to Werner, who laughingly tucked the stem through the night-fighter clasp on his tunic. From the civic centre they drove with the twins and Arnold to the inn. Werner went back to collect the twin's mother and uncle. Their father was working and was not expected until the evening.

The twin's aunt had stayed at the inn to prepare a simple wedding meal. Arnold had broken into the last of his reserve stock of wine and had placed the bottles in buckets of snow.

Ilona's father had telephoned from Nuremberg that morning to say the train which he'd hoped to get had been delayed with some mechanical trouble and he would not arrive until the evening.

Werner arranged to drive from the village to meet him at the railway station. By eight o'clock all the guests had arrived and Walter Stroheim took his daughter and Werner aside. "One cannot get gold in Germany these days and I suppose I should've been a good patriot and handed it in for

159

the war effort. Somehow I never could." He produced a plain gold band and handed it to Werner.

"It was her mother's. She'd have liked her to have it," he said quietly. Werner took Ilona's hand and gently removed the gilded metal ring he had placed on her finger and slipped the gold in its place.

He raised her hand to his lips and kissed the ring. "Thank you, Herr Stroheim. It shall always stay there."

The old man smiled. "Now you're my good son you must call me Walter."

They danced, sang and drank to Arnold's accordion well into the night. When all the guests had gone and only Arnold and Walter were left, Ilona said. "We've had such a wonderful day."

Arnold puffed thoughtfully at his pipe. "Your father and I have not seen each other for a long time. We'll sit here awhile and talk of the old times. God give you love and concord," he said as they made their good-nights.

Two days later, on the Sunday, Werner took a long farewell from his bride and drove to the neighbouring airfield. He had arranged with Arnold to pick the car up at some convenient time. That afternoon Ilona and her father took the train to Nuremberg. They had barely two hours in the old historic Bavarian city before Ilona caught the transport to the sectional control room some forty miles north-east of Nuremberg. It was outside the town of Bamberg she later discovered.

The control room was in the centre of a wood and was a small scale copy of Treuenbrietzen. Like the Berlin 'battle-opera' room it was deep underground. Its radar masts and aerials skilfully blended with the tree tops.

As the map grid references came over their headsets the girl plotters moved the black arrows representing the bombers in well defined tracks. It was almost the same system as she'd been used to. The radar stations which controlled the fighters – usually two at a time – were marked by small blobs of yellow light.

She was told that the control room, under the master 'opera room' at Schleissheim, vectored the 1st Gruppe of Me 110s at Mainz-Finthen and the 2nd Gruppe at Echterdingen to their targets. On a wall, alongside the massive illuminated glass map, weather charts were constantly altered as the latest Met reports came in. Beside the charts was a huge oblong board which showed the state of readiness of the night-fighter squadrons and the Zahme Sau (Wild Boar) – the code-name for the three or four night-fighters which flew in close formation and were then sluiced simultaneously into the enemy bomber stream by the control room.

So Werner was probably right when he said some night she might be passing him orders. He wouldn't know the call sign of his night-fighter until he reached Mainz-Finthen but she was sure she would recognise his voice even if it was distorted by the jamming devices of the bombers. But to help her identify him he said he'd call 'waterfall' . . . now and then, if he was operating in her area. She would not dare to answer him or hint at her identity. That was rigidly forbidden. But she'd try to slip the word 'Fiss' . . . the first letters of the village in, then he would know.

Control's main radio beacon, over which the fighters would circle awaiting instructions, was code-named Otto. It was a few miles north-west of Frankfurt and near his airfield.

The young Leutnant who was showing her round pointed to a grim faced Hauptmann who was talking to the Operations Officer and said, "That's Karl Richter, the Chief Controller. You may sometimes have to relay his orders."

"Ah, the coffee is coming round. It's pretty watery but I'll get some. Excuse me."

He came back with two steaming mugs and handed one to her. "I see from your papers you were at Treuenbrietzen?" She nodded and he said, "You'll find it a lot quieter here, although we've been told that the huge losses over Berlin mean the British may switch their bombers to southern Germany . . . then we'll be in it."

Ilona sipped her coffee. "My father's a journalist in Nuremberg. He told me that at a press briefing they too were warned that towns in the South could be next."

"They're murderous brutes who don't bomb military installations but women and children. I often wish I was up there taking them down."

Ilona did not answer. The Leutnant, she considered, looked young and fit enough to fly if he really wanted.

Wolfgang was waiting for him at the airfield, on the outskirts of Paris, when his Junkers landed. They had not seen each other for close on three years and Wolfgang, he thought, was running to fat. They'd hardly exchanged greetings when his brother asked, "Did you bring the cases?" He shook his head and Wolfgang said a trifle irritably, "Berlin got another pounding the other night. My flat could well have been destroyed."

"The cases are safe. I took them with me but had to leave them with Raufft in Feissendorf. I had to fly here and they were strict on the baggage I could take. I had to beg even to get my luggage aboard."

Wolfgang looked relieved. "Good, there's a transport leaving the day after tomorrow for Nuremberg. I'll arrange now for a seat on it and go and get them."

Werner watched his brother stride to a room marked Senior Transport Officer and walk in without knocking. He shook his head. A visit from a Hauptmann in the Gestapo could well give the fellow a heart attack.

A few minutes later he came back. "It's fixed. He'll be

sent the official notification tomorrow. But I wanted to be sure of a seat."

Werner smiled thinly. "I suppose you could always have had some one thrown off had it been full."

Wolfgang laughed. "But of course." He put an arm affectionately round Werner's shoulders. "You're an ace and I'm proud of you. So you go back tomorrow?" Werner nodded. "You'll stay at my flat tonight. I'll have a car run you to the airfield. What time does your 'plane take-off?"

"0900 hours. It's the same one I came in but it's going on to Mainz-Finthen and then Loan-Athies with spares."

As they walked to the Hauptman's car, Wolfgang said. "We'll go to the flat so we can have a wash-up. Then I'll take you to an excellent place for dinner. I've a surprise laid on." He winked and Werner knowing his brother of old knew he must mean women.

"I'd better tell you I've just got married."

"Married?"

"Ilona and I were married two days ago in Feissendorf."

"Why didn't you let me know. I'd have come down."

"There was no time. I was going to tell you over the 'phone last night but we were cut off before I got to it."

"Well, well, so you've married Ilona." Wolfgang laughed. "You two were always for each other, even in school. I was surprised when she married Johan."

When Werner did not reply his brother slapped him hard on the shoulder. "She's a nice girl. I hope you'll both be very happy but is it wise for a night-fighter pilot to marry?"

Werner shrugged. "Soldiers in the trenches and men in the U-boats marry. Why not?"

"Why not," his brother echoed. He dug Werner slyly in the ribs. "Married or not you'll like where I'm taking you tonight."

"If it's women, I'm not interested."

"Don't be a bloody prude, Werner. You can at least look." As they settled in the back seat Wolfgang snapped at

163

the drive. "To my flat and let's get there a bit faster than we got here."

"Yes, Herr Hauptmann, Sir."

Wolfgang's flat was luxuriously furnished. Two big bedrooms ran off a long corridor which led to a spacious lounge and then a comfortably furnished dining-room. There was a large bathroom, equipped with shower and the inevitable bidet. Throughout the flat there was thick, almost new, carpet.

Wolfgang went into the kitchen, opened a big refrigerator which Werner could see was well stocked with champagne. He brought in two glasses and poured out the champagne. "We'll drink this and perhaps another bottle. Then you can have a bath."

Werner sipped the champagne. It was undoubtedly vintage. The last time he'd tasted champagne as good was after the fall of France.

He waved an arm round the room. "This is real luxury, Wolfgang. How do you do it?"

Wolfgang lowered his glass. "I don't take bribes if that's what you're thinking. I'm in security and things come our way. And frankly, I'd be foolish if I didn't sort of feather my nest while I can. I don't intend to be poor after this war's over. Far higher than me are . . . let's say, collecting items of value. Mostly it's from the Jews so no harm is done to anyone."

He looked thoughtful. "Most of it goes into the state coffers but some goes elsewhere. Surely you don't blame me if I take a little cut?"

"While we're on this, Wolfgang, why were you so anxious for me to bring those suitcases from Berlin? More loot?"

Wolfgang frowned. "I don't like that word. Since you're my brother I'll tell you. One suitcase is full of antique silver. Some of it very valuable. The other contains an almost priceless tapestry. I've wrapped it well in a sheet and packed it in cellophane. I hope you kept them out of the rain. I would hate the colours to run. They are rather beautiful." He laughed but there was no mirth in it.

"Where did you get them?"

Exasperation crept into Wolfgang's voice. "As I've said they were . . . er . . . collected over a number of years."

"Beginning with Asaph's silver?"

Wolfgang flushed with anger. "He was a dirty old Jew. He taught rank treason and propaganda in school. I was the only one to stand up and contradict so he took it out on me, the old bastard. He's no way different from the rest of his race. They bled us white before the war. We're merely putting the balance right and taking back our rightful heritage."

"He wasn't a bad old fellow," Werner said.

His brother scoffed. "You were always one of his favourites. I suppose you say the same . . . 'oh, they weren't bad fellows' . . . when you take down a Terrorflieger crew?"

"They've a job to do, the same as our bomber crews did over Rotterdam, Warsaw and London."

"Mein Gott! Are you becoming an Englander lover or a bloody pacifist? Such talk would be very dangerous outside this room. I warn you." Werner drained his glass and Wolfgang refilled it along with his own.

"No brother, I'm no pacifist and no lover of the Englanders. You forget our mother and my wife and child were killed in one of their raids but I try to face facts. They too are fighting for their lives, however wrong their cause."

Wolfgang took out a gold cigarette case and proferred it to his brother.

Wolfgang drew heavily on his cigarette and said, "I'd two R.A.F. men, an officer and a Sergeant, shot last week." His voice was matter of fact, as if he was commentating on the weather.

Werner jerked forward in his chair. "You had them shot? Why, man?"

"The French underground made contact with them and were passing them along their escape route to southern France, then to Spain. A collaborator tipped me. We caught them and the resistance red-handed. They attempted to shoot it out. The officer tried to pick up the gun of one of the dead resistance men. We shot him and then the other." He paused. "We fight a different war from you. It's a dirty war and there's no rules. We shall not advertise it. The British aircrew were not prisoners of war and there'll be no record of them. They evaded capture and linked up with the resistance. They were foolish men. They'd be alive now had they the sense to walk into the nearest police station and given themselves up."

"And the resistance men?"

"We took only two of them alive. They were on the verge of talking when I visited them last night. Unfortunately, the fool I left in charge of them was over-keen . . . they died this morning without regaining consciousness. It's unfortunate."

He ground out his half smoked cigarette with studied deliberation. "Major-General Josef Kurt Höwenhoff was very angry when I explained the position to him."

A cold smile creased his lips. "But I'm his blue-eyed boy. I see he gets handsome souvenirs and I see there's nothing he goes short of. He understands it was over zealousness on part of one of my subordinates. It won't affect my Colonelcy . . ." He shot a side-ways glance at Werner.

"You looked surprised. Colonel Wolfgang Franz." There was almost a purr in his voice. "Sounds good, doesn't it, brother?"

"My congratulations, Wolfgang, or are they a bit premature?"

"I shouldn't think so. I'm waiting for confirmation. The General recommended my promotion some time ago. It's only a matter of the promulgation."

He closed his eyes and massaged his forebrow. "It's not

an easy job I have. A good security officer is only as good as his er, informants. You find a good collaborator, either by coercion, bribery, or perhaps his lust for certain privileges but sooner or later they're found out by the resistance. Then we have to start again. The one who informed on the British airmen was a good one."

Wolfgang laughed. "He had to be, we had his wife and child in our care. But it is only a matter of time before the resistance find this out. He'll be a natural suspect. Enough of this. Take a bath and freshen up. Then I'll take you to a good place to eat, one of the best in Paris."

Werner reached for the half empty bottle of champagne. "Do you mind if I take this with me? I feel I need a drink."

"By all means. There's more if you want it."

The meal was the best Werner had had for years. The restaurant was packed and Werner noted it was mostly full of German officers none, as far as he could see, below the rank of Major. Most of them had strikingly beautiful women with them. Women, he thought, who were prepared to sell their bodies and risk retaliation by the underground in return for the easy life as mistresses of the conquerors.

After they had finished their brandy, Wolfgang called the waiter and to Werner's surprise just signed the bill. "The proprietor owes me some favours. It's one of his ways of repaying them," he explained. "Now I'll take you to the surprise of the evening."

The Staffelkapitan leaned forward. His voice was low and earnest. "Look Wolfgang, if this is some high class brothel you want to take me to, I'm not interested."

Wolfgang looked positively hurt. "Please Werner, you offend me with such crudeness. I doubt if the clientele of this lady's salon numbers more than eight. It's an elegant place and the champagne is very good."

They had been driving for nearly an hour when

Wolfgang ordered the driver to swing off at the next turning. The Mercedes purred along a tree-lined road which branched to the west. He slowed down as his headlights picked out two stone pillars, barely discernible in the shadows thrown by the arching trees.

The driver braked in front of heavy ornamental iron gates, embedded in the pillars. Wolfgang climbed out. Werner watched and saw that instead of pressing the push button, sunk in the right hand pillar, he fiddled with something behind the lock. He pulled out his cigarette case, lit a cigarette, and strolled back to the car. He had barely settled in his seat when the gates swung open. Werner decided they must have been electrically operated from the big house he could glimpse through the tree-lined avenue.

They parked at the rear of the heavily shuttered mansion and Wolfgang told the driver, "Get a rug from the boot and have a nap." Then winking at Werner, he added "We're likely to be some time."

"Ja, Herr Hauptmann."

As they came up the steps to the mansion a door half-opened and they stared into the saucer shaped eyes of a very pretty young girl of about twenty. Her breasts stuck out from her thin, almost transparent, green silk blouse. Her short red skirt clung tightly to her thighs.

She smiled sweetly. "Please come this way." They followed her down a long corridor to a cloak-room where she took their great-coats and then led them up a flight of stairs to another corridor leading to a room with high double doors. She knocked and opened the door. As they entered the door closed behind them and they heard the click of her heels as she retraced her steps along the marble flooring. A fat, jovial woman in her forties rose from a desk alongside one of the shuttered windows and waddled towards them. She held out her hand to Wolfgang, who clicked his heels and kissed it.

"How very nice to see you again 'Wolf'. I was beginning

to think you'd forgotten me until I got your telephone call."
She looked enquiringly at Werner. "So this is the brother
you were telling me about. He's very handsome and I see a
night-fighter."

Werner felt uncomfortable as her eyes fixed unwinkingly
upon him, sizing him up.

"This is Madame Rochelle, an old friend."

"A very old friend," she corrected and her voice was liquid honey. "Now, you must have a drink." She moved to
her desk and stabbed a button.

A few minutes later the girl, who had ushered them into
the room, came back with an ice bucket in which rested two
bottles of champagne.

She went over to one of the oak-panelled walls, opened a
panel and brought out a tray of glasses. She laid it on a
table flanked by four deep upholstered arm chairs, bowed
and left the room.

Madame Rochelle took one of the bottles from the bucket
and handed it to Wolfgang. He deftly thumbed the cork
and filled three glasses.

"To your coming promotion," she said to Wolfgang.
Werner decided the two must have known each other for
some time from the easy relationship between them and her
knowledge that he was about to be made a Colonel.

Werner raised his glass and studied Madame Rochelle.
She wore a pearl-grey dress. Her dark brown hair was
streaked with grey. Through the dim, shaded lights of the
room he could discern wrinkles round her incredibly blue
eyes.

Ten years ago, he conceded, she must have been a beauty. They drank and talked for a while and after they finished the champagne, Madame Rochelle rose and said, "I've
two new girls since you were last here. I think you'll like
them. Your usual room has been prepared."

Wolfgang shook his head. "I'm afraid we'll not be able to
stay the night. My brother has to leave in the morning and

169

I'm taking him to the airfield."

"Very early?" she asked and there was emphasis on 'early'.

"I'm afraid so."

She held out her hand and as Werner kissed it, she said, "Till we meet again, 'Wolf'."

She went over to the desk and jabbed the button. When the saucer-eyed girl came back, she said, "Shari and Marika are expecting them."

The girl took them along a narrow corridor which opened on to another double-fronted door. She closed it quietly behind them and left. The room was oval shaped with a deep pile mustard carpet. Two walls were panelled in gleaming black glass. Rose tinted lights, set in the glass, shed a warm illumination throughout. On one wall there was the outline of a life-sized nude. Two girls sat on high stools, alongside a black-glass cocktail bar at the far end of the room.

On each side of the nude was a discreetly framed door. As they moved across the room Wolfgang whispered, "Madame Rochelle is the guardian of some of the loveliest Jezebels this side of hell."

Werner looked at the girls, who turned and smiled invitingly. One was a slim, shapely girl whose dark eyes coolly observed him. Her lips were full and teasing. Her teeth perfectly white and even.

Her companion ran a hand over her loosely hanging black hair and slipped from her stool. She came towards them with a lithe, swinging panther-like movement. Fire smouldered in her brown, sloe-eyes. She lowered her long lashes and her lips parted in a soft, almost enigmatic, smile. Her lovely face expressed some of the mystery and allurement of the East. Werner was certain she was either of Burmese or Indonesian extraction. Both were dressed in diaphanous negligees which revealed much of their charms and heightened the senses by suggesting more.

The sloe-eyed girl took their arms and led them to the bar. She laughed a low, musical laugh. "I'm Shari and this is Marika. Which of you is Wolfgang?"

The Hauptman bowed. "And this is my brother, Werner. Madame Rochelle tells me you're new here."

They smiled and Marika looked directly at Wolfgang and asked, "Champagne?"

They nodded and Werner watched the intensity with which his brother was looking at Marika.

She filled four glasses. Shari seated herself beside Werner and languorously eyed him through half closed lids. With a slow, sultry smile, Marika leaned over the bar. There was a faint click of a switch. The wall lights dimmed and the shape on the black glass in front of them glowed in a rich alabaster hue.

Werner started as the full length figure of a beautifully proportioned nude appeared silhouetted against the dark glass. He gazed at it hypnotically as the illumination shone in all its shamelessness, revealing a figure of submissive beauty. But it was the downcast face of the naked figure that rooted him to his seat. His mind was speculating on whether it was the most artistic mural or the most outrageous piece of obscenity he had ever seen when he felt the pressure of Shari's fingers on his arm.

He turned as she slid noiselessly from her stool. Somehow she had slipped out of the light filmy thing she wore and, breasts thrust out, was posing proudly before them sensously slim, invitingly naked. Marika brushed against him and he heard again the click of a switch. The room was plunged into darkness. His lips were dry and he moistened them with his lips. There was another metallic snap. He swung round on the stool. The black glass glowed again as the nude reappeared. Marika had gone from the room and so had Wolfgang.

Shari came and seated herself beside him. Her negligee was now carelessly draped over her shoulders and parted to

171

reveal a smooth rounded thigh. She crossed her long, elegant legs and looked at him with a promising glance. She smiled and brushed her hair from her face. She placed her hands slowly round his neck and pulled his head down and kissed him lingeringly on the mouth. Reluctantly, he disengaged himself.

She frowned. "What is wrong, cherie? Didn't you like it?"

Before he could answer she slipped from the stool and darted through one of the doors to the side of the nude.

The lights went out. The room was in darkness once more, except for the flaming naked figure on the wall. From somewhere behind him came a slow, pulsating rhythm. Werner fumbled for his glass. The music played on his taut nerves and he felt his heart beat faster. It was the same feeling he had when he came in for a bomber 'kill'.

The music reminded him of the throbbing of jungle drums and conches. The lights came on and Shari reappeared in a white gossamery ballerina dress and a short, sleeveless brocade jacket. On her arms were elbow length black gloves. Her long, black silky hair streamed over her shoulders. Round her brow was a filmy headdress. She began to sway her body in undulating, tantalising movements that surged from her toes to her head. Slowly she raised her hands above her head and spun in a savage turn that sent her dress billowing from the waist, to reveal her naked buttocks.

The tempo of the music suddenly changed. It was louder and distinctly barbaric. Her dance became faster, primitive and lustful. Enticingly she swayed her hips, undid her jacket and tossed it carelessly into the air. Her head thrown back, her lips half-open in expectation and with her long hair flowing in wild disorder, she surrendered herself with wild abandonment to the frenzied rhythm of the music. Her stomach and buttocks undulated faster in studied sensuous circular movements. Her hands flashed down to her hips,

172

unhooked her billowing skirt and swept it from her.

She danced towards him, laughing, twisting, turning and swaying. There was a clash of cymbals, a click, and the music ended as suddenly as it had begun. With a perfect sense of timing she sank to the floor. Then with the speed of a snake, she wriggled to her feet and posed before him in challenging imitation of the nude on the wall. Wherever his staring eyes alighted, the black glass reflected every line of her lithe, exquisitely formed body . . . mocking, shameless nakedness, which tormented him with a wild ecstasy.

Her eyes were taunting him and her bold lips parted invitingly. She came up to him, pushed her body against him and her arms went tenderly round his neck.

"Have you ever seen someone dance like that?" Her eyes were earnest and her tone held a hint of challenge.

He disengaged himself from her tightening arms. 'No," he said. "That was the most sensuous dance I've ever seen."

Her eyes became soft. "Night-fighting must be very bad if it leaves a man like you . . ." she shrugged.

He took one of her hands. "You're a beautiful and tantalising woman, Shari. But it's not what you're thinking. I'm married."

"So!" The words were almost hissed.

"I was married only a few days ago and I am very much in love with my wife."

"Excuse me a moment." She went through the door she had earlier come from. A few minutes later she was back, this time with her negligee wrapped round her and tied at the waist.

She pulled the bottle from the ice-bucket and refilled their glasses. She looked at him intently. "You're a nice, man, Oberleutnant."

"Are you French?"

She smiled. "Half-and-half. My father was French, my mother Indonesian. I came to Paris shortly before the war."

He glanced at his watch. "I must leave within the hour. Could you remind the Hauptman of that?"

She handed him his drink. "Give them another half hour. I don't wish to upset him. He's a man of much influence and I like working here." She paused and her eyes looked straight at him. "There's worse things," she added.

They talked and drank for a little over half-an-hour. Then she went over to the door on the other side of the nude and knocked. He heard her whisper something.

She came back and gave a shrug of her shoulders. "He says you've plenty of time but he'll be with you shortly."

"Tell him I'll be waiting in the car." As he rose from the stool she put her arms round him and quickly kissed him. He reached into his tunic pocket but she placed her hand over it and shook her head.

"No, it's not necessary. You're a nice man."

She raised her glass and a sweet, sad look came into her eyes. "To a gentleman and a gallant night-fighter." She smiled ruefully and downed her drink. "Safe landings, Werner."

Chapter Eleven

Oberleutnant Franz arrived at Mainz-Finthen to find his crew already there. Petz had checked in two days before having completed the short course on the new Lichtenstein SN2. He was enthusiastic about its capabilities and eager to try it out on the bombers.

Kromer, their gunner, had arrived a few hours before him. Franz reported to the Staffel Commander and later that day went down to the aircraft which had been assigned to him – B1. His call sign, he was told, would be Berta One. Two other aircraft B2 and B3 would operate with him and their tactics would be Zahme Sau.

He was told that apart from the big raid on the capital, when he was on leave, there had been no other major operations by the heavies of Bomber Command. He clambered into the pilot's seat of the Me and the familiar smell of oil and petrol tickled his nostrils. For a brief moment he was glad to be back.

Then he remembered Ilona and wished he was back in the village. As he listened to his two crewmen making their pre-flight checks the fantastic dance of Shari flashed through his mind. It was a night he'd always remember. Wolfgang had flown early that morning to Nuremberg to collect his precious cases, but he doubted very much if he would get a warm welcome from Raufft. The old inn-keeper would be coldly polite. One did not cross a Hauptmann in the Gestapo, especially if you had watched him grow up.

Franz went through his cockpit drill and taxied the night-fighter on to the runway. He ran the engines at full revolutions for almost a minute and eased back the throttles. The engines seemed to be better than those in the aircraft at Parchim. He fastened his harness straps and called his crewmen. "We'll do a half hour airtest and Petz can get a little more practice with his new toy. Half-an-hour enough?"

"Ja, Herr Oberleutnant. That'll be fine," his radar man answered.

He slammed shut his side window and with his feet on the brakes opened the throttles. The fuselage shuddered and vibrated madly. He glanced expertly over his instrument panel and swiftly noted the readings. The main instruments were in different colours for speedy recognition: brown for oil, yellow for fuel and blue for air.

He scanned them again, his eyes alighting on the rev counters. They were working as they should.

He automatically went through his take-off drill. Flaps up, mags off, undercarriage locked, full fuel pitch, radiator gills closed and oxygen flowing. He had already tested the controls by waggling each control surface and was satisfied they were unlocked.

He called control. "Berta One – permission to take-off."

Control gave clearance. Werner released the brakes and smoothly pushed the throttles through the gate. The Me roard down the runway in an arrow straight take-off. He pulled up the undercarriage and climbed steadily towards the west. He checked his transponder, the instrument which enabled the ground traffic controller to identify B1 instantly on his radar screen, and saw it was functioning. The sky was grey and ashen. Below them was a brownish-greenish patchwork of fields and furrowed ground.

"Permission to test guns," Kromer said.

Werner banked to port, then to starboard and saw that the sky they were in was clear. "Go ahead!"

176

Petz thumbed the firing button of his twin-barrelled heavy machine-gun and the sweet-sour smell of cordite fumes wafted through the cockpit. He stopped firing and reported the guns were acting as they should.

"Now I'll test my guns," Werner said.

He glanced into his reflex sight and fired his two 2cm drum-fed cannon, each of which was loaded with seventy-five rounds of ammunition. A half second burst and he was satisfied they were in good order. The guns, built-in at the back of Werner were swivel guns, aligned to shoot vertically at an elevation of between eighty and eighty-five degrees and they were comparatively new to the aircraft.

Hitherto, Me 110s had been armed with two 3cm cannon. Werner knew from experience of them that they had three big drawbacks. They jammed easily and their muzzle-glare was such that they temporarily blinded the pilot and destroyed his night vision.

And their explosive power was so great that the debris from a bomber frequently endangered the night fighter. The new vertical cannon minimised that risk. It also had a low consumption rate and this allowed the pilot to attack from below and to the side of a bomber – a position from which he could seldom be seen. It was a distinct advantage and Werner reckoned a skilled night-fighter pilot could bring down five bombers with a drum of seventy-five rounds before having to reload the cannon.

Kromer, sitting in the gunner's glasshouse common to Me 110s, had the basic job of scanning the sky behind and above for signs of a sudden attack. This, experience had taught Werner and the other night-fighter crews, was the air-space from which the R.A.F.'s long-range intruder Mosquitos would be most likely to swoop on them.

Werner scrutinizing every sector of the sky in methodic sweeps saw an old Junker's transport ahead and about 1000 metres above them. He called Petz to tell him he had a 'target' to practice his radar on and was irritated when Petz

replied, "I've already been vectoring him, Herr Oberleutnant."

"Then why in hell didn't you tell me. That's what this
exercise is all about."

"Sorry, Herr Oberleutnant. I was about to alert you but
I wanted to get a bit closer."

For five minutes they played out their stalking, Petz
bringing the fighter into the 'kill' position. Werner peeled
off to port after he had made his theoretical 'shoot-down',
and swung the fighter on course for base. Light was failing
and he was anxious to get down before dusk and bathe
before dinner.

Exactly thirty minutes after taking off Werner brought
the Me down on the runway at Mainz-Finthen in a landing
that was as smooth as his earlier take-off.

Hauptmann Wolfgang Franz was not in the best of
moods when his car pulled up at Raufft's inn in Feissendorf. He had arranged before flying from Paris for a
Gestapo car to meet him at the airfield outside Nuremberg
but had found because of some misunderstanding it was not
there. He immediately got on to the local Gestapo Headquarters and after some heated exchanges, and a wait of
nearly an hour, a car arrived.

Raufft had seen him get out of the car with an overnight
bag and Wolfgang was quick to note there was no warmth
in the inn-keeper's welcoming smile. He could have been
some ordinary traveller seeking a bed for the night for all
the old man seemed to care.

The man hadn't even the courtesy to take his hold-all
from him as he entered the inn. But then, Wolfgang
reflected, Raufft had always been a dour one and at times
could even surpass the old Jew in rudeness.

He looked critically at the inn-keeper. "You were expecting me?"

"Yes, Werner told me you were coming but I didn't expect you so soon."

Wolfgang grunted. "We don't waste time in the Gestapo."

Raufft eyed him stonily. "So I see. You're a Hauptmann now."

"I shall be a Colonel by the time I get back."

"How long do you intend to stay here?"

"Tonight and tomorrow night. I'd have liked to have gone tomorrow morning but I can't get a flight back to Paris until the day after."

"I shall try and make you comfortable."

"If it's not too much trouble." There was unveiled sarcasm in the Hauptmann's voice. The inn-keeper ignored the remark and Wolfgang said, "Where are the cases Werner brought from Berlin?"

"They're in the cellar."

"I hope it's not damp there?"

"No, it's not damp but cold. I store my wine there."

"But why in the cellar?"

"It's better for the wine."

"I'm not talking about the bloody wine. I'm talking about the suitcases."

"I thought they'd be safer there in the event of an air-raid." The sarcasm in the old man's voice was lost on Wolfgang.

He shook his head and began to laugh. "Do you seriously think the English would waste valuable bombs on a place like this?"

Raufft shrugged. "Strange things happen in time of war."

Wolfgang spluttered. "The R.A.F. are not that mad. What in hell is there to bomb here? The place is so insignificant it's not even on our maps." He shook his head in utter bewilderment. "You've some wine down there?"

"I think we drank it all at the wedding. But I shall look."

179

"I'll come with you. I want to see the cases."

He followed the inn-keeper through a broken door with a glaring gap at its base, and down a short flight of stone steps.

Raufft switched on a light and walked to one of the wooden racks. He lifted some straw and took out two bottles of wine.

Wolfgang looked at him curiously. "I thought you said there was no wine left."

"I'd forgotten about these."

"Well, take them upstairs and open them. They'll be paid for."

Raufft hesitated as Wolfgang knelt over the cases and fumbled with his key ring.

He looked up sharply and arched an eye-brow. "Well?"

Raufft turned and shuffled up the steps.

A little later Wolfgang joined him in the kitchen. "I'll leave them in the basement for the present."

Raufft handed him a glass of wine. He sipped it and grimaced. "No bouquet and no body."

"Werner liked it."

"Huh, then he has no taste for good wine. It's as well I brought some good brandy with me."

He drained his glass. "Is it possible to have a bath?"

The inn-keeper shook his head. "There's no hot water."

"Surely you've got wood?" Then nodding his head towards the window, he said, "There's enough timber out there."

"It would take too long to heat."

An incredulous look came into the Hauptmann's eyes. "Well, is there any food?"

"Not much, perhaps some cheese, sausage and bread."

Wolfgang grinned crookedly but there was no humour in his smile. "Did they have that for their wedding feast?"

Raufft shook his head slowly. "It was a simple meal. They brought their own rations." His voice was blunt and toneless. Wolfgang stroked his chin in silent exasperation. It was pointless pursuing anything with the old man. He resigned himself to having to rough it for the two nights he'd be in the village. He swore lustily under his breath. He'd been glad to leave the village at the outbreak of war and he'd be even happier to leave it this time. He opened his hold-all, took out the brandy and poured himself a large drink. There was only one bright thing about his trip to Feissendorf. The contents of the suitcases were intact.

Wolfgang woke with the dawn. The old man had lit a fire in his room the previous night and he had stacked it up with logs before going to bed. The embers were still smouldering. He got up and put some more logs into the big grate and watched as they crackled before storming into a blaze. He went to the window. The sun was rising in a red-orange hue in the east spattering the sky as it crept from its sepulchre behind the vast chain of mountains.

There was a light wind he noted with strata cumulus cloud beginning to form over the peaks and down over the valleys with the promise of mist later in the day. The thaw was quickly setting in and from his window he could see the stream had swollen into a fast moving torrent of water.

He pulled on his trousers, threw his tunic over his shoulder and went downstairs where he found Raufft brewing some coffee.

The old man nodded towards a big iron pan on the stove. "There's hot water for a shave."

He grunted his thanks and took the pan upstairs. He shivered. The room was still cold although the logs were well ablaze.

After he had washed and shaved he dressed meticulously and made his way downstairs. Hell, he thought, another boring day and night here then he'd be gone. And there would be bloody hell let loose if the transport that was to take him to the airfield the following morning did not arrive in time.

As Hauptmann Wolfgang Franz sat down to a breakfast of coffee, cheese and bread the code-word Tampa clicked over the teleprinter at the Pathfinder airfield at Wyton, near Huntingdom. Bomber Command Headquarters were calling on Meteorological Flight 1409 for a report on the weather conditions in Southern Germany.

A little later a Mosquito, stripped of its guns to give it even more speed, screamed down the runway.

Air Ministry records show that the Mosquito flew as far as Aachen but comparable German sources indicated that it penetrated as far south as Leipzig. Be that as it may, the information its crew brought back was immediately transmitted to Bomber Command Headquarters.

A conference of the Command's top Meteorological experts considered the report, along with other Met data that had come in from other sources, and reported that the night would be suitable for operations from all the bomber groups. For the outward flight they predicted there would be broken cloud everywhere except in southern Germany, where it was expected to be layered.

Over Nuremberg they forecast there would be strata cumulus to 8,000 feet, with patchy cloud at 15,000 to 16,000 feet. They thought, too, that there was a chance of a crescent moon. At High Wycombe "Bomber" Harris, reading the Met reports, decided that the target for the night would be Nuremberg. The city had for some weeks been high on the list of the Cabinet's Combined Strategic Targets Committee. The ancient Bavarian capital would be the first southern German city to feel the full fury of a mass saturation attack.

His desk calendar gave the date as 30th March 1944. He

summoned a conference of his advisory staff in the big underground operations room and announced the target. Shortly after midday the master teleprinter at High Wycombe clattered out the first alert signal to Bomber Groups 1, 3, 4, 5 and 6 and also to Pathfinder Group 8. The message to the Group Commanders was in code and the accompanying order was terse: "Maximum Effort . . . All aircraft to operate."

In turn the battle order was passed from the Groups to the squadrons. All incoming and outgoing telephone calls to the outside world were blocked . . . the security curtain had fallen. Their only contact now was by teleprinter and 'scrambler' telephone with their respective Groups.

Babies could be born and parents dying but such mundane daily occurrences would have to wait until the bombers got back and the telephone black-out lifted.

At Pathfinder Headquarters the Pathfinder chief drew up, on a huge glass-covered table, a detailed flight plan for the bombers to follow. The finalised result would then be transferred to another great map which took up an entire wall. It was a typical Pathfinder flight plan, replete with 'dog-legs' – zig-zagging manoeuvres from the direct line of flight – and other tactical feints aimed at confusing the enemy and making the task of night-fighter interception as difficult as possible. Much of it was based on the meteorological findings brought back earlier by their Mosquito.

As was Pathfinder plotting custom the route was worked out backwards from the target. It was influenced by their preference to attack down-wind – past experience having proved that the tendency in a bombing attack was to 'creep back' from the aiming point or drop the bombs short of the target.

This was even more likely when the bomb-run was made into the wind. Because of the uncertainty of the weather and the likelihood of thick cloud over the city, the

Pathfinder chief decided that sky-marking techniques would be used. This, he was aware, was the least accurate of methods but the only possible one if a target was covered by cloud.

The route was sent to High Wycombe and to the utter astonishment of the Pathfinders was rejected by Bomber Command Headquarters. The route that had been decided on, they were told, would be a straight run-in with no 'zig-zags', feints or minor raids on diversionary targets. But in what the Pathfinders took to be a half-hearted bid to fox the German controllers, a small force of Halifaxes were to lay mines off Texel and in the Heligoland Bight.

In addition, they were informed, a fifty strong force of Mosquitos from No 8 (P.F.F.) Group were to attack ten other targets, mostly in the Ruhr, some of them with orders to shoot-up night-fighter airfields in the area. The Pathfinder master bomber who was to lead the attack stormed into his chief when he learned of the route and angrily warned that if the flight plan was not altered the result would be Bomber Command's biggest ever 'chop' night.

Patiently the Pathfinder chief took his Wing Commander aside and explained that he had already protested to Bomber Command H.Q. but had been over-ruled by a vote of the Group Commanders. There was nothing else to do but follow the route they had been given.

He went on to explain that the main-force commanders wanted to test their theory that the German controllers would be unlikely to believe that the bombers were in fact flying straight and true to their target.

Detailed orders of the attack tactics were transmitted to the Groups. They were informed that the duration of the raid would be from 0105 hours to 0122 hours, during which time Nuremberg was to be saturated with high explosives and incendiaries. The weather forecast given to them warned Groups 4 and 6 to expect valley fog when they returned.

Over Germany they expected a heavy, overcast sky with thick layers of cloud over the target. They were also advised they could expect large amounts of strata cumulus to 8,000 feet, with a risk of patchy medium cloud to 16,000 feet.

On 187 Squadron the mess orderlies were preparing the tables for the evening meal when the loudspeaker system blared, "Attention! . . . Attention! . . . All pilots, navigators and bomb-aimers to report to navigation briefing room at fifteen hundred hours . . . Attention! . . . All pilots . . . "

The repeat of the summons was drowned in the babble of conversation it had triggered off.

"Je-sus, bloody Christ! We're fuckin' well on again and it's Berlin for sure!" Burrowes, S-Sugar's rear-gunner, exclaimed.

Mackay drained the last of the beer from his glass and looked at Mitchell. Their eyes held and Mitchell said, "This is our last 'op'."

"Correction. It's the last 'op' of this tour," Mackay said quietly. On the way to the navigation briefing Holton whispered to Mackay, "Mac, I'd like a word with you."

They slowed down their pace to allow Mitchell to walk ahead and Mackay said, "What's up. Want a loan?"

Holton's face was drawn and intense. "I wish it was only that." He hesitated for a moment and then he blurted out. "Remember what you said the other night about a dose? I think I've got a present from that bitch. What's the symptoms? You've been around."

Mackay shook his head. "I've never had it. But I've known one or two who got it and they told me that if it's 'gon' you feel a sharp pain when you piss."

Holton paled. "I've felt it for a couple of days. Each time I urinate it gets worse."

Mackay knew that it was superfluous for he'd have known if his navigator had been with another girl. Yet he asked, "Sure you haven't been with anyone else?"

"No one. I swear."

Holton stopped and said firmly, "I'm going to the Doc, now."

"No," Mackay said firmly. "Don't be a fool. Wait until tomorrow. If you go now, you'll be whipped off for tests. After tonight we're finished. You don't want to come back in a few months time and have to fly as a spare with some 'sprog' crew to complete your tour. You might even have to start the lot again."

"You think they'd do that?" Holton's tone was sheathed in anxiety.

"Listen," Mackay said, "My advice is good. Finish this tour. Then report tomorrow. You've nothing to lose."

"Supposing we don't get back?"

Mackay laughed. "Then you've nothing to worry about, have you?"

"I didn't mean it like that. I mean supposing we have to bale out. Then what."

The Scot grinned. "Don't think it's a disease peculiar to the British. The Krauts get it too and their medicos are pretty good. They'll probably laugh their heads off at you descending on their hospital with a 'brolly' above you. But they won't charge you."

Holton grinned sheepishly. "I dunno Mac, but you make me feel better."

The Scot placed an arm round his navigator's shoulders. "Stop worrying about it."

"Mac!"

"Yeah!"

"You were right. She's a cow. I should've listened to you from the start. I'm sorry for what I used to say."

"Forget it."

They joined Mitchell in the briefing room. He seemed oblivious to the fact that they had not come in with him. As always the tension was electric and tense enough to send nerves already raw from the previous Berlin operations tingling with knife-edge apprehension.

It was always like that, Mackay thought, as he lit a cigarette. He mused that they had the advantage of knowing where they were going before the rest of the crew. For the navigation briefing always preceeded the main briefing so that the navigators and bomb-aimers could work on their charts and have everything ready. He looked round the huge Nissen hut. There was a sea of blue splashed with the heavy white woollen polo neck sweaters the crews wore under their battle-dress tunics.

They were getting younger, he decided, but their faces were prematurely old. Some were so boyish looking that they must have come straight from school as, he knew, many of them did. It was the same sort of youth, he supposed, that were slaughtered so needlessly on the Somme and the other vast killing grounds of World War 1. He saw faces he had not seen before. They must be the new crews, the replacements for those who had not come back from the Berlin raids. They looked lost and utterly bewildered as he had done that first day on the squadron.

The veterans had long since trained themselves to show the minimum of emotion. Christ! he thought, Q-Queenie and themselves were the last of the originals. He knew the squadron always betted on which of the 'finalists' would come through. He wondered what odds they had placed on themselves. They'd not yet had a replacement for Wing Commander Brewis. His role had been temporarily taken over by Squadron Leader Roberts who had been posted to them only a few weeks ago. Roberts had spent most of the war instructing in Canada and was honest enough to have admitted once to Mackay that his posting to the Squadron was the worst news he'd ever had.

But he was putting on a brave show. He jerked the cord attached to the curtain concealing the wall map. It slid easily across. Sixty pairs of eyes slanted towards Berlin and slanted away as they realised that the thick black cotton marking the route was going southwards not eastwards.

From the wooden bench behind them, Cotton said in his Yankee drawl, "Gee, say can you make out from here where we're going?"

His navigator's answer was swept away when the Squadron Leader's voice rose above the babble of conversation. "Okay chaps, settle down and listen. The target tonight is Nuremberg. It'll be a change from Berlin and we're going to flatten the city with eight hundred bombers."

"Jesus Christ!" Mitchell exclaimed, "That's a long way down. It could be bloody sticky."

Around them there were some curses but most of the crews were silent. There was nothing they could do about it. That was why they wore wings. And tonight, like other nights before, they would race in the sky with the reaper.

The Squadron-Leader cleared his throat. "A small force of Halifaxes will be on a 'gardening' operation off the Heligoland Bight and Mosquitos will be shooting up some of the night fighter fields. So if you see anything twin-engined be a bit careful. It could be one of ours."

"Fuck that," said Mackay. "If anything with twin engines sniffs around us . . . he gets it. A hundred to one it'll be a fighter."

The Squadron-Leader turned to the map and pointed with a billiard cue at the route. "It will be a straight run in, with no 'zig-zagging' or feints and . . . "

An angry, disgruntled murmur that rapidly swelled in pitch rolled through the briefing room.

"What fuckin' chairborne genius thought that one up?" an Australian at the back shouted.

"Take it easy lads," the Squadron Leader said. "It should be a lot easier than Berlin or Leipzig and the Hun is unlikely to think we've switched from the Big City. Now, let's get on. You'll be carrying a full bomb-load of four 1,000lb high explosive and between 2,000lb and 3,000lb of incendiaries. The Lancs will be carrying one 4,000lb high explosive 'cookie' and between 5,000lb and 6,000lb of incendiaries. The incendiaries will be made up of 32lb oil-bombs and caskets of stick incendiaries." He went on to tell them that the duration of the entire attack was planned to be from 0105 hours to 0122 hours, with the main onslaught between 0110 hours and 0122 hours. Zero hour for the main force was to be 0110 hours. But five minutes before that, twenty-four Pathfinder Lancasters – their bomb-aimers using H2S – were to release target illuminators.

Following them would be a sixty-seven strong wave of supporters, who would spray Nuremberg with more target indicators. Backers-up would continue exposing the target with more illuminators from 0109 hours to 0122 hours.

The Squadron-Leader went on to say, that Nuremberg was an important city with a population of around 350,000. In this centre of general and electrical engineering was the famous M.A.N. works, which produced land armaments ranging from heavy tanks and armoured cars to Diesel engines."

Mitchell nudged Mackay. "He's going well beyond the usual navigation briefing. We usually get this 'crap' at the main briefing."

Mackay nodded. "He's new to the job and obviously wants to tell us everything he knows."

The Squadron Leader turned towards the station's navigation officer, who was standing on the platform beside him. "Bill, here, will put you in the picture on the Nav side."

The navigation officer, a round faced, stocky man with the D.F.C. on his tunic, began talking. "The turning points are listed separately on this," he tapped with his billiard cue a white piece of paper pinned below the map and went on, "but I'll run through them swiftly."

He paused. "A word to the bomb-aimers. The forecast wind speed is sixty miles per hour at 21,000 feet over the target in direction 280 degrees so you'll have to be snappy and pilots, you can expect the wind speed to increase to seventy miles per hour over the French coast on the way back. Visibility is likely to deteriorate on the homeward trip so you'd better waste no time."

He scanned the intent faces below him and went on: "Before the main force reaches Nuremberg, a small force of Mosquitos will make a feint attack on Cologne between 2355 hours and 0007 hours. And a second force of twenty Mosquitos will drop spoof fighter flares, 'window' and also target indicators on Kassel between 0026 hours and 0028 hours. It is hoped this'll confuse the Germans into thinking we're after somewhere in the Ruhr and so lead them to order the bulk of their fighters there. That's about all. Any questions?"

"What's the chance of a 'scrub'?"

The Navigation officer smiled thinly. "The weather's bad but I wouldn't hold out any hopes of the operation being cancelled. Right, if there's no more queries get to work on your charts. See you at main briefing."

"It's a bloody long way down," Mitchell repeated as he watched Holton and Mackay get to work on their charts.

Holton laid down his dividers. "With winds like that behind us – providing the forecasts are correct – we could hurtle down on Nuremberg with throttles wide. Our speeds would baffle the flak batteries and amaze the night-fighters."

Mitchell said, "We'll have to keep to the speeds laid down otherwise we'll be a lone 'blip' ahead of the rest and easy to be picked off."

They finished their pre-flight charts and tumbled out of the briefing-room to find that the rest of their crew were disconsolately waiting for them in the drizzling rain.

Mitchell felt a great sympathy for them. They'd never bothered before to wait outside the navigational hut knowing that it was strictly forbidden for pilots, navigators and bomb-aimers to divulge to anyone what the target was until it was generally announced at the main briefing. But this was their last trip and curiosity burned in their eyes.

At last Smythe, their engineer, could no longer contain his apprehension. "It's Berlin again, isn't it?"

"You know bloody well we can't tell you," Holton said irritably.

"The flights say it's a full fuel load, so it must be deep," Davis, their mid-upper, chipped in.

Mackay looked at Mitchell and their eyes locked knowingly. "Since this is our last 'op' . . . " Mitchell corrected himself . . . "the last of the tour, I'll tell you but swear you'll pass it on to NO ONE." He deliberately emphasised 'no one'.

"We swear," they said in almost one voice.

"It's Nuremberg."

"Christ where's that?" Burrowes ejaculated.

"It's a helluva long way, in the southern tip of Germany Bavaria," Mitchell said.

"Holy Mary! That's further than Leipzig, and look at the 'chop' rate we had there," Parke said.

"Not to worry. We'll get there and we'll fuckin' well get back too," Mackay said with a confidence which belied his inner feelings. Oh, Christ! he told himself, why give us an unknown like this with an arrow straight course from Charleroi in Belgium until we hit our only turning point at Fulda north-east of Frankfurt. Not until then would they swing on to a south-easterly heading for the bomb-run on Nuremberg. Nearly 250 miles of dead straight flying. He had already written off the 'gardening' division. There would be too big a difference in the blips the enemy radar would pick up. Too startling a gap in the span between the two forces.

Mackay fumbled for his cigarettes. If the enemy controller decided the mine-laying was a 'fox' and sent his Ruhr night-fighter force airborne they'd be intercepted on the turn at Charleroi.

As they walked to the mess they could see the petrol bowsers and the bomb-trolleys roll laboriously towards the dispersal bays of the Halifaxes. None of them said it but they knew deep in their hearts there'd be no 'scrub' to the night's operations. Their appointment with the Luftwaffe was on.

Chapter Twelve

The giant German Freya sets, their huge bowls constantly scanning the eastern coast of England, from the Wash to Harwich, flashed the first alert of intense enemy air activity off the Naze. The shorter range Würzburg detected it some time later. The Freya with twice the range of the Würzburgs invariably made the first contacts. The Würzburgs with their thinner but more accurate beams, were used to direct the night-fighter near enough to the bomber until its radar man could pick it up and vector his pilot to it.

The normal drill was for the night-fighters to work in pairs. Fighter No 1 being directed by the Würzburg operators while Fighter No 2 circled the radio beacon assigned to it until the first made contact. Then the second fighter was taken over by the Würzburg. Once the fighter picked up the bomber, with its own radar eye, it would fly slightly lower to it so that the enemy was silhouetted against the upper starlight. On visually identifying a bomber the fighter would stay below it, either to port or starboard, and fire into its wings setting the petrol tanks ablaze. Then it would dive sharply to avoid the tremendous concussion of the exploding bomb-load. Their range on a dark night could be anything from one hundred to one hundred and fifty metres. On a bright night it might be more than two hundred metres.

The Freya and Würzburg radar formed a strategic listening arc from northern France, through Belgium and Holland, tailing eastwards across Denmark and Germany. Those in Holland and Belgium began to report enemy jamming.

At Treuenbrietzen the controller studied the radar reports on the force of Halifaxes approaching the Heligoland Bight. It could well be Berlin again, he considered. There had been no let-up on the attacks on the capital and there was no reason, apart from their huge losses, for the British to switch suddenly elsewhere.

One of the Luftwaffenhelferinnen auxiliaries handed him a teleprinter flash . . . "Mosquitos making low level attacks on night-fighter airfields in Holland."

He called for the latest Met reports and read them rapidly. They forecast a clear, starlit night with a quarter moon. There was a promise too that very soon the moonlight would get brighter. Ideal conditions for hunting the Terrorfliegers, he mused.

More reports from the Freya and Würzburgs were handed to him reporting that a heavy force of bombers were nearing the coast on a heading which would take them over Bruges. He hesitated no longer. His staffels would intercept the bombers as they came in. The sky was clear of cloud from the coast inwards, and his pilots – once they were vectored into the bomber stream – would have ample opportunities of visually making contact.

He dismissed the earlier Heligoland sightings as either a diversion or a mine-laying operation and gave the order for the first of his Gruppen and Staffels to take-off.

The Freya sets were now picking up the impulses from the bombers Gee and H2S radar in a steady and constant stream. It confirmed to the controllers that a massive air attack was being mounted by the British Air Chief Marshal. Treuenbritzen sifted the latest reports and plotted the enemy bombers passing over the regions of Antwerp and Brussels to the position Luttich, Florennes, where they suddenly swung on to an easterly course. He glanced at the huge wall clock . . . 2312 hours. Fresh reports were handed to him that Mosquitos were making low level attacks over a wide area of the Ruhr. He looked into the eyes of the girl auxiliary and noted the look of undisguised admiration in her face. He read the message she handed him . . .

"Spearhead of enemy bombers has changed course at Charleroi . . . now flying sou'westerly heading . . . height 5,000 to 7,000 metres." The battle situation was still too fluid, still too confused, for him to commit himself unreservedly but everything pointed to a target in southern Germany.

His eyes critically surveyed the plot before him. It was taking a very definite shape. If the bombers held to the course they were now flying they would cross the Rhine directly over radio-beacon Ida, where the vanguard of his fighters was orbiting. To the south of Ida was radio beacon Otto, where more of his fighters were circling. He could hardly contain his excitement. It was unbelievable they were playing right into his hands. This, he assured himself, would be a massacre of Harris' heavies. They would break the bomber stream.

He turned to his deputy and ordered him to alert Schleissheim. Frankfurt . . . Würzburg . . . Mannheim . . . Karlsruhe . . . Nuremberg . . . Augsburg . . . Munich. Any one of these cities could be their objective. When they swung off he would know . . . for from past experience he knew that the R.A.F. never flew directly to their target.

In the blacked out navigation compartment of Q-Queenie, Pilot Officer Tresland laid down his protractor and snapped on his intercom.

"Nav, to Skipper. The Met forecast winds are all cock. We've an amazing ground-speed because of terrific tail winds. We'll have to dog-leg otherwise we'll be far ahead of our E.T.A. at Charleroi. First dog-leg coming up."

Cotton braced himself in the pilot's seat. He hated to dog-leg for it meant flying 60 degrees port for one minute and then swing 120 degrees back, flying two sides of an equilateral triangle, and there was always the risk of a collision.

He looked out ahead. The great pyramids of cloud through which they had been flying were fast breaking up. Before them were broken patchy formations and visibility was rapidly improving.

Warrant Officer Mackay rose from the navigation bench of S-Sugar and lumbered into the nose and cursed at what he saw. The moon was coming out and wiping away the sheltering and comforting cover of darkness. He could see without difficulty other bombers around him but what really worried him was their tell-tale vapour trails.

Ahead and below were the waving, groping arms of the searchlights. They had just made the course change at Charleroi and as they skirted clear of Aachen he searched the sky again. It was unusually bright, brighter than it had been on the Berlin raids. Hell, things didn't look good. Almost naked in that pale shimmering moonlight. He cursed the failings of the Met men.

The flak was coming up in steady, bewildering patterns of technicoloured light. Some of it was bursting in neat groups of threes and, he knew, it was predicted radar fire.

Over the intercom Sergeant Davis, in the mid-upper turret, announced in an almost petulant voice, "Combat. Star'd quarter!"

Holton cursed. They had nearly 250 miles to go and a fighter was already among them. Air-to-air tracer ripped across their port quarter. Seconds later there was a dazzling splash of fire, followed by an explosion. Another ball of fire blossomed above and ahead of them.

Mitchell switched on his intercom. "Skipper to Navigator. Log on chart two bombers going down in quick succession." The disquiet he had been feeling ever since he had seen the flight plan increased as he saw more bombers falling, fire trailing from their wings.

He stifled his unease and calmly dictated the details to his navigator. Another fiery cross hung in the sky some three hundred metres ahead. He reported it but this time said, "That'll be our last shoot-down entry. They'll know without us having to tell them how many have got it tonight because of this fuckin' stupid route."

The intercom crackled. This time it was engineer Smythe, in the astrodome. "Unidentified aircraft coming towards us port quarter."

Mitchell's hand tightened on the control column and he braced himself in his seat to throw the Halifax into a cork-screw, when he saw the massive shape of another Halifax as it zoomed over them with twenty metres clearance.

"Je-sus, that was close and it was from the squadron! I could clearly make out its marking," Davis exclaimed. Bomber Command was scattered and bewildered by the fantastic winds it had encountered and was now strewn out in a wide, vulnerable stream unprotected by concentrated 'window'. Enemy radar easily penetrated the loosely and thinly spread layers of 'window' and the deadly predicted shells crashed into the widespread 'box' they were flying. In the fifteen minutes or so after the bombers had changed course at Charleroi for the straight four-hundred-kilometre run to Fulda – their final turning point – the Command had lost twenty aircraft.

The incredibly strong winds were playing havoc with the navigation of the less experienced crews, who found themselves well off trace and easy prey for the German radar. The range-finders of the guns had little trouble in locking on to them and predicted fire took its toll of more and more bombers.

Never had the ground defences known such a night. Usually, in their duels with Harris's heavies, the gunners had only a few minutes to throw up their barrage before the concentrated pack of bombers flew out of their sector; and if they brought down two or three they were elated. But tonight it was The Kill. Halifaxes and Lancasters droned across their sights for nearly an hour, and they fell one after another to the radar accuracy of predicted fire.

Sergeant Burrowes, guided by directions from the Fishpond set Parke was working was the first to glimpse the night-fighter. "Corkscrew port!" he shouted. A staccato shudder hammered along the fuselage as he opened up with his four Brownings. Seconds later a new vibration rattled the Halifax as Davis in the mid-upper turret fired.

Mitchell had already kicked on full left rudder. Now he threw the control column forward. The heavy bomber plunged into a twisting dive as a stream of cannon fire trace flashed above, missing them by micro-seconds. Burrowes reported they had lost the fighter. Mitchell levelled out of the corkscrew and wheeled the bomber back on course for Fulda.

Oberleutnant Fpanz in Messerschmidt Berta-1 was orbiting radio beacon Otto waiting for directions from ground control. Petz, who had already tuned their radio to control, heard their call sign come over.

Franz acknowledged and the controller said, "Berta 1 to Grid O.R." He swung the night-fighter onto course, checking the map strapped to his leg and a little later saw the first of the fighter kills flare in the sky to the east. Petz had his eyes glued to the two cathode screens of the Lichtenstein SN2 radar. One gave the height and the other the bearing of the enemy aircraft. Two blips crept into the far edge of his range finder. They were about five kilometres away. He gave instructions to Franz to turn port and fly on a south-easterly course, maintaining height at 5,200 metres.

Petz adjusted his range detector knob and his eyes puckered in astonishment. One of the blips had an extraordinary look about it. It was much larger than the other contact and was moving at a fantastically high speed for a heavy bomber. He called Franz. "Two contacts. One of them's very odd. It's bigger and faster than anything I've ever picked up."

"Vector me to it," Franz replied.

"Vector Seven," Petz said.

Franz thumbed off the safety catches and set his guns to 'fire'. Petz had on rare occasions picked up enemy aircraft flying in close formation but seldom at night and then only for a few minutes. Often they had been bombers that had joined forces by chance but the strain on both engines and pilots was too great, he knew, to make the effort worthwhile.

His mysterious trace climbed sharply and its speed was such that he had difficulty in keeping up with it. "You'll have to increase speed, Herr Oberleutnant."

Franz rammed the throttles and gradually narrowed the gap.

"Vector Four . . . Five hundred and fifty metres . . . five hundred metres . . . " He broke off. The SN2 could bring a night-fighter no further.

"Vector ZERO," Petz said. It was now up to his pilot to pick it up. Petz reached for his night-glasses.

"I see it. Two Lancasters in tight formation". He eased back on the throttles and could now clearly make out the fingers of reddish-yellow light from the bombers' exhausts. Cautiously Franz brought the Me 110 under the Lancaster on his port side and manoeuvred the fighter to within fifty metres of the bomber. He lifted the Messerschmidt's nose.

He was below the bomber and could make out the egg-shaped scanner of the Lancaster's H2S radar. There was no sign that they had been seen. Juggling with his controls he aligned the port wing of the bomber in his sights. He pressed the button and the Messerschmidt shook violently as its 2 cm cannons blazed.

Flames lept from the port inner engine of the bomber and lanced along its wing. Another tulip of fire bloomed from its port outer engine. He tapped on starboard rudder and flew crabwise under the second Lancaster and raked it with his side cannon. Kromèr, their gunner, watched fascinated as the two burning bombers flew on side by side, still on their original course.

Franz positioned the night-fighter well to their starboard and out of range of the Lancaster's puny .303 guns and saw the first bomber he had attacked slip into a floppy dive to port. The second Lancaster curled to starboard. They crashed north and south of the Rhine with mighty explosions. Cascades of red and green target indicators showered from their wreckage.

Franz was highly elated. "That's two Pathfinders we've downed. We must be in the spearhead of the Terrorfliegers." Franz called his controller and reported the 'shoot-downs' and the courses the Pathfinders had been flying.

Control came faintly through the static and the jamming by the bombers. He had difficulty in hearing. "Achtung: Order proceed Argel Two – Band three."

He acknowledged and told his radar man that they were being taken under the control of Schleissheim's number two control. There would be less jamming and the wave-length would be clearer for they were nearly out of range of their original controller who was anxious to pass them on and take over the other fighters circling the Otto beacon now they knew the heading of the bombers. He set the new course and tapped on rudder swinging the Messerschmidt into a turning climb.

The flak burst hit Q-Queenie under the port wing some minutes before they reached the final turning point at Fulda for the bomb-run on Nuremberg. The Halifax bucked like an unbroken horse. Its nose dropped in a sickening motion which twisted their stomachs. Sergeant Hartley felt the shrapnel burn into his left thigh and side as he was hurled against the H2S set.

Cotton recovered fast from the initial shock of being hit and brought the bomber from its dive. A banner of flame fanned from the port inner engine now whining like a wounded buffalo. Quickly he feathered it and gasped with relief when the airscrew lazily whirled to a stop. The fire had no time to get a hold. The howling wind that had been battering them and playing havoc with their navigation now snarled in their favour. The feathering doused the fire in the stricken engine.

He was about to call his crew to report damage and casualties when Orly in the rear-turret screamed, "Corkscrew, star'd."

Simultaneously with his order a burst of cannon and heavy machine gun fire punched along the rear fuselage. Cotton flung the bomber into a blood-draining screw to the right, then twisted it into a dive to the left.

He tested the controls. They were still firm although the trim was ragged. "Okay, Skip. Think we've lost him."

Cotton called his crew. He did it methodically asking each one if he'd been hit.

Hartley reported he had and from the pain in his voice they knew his wounds were serious. They had all answered except the mid-upper. He called him again.

But Hopkins would never again hear his voice called on the intercom. Two cannon shells had hit him where his

201

neck joined his shoulders practically decapitating him.

Batten, the engineer, thought it was only the padded head-rest of his Mae West that kept his dangling head from falling off as he dragged him from the turret.

The warm blood of the dead gunner oozed over his battle-dress, staining the orange coloured life jacket with splotches of dark red as he lowered him to the fuselage floor. Oil, from the hydraulics of the shattered turret, had mingled with the blood on the gunner's mangled face giving him a grotesque appearance.

Batten plugged his intercom to one of the spare sockets in the body of the Halifax and leaned heavily against one of the spars. He felt shocked and sick. His heart thumped madly as he gulped in the oxygen.

He called Cotton. "Ted's bought it. His head's practically blown off. There's a bloody great hole in the turret and one in the fuselage where I'm standing."

"Anything else damaged?"

Batten made his inspection. He flinched as he saw the crouched form of Orly swing his turret in sweeps from port to starboard. He expected him to be dead.

"Engineer to Skipper, Mick's been damned lucky. There are holes in the fuselage behind him. The burst started just behind him and ended a couple of feet beyond the mid-upper."

"Right, come back and see what you can do for the bomb-aimer," Cotton said. The American again checked his controls and decided to push on to the target. Bomber Command's orders, he knew, were explicit. No turn backs when just one engine had gone. Anyway, Cotton mused, they'd have a better chance in the main stream than as a solitary blip wheeling on course for home. He clicked his intercom switch and called Batten. "How's Hartley?"

"He's in bad shape. I've given him some morphia and dressed his wounds. He insists on doing the bombing."

"Does he need a tourniquet on that leg?"

"Not for the moment. I'll check later." Tresland came through. "Skip, Pathfinder flares should be seen in two minutes." Hartley limped into the nose and painfully lowered himself along the bombing mat. "Target ahead . . . swing four degrees port," he said as he saw the skymarkers go down. "Right . . . stea-dy. Touch port . . . hold it." He pressed the bomb-tit and the bomber reared as it left its load. "Jettison bars across . . . close bomb-doors and let's get the hell out of here," Hartley said. Cotton wheeled the Halifax onto the homeward course. Hours later, physically and mentally exhausted, he swung Q-Queenie into orbit over Merton Wold and requested priority landing. He was not all that surprised when they told him to orbit. They had flown through fog and snow to reach base and over his R/T he heard dozens of desperate 'Mayday' calls from crippled, stricken bombers, with wounded and dead aboard. They gave Hartley another shot of morphia as they circled waiting the order to 'pancake'

It was exactly 0056 hours when Franz saw the first of the enemy's sky-markers splash in dull greenish hues in the sky to the east and he knew beyond any lingering doubt that the bombers' objective was Nuremberg.

Specially equipped aircraft, with complicated and sophisticated transmitting and receiving sets, were flying in the bomber stream, their German speaking operators confusing and infuriating the night-fighters and their controllers with false orders and countermanding instructions. It was difficult to know who was the genuine controller.

Franz then was not unduly surprised when a woman's voice came over his head-phones. 'Argel Two to Berta 1. Order-Grid C." The voice was calm, unhurried and clear. He thought it could be Ilona's. He had never heard her voice on the air and the static around could have distorted

203

it. It was worthwhile, he considered, slipping in their pre-arranged code word.

"Berta One. Acknowledge . . . waterfall."

To his immense pleasure and delight the voice answered. "Argel Two. Fizz. Steer 145."

He swung the night-fighter in a tight bank. Tonight the next 'kill' would be hers. They flew on in silence. Franz switched his oblique gun safety-catches back to 'fire' and checked his instrument panel. Petz turned from his radar and scanned, with his powerful night-glasses, the sky around him.

"Argel Two to Berta One . . . ten degrees port. Up height 800 metres." Ilona's voice, he detected, had lost some of its crispness.

Petz lowered his binoculars and turned again to the radar. He saw a blip slip onto his outer range circle.

"Contact. Steer 140 . . . eight degrees port," he ordered. Franz touched the rudder and lightly juggled the control column.

"Seven hundred metres . . . five hundred and fifty . . . five hundred . . . right a touch . . . stea . . . dy . . . up a little . . . stea-dy. You should see him."

Franz searched the sky ahead and above . . ."Got him." Pinpoints of reddish light stabbed the darkness. He nursed the Me towards the bomber's exhaust flames.

Petz rose from the radar and framed the exhausts in his night-glasses. "Lancaster! . . . Lancaster!" he said.

Franz saw the bomber was weaving gently to starboard and then to port. He edged the fighter to a position seventy metres below and to starboard of the bomber. Franz raised the nose of the night-fighter, glanced into his sight . . . eighty metres . . . sixty metres . . . fifty.

He fired a long burst and saw the bomber's starboard inner engine drag a streamer of fire. Flames lanced from its starboard outer and the Lancaster's nose.

He threw the Me 110 into a tight diving turn to starboard. The cloud below was plastered with Pathfinder flares and he reckoned he must be over Nuremberg. His eyes searched for the bomber, which he thought could well be another Pathfinder. As if reading his thoughts Petz called: "It's going down. I've seen two parachutes. One 'chute's got caught on the tail."

"Is it likely to fall on the city?" The Oberleutnant's voice was sheathed in anxiety. He knew if it was a Pathfinder and it crashed on the city, its flares would detonate and would be visible through the cloud. The other bombers would then bomb on them.

"It's maintaining height, but very slowly. Reckon it'll over-shoot the city and crash miles past it."

"Good," Franz said and began to put on the height he had lost in the attack. He reported the shoot down to control. Petz, from the light of an explosion to their port, sighted the silhouette of another four-engined aircraft. It looked to him like a Halifax.

Franz also spotted it. It was below and ahead of them. If he was not to lose the bomber there would be no time for the attack tactics he preferred, from below and to the side of his prey. This time it would have to be a more dangerous approach – a diving attack – which would expose him to the bomber's rear-gunner. He hauled the Me round and checked his fuel gauges. There was enough for one more attack but it would mean landing at an airfield near the target. There was not enough fuel to get to his own base.

He found himself sweating and a tremor of a shake went through his body. No, he'd had enough. He'd break off. He had already taken three. More than a good night's hunting. Now he was amidst the flak and it could not differentiate between enemy or foe. He wanted to get clear of it. He was about to announce he was to land when Petz said, "There's the bomber . . . ahead and below. Throttle back or you'll miss it." The voice was very, very calm.

He cursed the radar man. It was the same bomber he had

seen a few seconds earlier. He would have to go in. He again cursed Petz and his extraordinary vision with the night-glasses. "I've already seen it, Oberfeldwebel," he snapped.

"Good! It should be a sitting duck, then." Franz was not sure whether his radar man's comment was over-zealous or thinly veiled sarcasm. He decided to ignore it.

Mackay had barely given the order to close the bomb-doors after bombing on a cluster of green sky-markers when a flak burst exploded some sixty feet below and behind them throwing up the Halifax's tail and rocking them violently. They heard some of the shrapnel rattle and splatter along their rear like stones thumping on a tin roof.

Mitchell thought he heard either a shout or a groan when the shell exploded. "Skipper to bomb-aimer. Nip back Mac and see what damage that one caused."

Then he called Burrowes in the rear-turret. There was no answer. "Hear that, Mac?"

"Yeah, I'll check on him."

Mackay knew when he rotated the hand lever of the turret door to get it back into the fuselage that Burrowes was either dead or badly wounded. His head was lolling about as the bomber pitched and rolled. He hauled the rear-gunner into the fuselage and saw that a piece of shrapnel had hit the gunner below the chin, taking half his face off and penetrating his brain. Death must have been instantaneous, he considered.

"Chris has copped it. Hole in his head."

"Man the turret till we get clear of this," Mitchell ordered.

Mackay dragged the gunner into the fuselage and eased himself into the turret and cursed as his head thumped a jagged hole in the perspex roof. He settled his tall frame with difficulty into a turret built for a short, stocky body and tested the hydraulics. The turret was miraculously still functioning.

"How's things back there?" Mitchell asked.

"Bloody cramped, draughty and generally fuckin' uncomfortable but the turret's serviceable. I'm going to test the guns." He checked and found the safety catch on 'fire' and thumbed out a half second burst.

"I can bloody well hear and for once it's a heartening sound," Mitchell replied. God, how he wished this night would end. He'd seen nothing but combats and bombers exploding all around ever since the straight run from Charleroi. The Halifax bucked in the slip-stream of bombers ahead and he had to fight the controls to keep her on keel. He looked out of his side panel. Everywhere the sky was pock-marked with spent A.A. shells and the bursting camera flares of the bombers.

Mackay peered from his turret and noted there were no great fires below. He'd been on too many saturation raids not to recognise that this was an utter abortive operation. The fighters, the flak and the high speed winds had transformed what should have been a tight concentration of bombers into a wide gaggle of aircraft fifty miles across — most of them battered and crippled. It was obvious from the haphazard shape of the bombing that many were just jettisoning their loads anywhere.

"WOP to rear-gunner. Contact eleven o'clock star'd quarter." Mackay dimmed the brilliance of his graticle sight and deftly swung the turret, aligning his four Brownings on the sector. He lowered the sighting angle to the deflection he needed to spray a fighter coming from such an angle. He again scanned the quarter, blinking his eyes now and then to sharpen his night vision which had been assessed in his early training days as 'above average'.

"Blip coming closer . . . same quarter. See it yet?" Parke's voice was anxious and eager.

He was about to answer when he spotted the dim outline of the fighter's nose and wings. He ringed them in his sight, thumbed his firing button in a long burst and kept it pressed as he shouted: Corkscrew star'd, Go!" A few seconds after his burst he saw tracer flash past and heard it whipcrack for'ard. He heard a shout of "Je-sus, I've been hit," as the Halifax tilted on its wing-tip before hurtling into the dive. He tried to keep his graticle sight on the fighter. He saw that some of his tracer flashed above and below it . . . but the broken lines of the trace proved that some had gone home. He smiled faintly into his mask as it flicked over, almost on its back, before banking in a dive. He glimpsed its glowing exhausts and in the split seconds of the action identified it as an Me 110. He thought he recognised a big 'B1' stencilled on its fuselage.

Mitchell jerked convulsively in his seat as the cannon shells ripped through the cockpit tearing jagged holes in metal and perspex, showering him with splinters and panel glass. He simultaneously felt a stabbing pain in his right thigh and shoulder. He heard himself say, "Je-sus . . . I've been hit." Yet the voice didn't seem like his. The pain was more intense when he hauled the Halifax from its evasive action.

Two cannon shells smashed into the navigation hatch and three into the bomb-aimer's compartment. One tore a nine inch hole in Holton's chest, the other crashed into the H2S set, where normally Mac stood. Engineer Smythe raised himself from the floor where he had been flung during the corkscrew and made his way into the nose.

Holton was lying on his back, one knee buckled under him. His eyes were open and staring like a small boy who had just picked a lucky draw from a school sweepstake. The hole in his breast blossomed like a flaming bud, whose petals were opening, prematurely, into a widening circle of deep red.

On the other side, Smythe thought, the hole must be even

208

bigger where the shell passed through. He pulled, half dragged, the navigator into the nose and checked the damage. He turned on the Gee set and sighed with relief as it came on in a greenish glow. Satisfied he switched it off.

Stumbling into the cockpit of the still pitching and rolling aircraft he saw the blood seeping from Mitchell's shoulder. He pulled out his first-aid dressing and cut away the arm of his pilot's battle dress, ripping the seam across the shoulder. The wound was deep and the blood made it impossible to see if there were any splinters in it. He pressed the thick antiseptic gauze over it and tightly bound it with its attached strips. He tucked the torn tunic around it and refastened Mitchell's life-jacket and harness.

Mitchell smiled faintly at him and murmured into the intercom, "What a bloody, bloody night." His pilot, Smythe noticed for the first time, was holding the control column in his left hand, his right was gripped over his right thigh. Blood was oozing through his gloves, down his leg and staining the rough cloth of his battle dress trousers.

He flicked on his intercom. "Look Skip, you'll have to get that leg fixed. Better get Mac out of the turret to take over while I dress it."

"No," Mitchell said. "The rear-turret must be manned and so must Fishpond. Anyway, where the hell is the navigator. Get him to help you."

"He's very dead," Smythe said.

Sergeant Davis, in the mid-upper turret, who had been silent throughout the attack, said, "Skip, the attacks are mostly coming from below. I'll move into the rear-turret and Mac can take over from you for a spell."

Mitchell considered for a moment and winced with pain. "Okay, that seems sensible . . . Hear that Mac?"

"Nuff of the chatter. If we're to make the switch let's do it . . . Now," Mackay said.

The Scot waited in the rear-turret until he felt Davis tap his shoulder. He laboriously extricated himself from the turret and watched the five foot three mid-upper nimbly settle in behind the rear guns before making his way back to the cockpit.

He helped Smythe to get Mitchell out of the seat and slipped in. He stretched his cramped legs until they rested comfortably on the rudder pedals. He braced his back against the armour plated seat and beckoned to Smythe to fasten the harness.

Mitchell handed him his knee pad and he saw that Holton had, as was his custom, taken the precaution of working out the course for home before they made the bomb-run. Jack was a good navigator, he reflected sadly. He would fly the course until they were in range of Gee. Then Mitchell could fly it while he navigated.

Smythe had the first aid box beside him and had ripped a great tear in Mitchell's trousers. He tied another antiseptic pack over the thigh wound, pulled out the morphia tube, unscrewed the tip protecting the needle, and plunged it into his pilot's thigh above the wound.

"Christ almighty! I didn't tell you to give me a shot. I've got to fly this fuckin' aircraft."

"It's only a quarter shot. It won't put you to sleep but it'll make you a bit drowsy for a spell. Anyway, it will ease the pain. You can have another later."

Mitchell, despite his pain, grunted. "Hell, we've got a bloody quack on board."

Mackay glanced at them and over the intercom said, "For Chri'sake shut up and get 'Mitch' into the 'dickey' seat beside me. Then man the mid-upper until we get clear of this shit. It's still coming you know."

"Pass my coffee flask, I need a drink." Mitchell's voice was almost slap-happy. Mackay put it down to shock. His pilot, he knew, sometimes laced his coffee with Scotch. Mackay had already made up his mind that Mitchell would get no 'snifter'. "Your flask is shattered Mitch," he lied. "You'll get a drink from mine later." He then called Parke.

"You keeping an eye on Fishpond?" That, and the alertness of the gunners, was what he would have to depend on.

"My eyes never come off it. It's saved us once and got you a fighter," Parke said.

"No," Mackay answered. "It was you who got it. I just followed your instructions and pressed the tit. Didn't see it go down in flames although I'm certain I hit it a few times."

"We'll call it a share Mac," Parke said.

Mackay juggled the rudders and moved the control column weaving the Halifax in an undulating motion to give the gunners' a better sweep. The controls were responding. Nothing crucial seemed to have been hit. He turned and winked at Mitchell. " 'Mitch' check and estimate our fuel."

"Okay, Captain," Mitchell said mischievously, but his face was drawn and the pain from his wounds showed in it. They flew on but the ninety-mile-an-hour winds that had been behind them were now in front, cutting their previous ground speed to an alarmingly low rate. And wherever their eyes alighted the sky was splashed with flak bursts and air-to-air tracer. More and more bombers were dropping from the sky, banners of flames dragging from their wings and fuselages, as the fighters darted in among the broken stream singling out their prey.

Davis, in the rear-turret, saw a bomber on fire far behind them. It was getting lower and lower and had well over-shot the target. It might have been a trick of the shell blasted skies around them but he thought he saw a parachute caught in one of its fins. He tore his eyes from the macabre scene and swung the turret in a starboard sweep.

The raid, intended as a mighty saturation attack, had become a rout with Harris's heavies being massacred as fresh staffels of night-fighters harried them on their homeward route. Many, who had misjudged the wind speeds, jettisoned their loads as the fighters darted in hosing them with high speed cannon and then veering off to come in again with furious persistence.

The burst from S-Sugar's rear-gunner sprayed Messerschmidt Berta One as Oberleutnant Franz was ringing the Halifax in his reflex sight. Through a combination of shock and instantaneous reaction he got a three second burst off before he flicked over his right wing and went down from a slow half-roll into a dive that took him clear of the bomber's rear-turret. He had felt something pound into his right knee-cap. At the same time a great pain hammered his head. Petz sitting behind him sensed a pluck on his sleeve and found that a .303 bullet had ripped through it without grazing the flesh. Kromer behind him was not so lucky. A .303 had made a hole in the centre of his forehead.

Franz pulled out of the dive and winced as the safety straps bit hard into his shoulders. He thought he had taken another bullet somewhere in his right ribs. Cold trickles were running from his brow into his oxygen mask. He brushed them and saw blood on his glove. His left hand was weak on the control stick. Smoke was bellying out of the cowling of the starboard engine. It seeped through the bullet holes in the cockpit before the windrush from the shattered wind-screen caught it and sent it skeining away. He heard Petz say something but his brain felt light.

"Are you alright?" he shouted.

"Ja, Herr Oberleutnant, but Kromer is dead. Just one bullet but it went into his head." The voice was clinical, as an operating surgeon's. A pause and Petz said: "And you Kapitan?"

Mein Gott, Franz thought, but he's a cool one. "I've been hit, leg and head. Perhaps also in the body. Had it been cannon shells I'd be dead and so would you. I must call for an emergency landing."

"I'll come forward and see what I can do for your wounds."

"Thank you Hans." It was the first time, he reflected, he had ever addressed his radar man by his first name while airborne. Petz had a similar thought. A smile creased his lips as he moved, almost double, towards his pilot. He undid the strap of his helmet and pulled it off. There was a deep gash which ran along Franz's forehead to the crown of his head. Icy air from the holes in the vision panel whipped through Franz's hair, like a wind-storm through a corn field. Much of the blood was already congealing and Petz decided it was a glancing blow that might have scraped the bone, causing slight concussion. He pulled a first aid dressing from his tunic, ripped the protecting cellophane cover and tied it over the wound. He brushed the blood from his pilot's eyes and slipped back his helmet. He fixed the goggles firmly over the eye and was about to examine his leg when Werner said: "There's no time to lose . . . must call Argel. See where the smoke's coming from?"

"The engine cowling but there's no fire."

Fumes rose in the cockpit but with his mask on he didn't notice until it stung his eyes.

"I think a pipe's been hit. I can smell fumes."

Franz nodded. The main damage, he thought, appeared to be in the engine. Apart from a jagged groove across the starboard wing and the shattered vision panel, he saw no other visible damage. His hands and feet moved instinctively on the controls. The ailerons and tail-unit seemed undamaged. The mast and aerial looked intact.

"Berta One calling Argel Two. I'm in trouble . . emergency landing. Over."

"Argel Two to Berta One. What trouble?"

"Star'd engine smoking . . . fumes in cockpit. I'm wounded in leg, head and body . . . one dead on board."

"Check instruments," came the calm but precise order.

Franz scanned his panel. "It's an oil pipe 'Bout half pressure."

"Argel Two to Berta One . . . you're five minutes from emergency field. We don't think you'll blow up, but your engine might seize, or catch fire. Better bale out."

"No I shall land . . . please track me." He looked at Petz, who nodded.

"Your Grid position is T.A. . . . . 010-49."

Ilona Stroheim trembled as the message came over her ear-phones. A man communications officer had taken over from her after the 'specials' of Bomber Command had stopped transmitting their impersonations of the German ground controllers and she was inwardly glad. Her mouth twitched nervously. She knew she was no longer capable of relaying cool, precise, and unhurried instructions. Her eyes, wide and fearful, saw through a blurred mist of starting tears the controller consult the illuminated map. His finger stabbed at an airfield on the outskirts of their control centre. Turning to his deputy he said, "Get on to Aepbach immediately. Tell them a crippled fighter is coming in. Order two guiding searchlights to be switched on and half minute flare bursts. Order a crash tender and ambulance to stand by."

He strode over to the communications officer and took the microphone from him. His tone was crisp and authoritive. "Argel Two to Berta One . . . Steer 188 degrees . . . Aepbach four minutes ahead of you and alerted to light up. Over."

Ilona heard a voice she scarcely recognised as her husband's. It was wrapped in pain. "My red lights are flashing . . . running out of fuel."

"Have they just started?"

"Ja."

"You're too low now to risk baling out. Steer three degrees port. You should see Aepbach searchlights." Ilona felt sick and faint. By an effort of will she stopped herself from dashing over and wrestling the microphone from the controller's hand and shouting to Werner that he must live . . . mustn't burn in the landing, but her legs were leaden. The routine sounds in the control room made her dizzy and it took all her strength not to collapse. Her heart was bursting. Her head ached. Closing her eyes she abstracted herself in memories of the week before, the village and their swift but marvellous marriage. It helped brace her emotions for the tense, terrifying minutes ahead for the two flyers in the stricken fighter.

Franz banked the night-fighter and saw the beckoning arms of Aepbach's homing searchlights. A green Very light burst between them. He looked again at the altimeter. It showed eight hundred feet. Smoke was tailing out from the engine in a long black wake. It was beginning to look like smoke that could blossom into a fire-burst. He put the Messerschmidt straight down, veering in from the south-east. His undercarriage functioned at the first attempt. He was lined up well, at three hundred feet. It would have to be a dead-stick landing. Cautiously he put on a little more throttle and glanced at the altimeter . . . 150 feet. He eased back the throttles. There could be no overshooting.

He flashed over the perimeter road at one hundred feet, side-slipping a little, then flattening badly until he got the nose down and steadied. He slipped again, flattening out with forty feet to go, his speed just above stalling but the drift was taking him too far to port. Ahead was the start of the runway. A group of huts and light A.A. guns entrenchments passed under him. He put the nose down more knowing that with the delicate balance between air speed and gravity he would never lift it again on an engine that was on the verge of erupting into flame.

He saw the fire-tender moving towards the end of the runway, closely followed by an ambulance and crash-wagon. Ground crew were running from the perimeter huts. The pain was coming in sharp, racking jabs through his body. Red-hot knives seemed to lance his knee each time he put pressure on the starboard rudder pedal.

He pulled hard back on the control with his right hand. His left was practically useless and had no power in it. The wheels hit hard on the concrete before the tail-wheel settled bringing the nose up and blocking his view. He thumped on the brakes and felt them biting. At the same time the aircraft swung to the right and hit the rough grass at the edge of the runway, its wheels ploughing into a ridge of earth. One leg buckled and collapsed. He was thrown against the straps. Then his head came back hard against the head rest.

Petz freed himself from his safety harness. Quickly he leaned over Franz and unfastened his harness. Flames were now curling from the engine, their tongues licking around the cockpit. Franz felt his legs numb and had difficulty in getting his feet from the rudder-bar straps. Men were clambering over the cockpit. He felt strong arms lift him and yank him clear as the fire-tender began to hose the flames. Petz was with him in the ambulance when the fire gushed in an orange flush. The fire-tender swung away, and roared clear, as the petrol tank of the Me exploded, showering the perimeter path with blazing debris and thick choking acrid smoke. He heard Petz say, as he slipped into unconsciousness. "There're not many who could've brought it in. I knew he could. That's why I stayed with him." There was no mistaking the pride in the Oberfeldwebel's voice.

Chapter Thirteen

The heavy fire from the Nuremberg defence batteries had
long since awoken Wolfgang and Raufft. The Hauptmann
swore. He had gone to bed early so as to make an early start
in the morning for Paris. The two nights in Feissendorf had
been uncomfortable if not dowright rough. The food had
been bad and so had the wine.

He pulled on his trousers and threw his great-coat over
his shoulders. He lifted what was left of his brandy bottle
and saw it was half full. He took it with him as he made his
way downstairs to the inn's kitchen. Raufft was sitting
huddled over the stove with a blanket draped over his
shoulders.

"They're bombing Nuremberg," he said in a toneless
voice.

Wolfgang scowled. "I'm not deaf. That's what bloody
well woke me." He went to the door, opened it and stepped
out into the cold night air. There was no mistaking where
the city lay. The distant clouds were on fire and below them
he could see the toppling arms of the searchlights as they
probed the cloud layers. Now and then he could hear the
crump of bombs from aircraft which had overshot the city
by miles and were unloading at random.

He closed the door and went back to the old man crouched over the stove. Raufft got up. "Where are you going?"
queried Wolfgang.

"Into the cellar. It'll be safer. Stray bombs could fall here," he said as an afterthought.

Wolfgang was about to scoff but the uneasy feeling came to him that the inn-keeper was not being needlessly cautious. "Very well. I'll come with you." He raised the brandy bottle. "Bring a couple of glasses and some blankets." He shrugged. "We might as well be comfortable until the raid ends. It shouldn't be long."

He opened the cellar door, switched on the light, and made his way carefully down the stone steps. A few minutes later the old man joined him, carrying a bundle of blankets and two glasses. They sat down on two rough wooden stools, the blankets over their shoulders. Wolfgang poured three fingers of brandy into the glasses Raufft held out.

They were on their third glass when the sound came to them. At first they heard it as a thump-throb-thump of un-synchronised engines which, as the aircraft came nearer and lower, rose into a whining crescendo of noise.

"It's either one of our night-fighters or a bomber being chased by one," Wolfgang said confidently. But he was wrong as so often he'd been in the past. The low flying air-craft was the Lancaster that had earlier been hit by Franz. And as Franz had surmised it was a Pathfinder – like the other two he had brought down – for the Oberleutnant had unknowingly intercepted the flare-droppers. All on board were dead except for the pilot. He had been mortally wounded in the action yet half dead he was attempting to crash land. He hadn't the strength to drag himself from his seat and bale out. He had not let this be known to the two surviving crewmen he had earlier ordered to the escape hatches.

He had no proper control over his tail-unit but then he could not know that one of his crewmen was still dangling from a parachute canopy draped round his tail. His port outer engine was trailing fire. The wind had put out the blaze in his port inner.

218

The Lancaster cleared the crags at the far end of the valley and passed over the village when its pilot saw the great jagged peak before him. He hauled back on the control column but his failing strength had now gone completely. The great bomber crashed head-on between the two waterfalls. Moments later there was an even more tremendous explosion as its 4,000lb light case 'cookie' went off, detonating the incendiaries and the target indicators.

The faulty fissure in the rock face which zig-zagged from the water fall at the mouth of the mountain top lake down to the lower escarpment was torn asunder. There was a thunderous, rumbling roar as the foaming waters of the lake crashed down on the waterfalls, tossing their natural sluices aside like bobbing corks.

Like a gigantic, ever lengthening python, it snaked down on the village tearing away huge rocks and up-rooting giant trees which it swept before it. The millions of tons of water rolled at 200 feet a second down the mountain and olbiterated the picture postcard village of Feissendorf in four minutes flat.

Most of the 150 odd villagers and their children were drowned as they stumbled from their beds, awakened by the Lancaster's impact with the peak. Those who had somehow got into the narrow streets, on hearing the detonation of the bomber's load, were tossed like puppets in the surging waves of the flooded waters as they swept over the village and roared down the valley.

Among the broken, drowned bodies that were to be found later by the rescue squads were those of the twins Heidi and Heiti. The icy cold waters of the deluge caught Wolfgang and the inn-keeper as they scrambled up the cellar steps. The heavy cellar door, torn from its hinges and propelled by fifty tons of surging, bubbling water sandwiched them against the stone walls. The rescue squad which found them considered they had died from broken skulls rather than from drowning. Later, much later, the Air

Ministry identified the pilot of the Pathfinder Lancaster and gave him a posthumous award for the 'single purposefulness with which he pressed home his attack on Nuremberg'. It was not until very much later that they learned, through their intelligence agents, that it was the mountain which had had the rendezvous with the aircraft.

"Jee-sus Christ Almighty! We've just got through a snow-storm now it's flaming bloody fog," Mackay cursed as he looked out on the writhing banks of flat, grey fog stretching over southern England in an impenetrable wall. "Is there no fuckin' end to this bloody night?" No one answered. They were battle-fatigued and listless. They had crossed the enemy coast low, twelve to thirteen degrees starboard of the Flight Plan and they had been too tired, too indifferent, to take much notice of the flak coming up. The effects of their benzedrine tablets had long since gone from their bloodstreams. Flagging spirits, momentarily boosted on crossing the coast, sagged with despair, and utter disbelief, that the weather was still fighting them remorselessly.

Mackay's eyes swept to the altimeter, on to the artificial horizon and back to the air speed indicator. They flicked to the repeater compass in its rubber suspension. He altered course three degrees port.

He glanced at Mitchell in the bomb-aimer's seat beside him. His pilot appeared to have got over the initial shock of his wounds. As if intercepting his thoughts Mitchell said over the intercom: "I'll take over now so that you can 'home' on Gee."

"Sure you're in shape enough?"

"The leg's stiff and bloody painful but it'll work." With the help of the engineer he slipped into the seat vacated by Mackay. His face twisted in pain as he stretched his legs onto the rudder pedals. Mackay took a series of rapid fixes from the Gee box and plotted them on Holton's blood-stained Mercator chart.

"Alter course eight degrees port and get down to five thousand," he said. A little later he said, "Start losing height until you get down to one thou'. We should be over base in twenty-two minutes."

Mitchell called base and was surprised when it came through so quickly and clearly. Three more aircraft were in the circuit orbiting at stepped-up heights and they heard control give the order for Q-Queenie to 'pancake'.

"The Yank's made it," Mitchell said. Cotton, he reckoned, had only one more trip to do. A little later control called them to land and Mackay moved into the 'dickey' seat to work the throttles. The Halifax banked into the funnel with the altimeter reading 150 feet. The light on the glide indicator path showed amber. Mitchell shed some height and the amber changed to green.

The indicator was steady on the green as the blurred outline of the boundary hedge flashed beneath them. The main runway lights twinkled on each side of them like big blue diamonds.

"Cut!" Mackay closed the throttles. The Halifax's great undercarriage slapped heavily on the black concrete, bounced and then the wheels slapped heavily again before settling. Mitchell's feet juggled on the rudder pedals and another jolt of pain shot through his leg as he stood on the brakes. The bomber rolled to a stop.

Mitchell was rushed in the waiting ambulance to the sick-bay. Holton and Burrowes were lifted into the canvas topped 'blood-wagon', with its scrubbed wooden floor boarding, and taken to the station's mortuary where they were laid out beside four other blanket-covered bodies. One of them was Sergeant Hopkins, Q-Queenie's mid-upper gunner. Group Captain Havilland came up to them as they filed into the de-briefing room. He smiled faintly. "When

you weren't first back I began to worry. You usually are."
He paused. "I'm sorry about your navigator. Halton wasn't
it?"

"Holton," Mackay corrected and thought he detected a
slight flush on Havilland's face.

"And Mitchell?"

"He'll live," Mackay said. The Group Captain pursed
his lips. Mackay, he considered, was being his usual rude
self. He was almost insolent. He could have phrased his
answer with more deference. He looked intently at the tall,
lean Scot and thought that he had the look of the old pirate.
He would not have been surprised if Mackay had walked in
one day wearing a gold ear-ring and a black patch over an
eye. He had little respect for authority. He had sometime
back turned down a commission as his pilot had. Neither,
he reflected, were really officer material. Formality re-
quired him to ask him again before he left the station. He
hoped Mackay had not changed his mind. He didn't think
he'd be an asset to an officers mess.

He cleared his throat. "You've finished your tour now.
Have you, er, any plans?"

"Pathfinders," Mackay said.

"Any particular squadron?"

"6-7 they're the best."

The Group Captain nodded. "I'll personally recommend
the posting but before I do will you reconsider taking a
commission? As a Warrant Officer, you'd go direct to Flying Officer rank."

Mackay shook his head. "Thank you, Sir. I prefer to stay
as I am."

The Group Captain turned to the rest of the crew. "What
are your plans?"

"I'm going with Mac on Pathfinders," Parke said.

"Sure?"

"Quite sure, Sir."

"Very well." Turning to Smythe he asked, "And you?"

"I'll take my leave and then opt for instructing." The Group Captain looked at Davis. "That's my plan too, Sir." The Group Captain moved towards another crew who had come in. Many aircrew had passed through his station and there would be many more. A few a pitiful few, would complete a tour but as the weeks dragged into months their names and faces would be just dim memories, superimposed on one another.

So far four of his bombers were missing out of the twenty that had gone out. A half hour later the tally was altered to five when it was obvious that the late aircraft was well over its maximum return time and fuel endurance. Three more had made crash-landings on emergency airfields on the south coast. Five had died in the crash-landings and six had been badly injured. It was without doubt the worst mauling the squadron had ever had. He wondered what the over-all Command loss would be.

There was a brooding silence in the mess at lunch time when the B.B.C. broadcast the terse communique from the Air Ministry: Last night, aircraft of Bomber Command were over Germany in very great strength. The main objective was Nuremberg. Other aircraft attacked targets in western Germany, and mines were laid in enemy waters . . . Ninety-six of our aircraft are missing."

Mackay skipped lunch and had two large whiskies instead. He didn't feel like eating. He had seen Mitchell and Hartley off in the ambulance which was taking them to a civilian hospital for surgery. Three times the ambulances of St Mary's had made the trip to the bomber base. But before Mitchell left the senior medical officer has assured him that his pilot would be alright, although there was a fifty-fifty chance that Hartley's leg might have to be amputated.

The station transport dropped him at the Swan shortly before lunch time. May fought the impulse to dash from the bar and throw her arms around him. Instead she went on pouring two pints for a couple of aircraftmen who had come in.

"Bit rough last night, Sir," one of them said as he came up to the bar. "A bit," he said and the ice in his voice dismissed any further conversation. They took their drinks and moved over to the fire.

May poured out a large Scotch and handed it to him. "Congratulations my love, you've come through."

"Jack and Chris are dead," he said.

"Oh, God!" She turned from the bar and poured herself a drink. Some villagers came in and called for service. As she began to serve them Mackay said, "I'm going along to the newsagents. Want something to read. I won't be long."

He was coming out of the shop when he met Maggie. "I've just been on to the station and they told me about Jack. How terrible." She hesitated. "I really wanted to know if you were alright. You've finished now, haven't you?" He nodded and her voice was low and earnest. "I do love you. Have always loved you. Can you please forgive me and take me away from here. I'll do anything you say . . . don't you know you're half of me, have always been since I first met you." He moved to get past her but she caught his arm. "Please, please . . . I love you." He took her arm from his and said, "Can't you get it through your head that it's over. Finished irrevocably when you went spade digging." He pushed past her and she shouted, "I'll kill myself . . . I'll kill myself." Mackay shrugged as he walked towards the Swan. He'd heard it all before.

He was half way to the Swan when he saw Flying Officer Cotton and Sue coming towards him. "Walking during drinking hours?" he said.

The American laughed. "We missed the transport to town. We'll get the next." He glanced at his watch and then at Sue. "The jewellers will still be open."

"Jewellers?" Mackay queried.

224

"I'm gonna get an engagement ring for my future wife and there'll be a double celebration tonight."

"Double?"

"Yep, the ol' man told me this morning that Q-Queenie is now 'screened'. We've finished our tour. There's no spare 'bods' to take over from Hartley and Hopkins so he's 'scrubbing' the one trip we've still to do."

"That'll screw up the betting book," Mackay said. "And I'm bloody glad."

"They'll put a plaque up. Two of us finish when the odds were on one. We were both very lucky, Mac." Mackay nodded and Cotton said: "I hear you've opted for Pathfinders. Tired of living?"

"Just couldn't stand the 'bull' on an operational training unit and you?"

Sue smiled and squeezed Cotton's arm. "He's transferring to the U.S.A.A.F. They've told him he'll get at least the rank of Captain and he's to return to the States. They need bomber instructors with experience," she added proudly.

Cotton looked a shade embarrassed. "My dad met my Mom over here in the first 'do' and I want Sue to come over with me. That's why we're to get married right away." His arm tightened round her waist and he added "We'd like you at the wedding, Mac."

Mackay shook his head. "Kind of you but I'm leaving tomorrow."

"Aren't you spending your leave with May," Sue asked.

"No, I've to go sooner or later, better sooner." He looked at Sue and for the first time she noticed that his eyes were gentle. "You'll like America. Good Luck." They shook hands and Mackay felt suddenly very tired as he entered the Swan. The sleep he had after the raid had been restless. He'd go upstairs and doze until evening.

Maggie went back to her two roomed flat. She slumped

into a tattered armchair and looked round at the dinginess of the room, its peeling wall-paper and dirty yellow paintwork. She buried her face in her hands. She longed for tears to break her pent up emotions but they had gone the previous night when she cried herself to sleep. Numbly came the realization that it was all over with Mackay. He would be gone from the squadron in a couple of days, probably by tomorrow. All her hopes, all her dreams, all her love for him were in ashes. Her stupid ploy to make him jealous had got out of hand disastrously. She should have known, she bitterly recriminated herself, that it was the wrong tactics to use with a man like him. She now knew finally that his assessment of her was nothing better than a cheap whore. She went over to the table, pulled a writing pad from the drawer and began to write. A little later she went into the bathroom she shared with the couple downstairs and filled the bath. The water was tepid as it always was. She looked in the cracked mirror and recalled how she had flung a shoe at it after one of her rows with Mackay. Slowly she undressed and extracted from her make-up bag the razor she used. She unscrewed it and took out the blade. She surveyed her body critically in the mirror. Many men had made love to it but none like Mackay. With the blade in her hand she stepped into the bath and stretched herself out. Swiftly, with only quick gasps at her slashing strokes she cut deep into the arteries in her wrists. She placed both arms under the water and the pain seemed to ease as the bath water changed from pale pink to a watery red.

Mackay felt someone shaking him awake. He stretched lazily on the big bed, yawned and looked into the soft eyes of May. "It's seven o'clock, Mac. You wanted me to waken you." She kissed him swiftly. "I must get back to the bar."

"Okay, I'll be down shortly."

He was downing his second drink of the evening when Constable Fulton came in. Mackay noted he was in uniform which he thought was odd at this time of night. He walked over and his face was stern, almost accusing. "There's been a suicide. A note was left addressed to you. Under the circumstances I opened it." He undid his tunic pocket and took out a letter which he handed to Mackay. Before he even glanced at the handwriting he knew that it had been no idle threat that she had made that afternoon. He read the note.

Fulton said: "She went into the bath and slashed her wrists. The folk downstairs found her. Have you her parents' address or next of kin?"

"No, they separated some time back and she was out of touch with them. There was a sister but she was killed in an air-raid."

Fulton rubbed his chin. "About the funeral. Will you arrange it?"

Mackay put down his glass. "Not my department. You people handle it."

Fulton spluttered. "But the note was left to you. Don't you even want to see her?"

Mackay shook his head and there was unveiled sarcasm in his voice. "Might tarnish the memories I have."

May finished serving three locals and came up to them, looking anxious. "Anything the matter?" Mackay handed her the letter.

"Don't know you should've done that," Fulton said.

"It's addressed to me, isn't it?"

"The coroner will want to see it."

"Great, he can bloody well frame it."

May's eyes widened as she read:

"I am going out of your life for ever. When you get this I shall be dead. You could not see to forgive me so there is nothing left for me now. Don't be angry with me. I love you and always have. Farewell, my only one. Maggie."

227

She handed back the note and Fulton noticed that her hands were trembling. He took the letter from her and the envelope from Mackay. He placed them in his tunic pocket. Carefully he did up the button.

"Oh, God! What ever made her do such a thing?" Someone called for service at the far end of the bar and she left them. Fulton turned on his heel and walked out. "Callous bastard," he said under his breath as he closed the door behind him. Much later that night as they lay in the big bed upstairs May said, "So you're definitely going on Pathfinding. You won't change your mind?"

"No, as I told you downstairs, I want to go."

"You knew this all along, all the time you were telling me you loved me and would take me to the mountains when your tour ended." When he didn't answer she went on. "You're going to go tomorrow then, just like that?"

"I couldn't tell you. I had to finish first before making any decisions."

She laughed bitterly. "All the nights I worried and cried when you went over. Don't you understand what a woman in love feels or has all the killing and the butchering left you totally insensitive?" He put his arm gently round her shoulders but she brushed it angrily away. "I'm left here as the scarlet woman of the village." She laughed again and the bitterness was sharper. "I used to laugh at that hackneyed phrase but everyone in the village knows we've been sleeping together. I didn't mind that for I was stupid enough to think you loved me."

"Stop it May. I do love you but you should know by now that when one completes a tour you either go for a period as an instructor or to the Pathfinders. Sooner or later you're called for a second tour. Better be sooner than later. Anyway, I'm not cut out to be an instructor." She pulled herself half upright in the bed and looked at him sharply. "Have you a death wish or something. You know damned well that the chances of coming through a tour is negligible

228

but two tours?" She laughed with the same bitterness. "Even a drunken bookie would know the odds on that are nil. You're truly mad."

When he didn't answer she said, "Who else is going with you?"

"Ted Parke."

"That figures, I always thought he was screwy. And 'Mitch'?"

"He plans to join us once the quacks fix him. By the time we get back from our leave he should be fit enough."

There was another long silence and she said, "You don't want me to come on leave with you?"

"I do but you know you can't leave the pub to run itself."

"That's why you bloody well asked me," she snapped.

"Not so May."

"You can spend leave here?"

He shook his head. "I must get away. I must have a change of surroundings."

"You mean a change of women"

"Don't be like that. It's just that they'd be going over at night."

"They will be at whatever Pathfinder lot you go to."

"That'll be different. I'll be up with them."

"Drop the heroics. It's out of character." She turned her back on him and bashed the pillow hard under her head.

Mackay woke well after daybreak had broken, stretched an arm out and found that the comforting body of May had gone. He got up, washed and shaved. He reached the bottom of the stairs when May, from the living room shouted: "There's some tea on the stove." He poured himself a cup and said: "I'm sorry you were so bitter last night. I do love you a lot. Try and believe this but even if I hadn't wanted to go I would still have to. It's their airforce, not mine."

He took another sip of his tea. It was as bitter-sweet as her voice.

"Can we have a farewell drink?"

"It's not yet opening time."

He laughed. "When did we ever worry about that . . . my love." She found herself smiling. She poured large whiskies into two glasses and took them into the back room.

She handed one to Mackay. He put his hands up in mock surrender and tenderly closed them round her waist.

"You'll spill the drinks and . . . "

His lips were soft and tender. The wild passion had gone and the thought surged through her that he did love her in his odd, strange way. He broke away gently, took one of the glasses from her hand and touched her lips with it.

"I shall never, never forget you." He downed the drink, slowly savouring its fieriness.

She took a sip from her glass. "Nor I you, Mac. You'll write?"

"I promise." He leaned over her and his lips brushed hers. He laid down his glass, put on his forage cap with its gold gilt wing with the tiny crown above it and hauled on his great-coat. He looked long at her and she thought there was love for her in his eyes as he pulled on his leather gloves. Gloves she had bought him with the last of her clothing ration coupons. He was always mislaying them.

"Don't lose them," she said.

He smiled. "It's the second time I've worn them."

"You're a beautiful· and a fantastic person May." He strode to the door and she heard it rasp on its latch. She crossed to the window, her drink still in her hand and watched as he walked to the lamp-post where the early transport from the town always collected up. Two minutes later her eyes were still on him as he clambered up beside the driver. There was a wave of a gloved hand. She wished he hadn't. It seemed such a tame, stereotyped ending to their affair. The transport moved off. She downed her glass and found that unconsciously she was fingering her wedding band.

She turned from the window. Other men would be flying over the village, as they had done for so very long now and each time the Halifaxes roared over, climbing for height, she would think of the man she had cried over so many nights. Never again, she vowed, would she ever get involved with bomber aircrew.

Ilona Stroheim had been given indefinite leave to visit her husband in the military hospital on the outskirts of Nuremberg when she told her controller that the pilot of Berta One was her husband. They had laid on special transport to take her to the hospital and arranged a room for her in the nurses' quarters.

They had operated on Werner within an hour of his arrival and the grey haired surgeon with the rank of Major had told her that he was still under the anaesthetic. He advised her that it would be better if she did not see him until the following day. He assured her that the operation had been satisfactory. The major wound was in the leg where his kneecap had been shattered.

"He'll be almost as good as new in a few months time. We've saved the leg but he'll always have a limp. But I'm afraid he'll never fly again," he said heavily.

She felt her heart thump with elation at the news. The night of the Nuremberg raid had been a torture she did not think she could endure again. Now Werner would never again have to fly against the Terrorfliegers. She went back to her quarters and for the first time for forty-eight hours sleep came to her easily.

It was mid-afternoon when they told her she could visit Werner. He was propped up in bed when she went into the ward and she noticed that his face was almost as white as the bandage round his head.

"Liebling, Ich liebe dich," she whispered as she bent over and kissed him softly.

"Liebe Ilona, how did you get here?"

"Remember my love, I heard everything. It was awful but now I am so very happy. You're going to get well. I am glad you will never fly again. My heart sings."

"Yes, they've told me." There was sadness in his voice. He stretched out his hand and she took it in hers. "Did they also tell you that I shall always have a limp and you will have a cripple for a husband?"

She laughed softly. "What nonsense, liebling. Your limp will always remind us of the hell you flew through. I am proud and happy, and so thankful that never again will you be up there."

"Will you light me a cigarette." She looked at him and he saw the anxiousness in her eyes.

"It's alright. The doctor said I could smoke a little." He smiled. "It's my leg not my throat, liebling."

He took a long draw on it and his eyes swept back to her. "They tell me that Nuremberg was not badly damaged. We broke the bomber stream. It was a massacre I'm told."

She nodded and he said, "But they bombed Feissendorf, hit the reservoir and the village was submerged."

"Yes," she said. "A Pathfinder aircraft crashed into the waterfall. The village had no chance."

He took another deep inhale from his cigarette and she noticed that his fingers trembled. "I think it was the Pathfinder I took down. I did not see him explode. He must have flown on, overshooting the city and gradually losing height until . . ."

"Shush," she whispered and placed a finger tenderly over his lips. "You mustn't think such things and you cannot know for sure. Pathfinders were being taken down all over."

"I've been thinking about the strange feeling I had when we stood at the waterfall. Do you believe in premonition?"

"I don't know. I think it was all a coincidence and we are apt sometimes to read too much into things"

He took a pull from his cigarette and handed it to her. As she stubbed it out he said, "Your father was alright?"

"Yes, he'll be coming to see you in a few days. And when you're better we shall go somewhere quiet for a rest."

He smiled faintly. "There'll never be another place like the village."

She pressed his hand. "There're other villages in the mountains."

"With waterfalls?"

"When you are fit again we shall look and perhaps we shall find one. But now you must rest. Go to sleep, liebling. I shall come again tomorrow." He watched her walk from the ward and his eyes became drowsy. He thought again of the Pathfinder and the strange twist of fate that had brought his brother back to the village. He closed his eyes and fell into a deep sleep.

THE CHANNINGS
OF EVERLEIGH
Margaret Maitland

BT51199 $1.95
Novel

They rose from prisons . . . Marcus Channing from an English jail, she from the New Orleans slum district known as "The Irish Channel". Together they would build an empire amid Louisiana sugar cane. At first the "old families" shunned them and their vulgar display of wealth, the lavish parties. But soon the Channings of Everleigh were too powerful to ignore. A BT Original.

SUPERSTAR
Barry Mazer

BT51200 $1.50
Novel

This is the story of Rick Lathem, a hard rock star who was born to lose. He was a superstar who relished in excesses—of groupies, money, drugs. There were those who hated him, those who used him, and those who would profit by his death. From wild parties at Malibu to the cocaine crash pads of Manhattan, this is the story of a superstar about to fall. A BT Original.

KATHLEEN
Amanda Hart Douglass

BT51201 $1.95
Novel

Kathleen Holliday was the most famous actress in America, but few knew her as Katie O'Dowd, daughter of a drunken thief and dying prostitute, waif of New York's most notorious slum. By brains, beauty, and ruthless ambition she rose to the pinnacle of success but carried the memories of her hellish childhood. She was attended by men of wealth and power who wished to possess her body and soul. But Kathleen could never be theirs. There was a part of her that no one could own. A BT Original.

TENDERFOOT   **BT51191 $1.50**
Zane Grey   **Western**

Never before published! Here is a new Zane Grey written at the peak of the great writer's artistic skills! This is the west as it really was—a time and place that have passed into legend.

ARIZONA JUSTICE   **BT51195 $1.50**
Gordon D. Shirreffs   **Western**

An ironwilled marshal rides into Llano meaning to bring back the terrible Donigan Brothers. They had killed many. Feared nothing. Sent men to their graves and men to the hills. But Rowan Locke meant to give it a try.

INVITATION TO   **BT51196 $1.25**
A HANGING   **Western**
Walt Coburn

For years Lee Jackson had been riding the outlaw trail, branded by a bounty for a crime he didn't commit. Now the law had him. He was sentenced to hang. And there was only one man that could clear him. The real killer.

THE PROUD GUN   **BT51197 $1.25**
Gordon D. Shirreffs   **Western**

Les Gunnell had cleaned the town up once. Now it was even more corrupt and mean. Now he rode into town determined to do it again. Could he?

THE RED DANIEL
Duncan MacNeil

LB477DK $1.50
Adventure

The Royal Strathspey's, Britain's finest regiment, are dispatched to South Africa to take command in the bloody Boer War and find the most fabulous diamond in all of South Africa—The Red Daniel.

SLAVE SHIP
Harold Calin

LB478KK $1.75
Adventure

This is the story of Gideon Flood, a young romantic who sets sails on a slave ship for a trip that would change his life. He witnesses the cruelty of African chieftains who sell their own for profit, the callousness of the captains who throw the weak overboard, and his own demise as he uses an African slave and then sells her.

A SPRING OF LOVE
Celia Dale

LB479KK $1.50
Novel

"A fascinating story."

—The Washington Star

"An immaculate performance . . . unsettling, and quite touching."

—Kirkus Review

This sweeping novel chronicles a determined young woman's search for enduring love. No matter where it took her, she followed her heart. The man with whom she linked her fortunes was said to be dangerous, but she knew there could be no one else.

TIME IS THE SIMPLEST THING
Clifford D. Simak

LB480DK $1.50
Science Fiction

Millions of light years from Earth, the Telepathic Explorer found his mind possessed by an alien creature. Blaine was a man capable of projecting his mind millions of years into time and space. But that awesome alien penetrated his brain, and Blaine turned against the world . . . and himself.

THE TAVERN KNIGHT
Rafael Sabatini

BT51128 $1.75
Historical Adventure

From the author of Scaramouche and Captain Blood!
A swashbuckling novel of revenge, romance, and
rebellion during the English Civil War, of Charles
Stuart and Oliver Cromwell, and of Sir Crispin
Galliard, alias The Tavern Knight, a drunkard,
debauchee, legendary swordsman, and former noble-
man who looks to revenge his murdered family and
regain his usurped title as Lord of Marleigh Hall
by the blade of his sword!

THE PATRIOTS
SEEDS OF REBELLION
Chet Cunningham

BT51129 $1.75
Historical Novel

The embers of rebellion that had been smoldering
now burst into flame with this second part of Belmont Tower's bicenntenial series! Ben Rutledge
had the most to lose . . . he also knew that war was
the only path to total independence. He was prepared
to risk anything.

THE LOVE GODDESS
David Hanna

BT51130 $1.75
Novel

A sizzling novel about one of Hollywood's greatest
stars—tempestuous, violent, sexually obsessed, and
all woman . . . a beautiful woman on a collision
course with triumph . . . and disaster.

THE VIENNA PURSUIT
Anthea Goddard

BT51131 $1.50
Mystery

Marta Fredericks had always believed her father
had been killed by the Nazis. At her mother's death
bed she discovers that he is alive . . . and had been
a Gestapo agent! She begins an adventure that soon
turns to nightmare and carries her from London
to Vienna to a deserted village on the Austro-Hun-
garian border.

THE ALDRICH REPORT ON MEN
Peggy Aldrich

BT51158 $1.95
Nonfiction

In the tradition of Kinsey and Hite, The Aldrich Report on Men further examines the origins of sexuality this time from the male point of view. Here are the private thoughts of men about their sexuality and interaction with women—orgasm, masturbation, intercourse, foreplay, homosexuality, and more. A BT Original.

THE GHETTO FIGHTERS
Translated and edited by Meyer Barkai

BT51159 $1.75
Nonfiction

First hand, authentic descriptions from diaries, memoirs, and other documents, recording the heroic battle of those who fought against the total destruction of Jews—freedom fighters in the ghettos of Warsaw, Vilna, Cracow, platoons of Jewish partisans roving the swamps and forests of Byelorussia, and fantastically brave breakouts from the concentration camps. Reissue.

DEADLIER THAN THE MALE
J.C. Conaway

BT51160 $1.50
Mystery

Four men had been beheaded with no clues, no motive, no suspect remaining. Novice Private Investigator Jana Blake finds her first criminal case a bizarre chain of killings with no real lead. Join Jana as she stakes her sleuthing from the subways of Manhattan to its breathtaking conclusion in the sky over the East River! A BT Original.

**Soldier of Fortune
OPERATION HONG KONG**   BT51161 $1.50
Peter McCurtin   **Adventure**

When a Chinese agent is sent into the port city to
disrupt daily life and instigate riots and street fighting, Jim Rainey is called in. He hand picks a team
of mercenaries. And for a time he is in charge . . .
Hong Kong, exotic port of call was his. A BT Original.

THE FOUR FEATHERS   BT51162 $1.50
A.E.W. Mason   **Adventure**

Here is a reprint of this classic of storytelling complete with suspense, honesty, loyalty, heroism, and
unswerving love . . . the story of Harry Faversham,
branded coward by three friends and the woman he
loves. Young Harry flees to the Sudan to devote himself to deeds of reckless daring and valor until he
can come home a hero. Originally published by Mac-
millan.

Lassiter/CATTLE BARON   BT51163 $1.25
Jack Slade   **Western**

Lassiter becomes a cattle baron when he inherits a
dead friend's ranch . . . and his wife! Against hus-
tlers, rustlers, a hanging judge, and a gunslinger,
he settles down to make it work. But when he is suddenly offered more than the ranch is worth he discovers his real inheritance—one hundred thousand
dollars hidden somewhere on the spread! A BT
Original.

SEND TO: BELMONT TOWER BOOKS
  P.O. Box 270
  Norwalk, Connecticut 06852

  Please send me the following titles:

Quantity	Book Number	Price
————————	————————	————————
————————	————————	————————
————————	————————	————————
————————	————————	————————
————————	————————	————————

In the event we are out of stock on any of your
selections, please list alternate titles below.

————————	————————	————————
————————	————————	————————
————————	————————	————————
————————	————————	————————

Postage/Handling ——————

I enclose . . . . . . ——————

FOR U.S. ORDERS, add 35¢ per book to cover cost of postage
and handling. Buy five or more copies and we will pay for
shipping. Sorry no C.O.D.'s.

FOR ORDERS SENT OUTSIDE THE U.S.A.
Add $1.00 for the first book and 25¢ for each additional
book. PAY BY foreign draft or money order drawn on a
U.S. bank, payable in U.S. ($) dollars.
☐ Please send me a free catalog.

NAME_____
              (Please print)

ADDRESS_____

CITY ——————————— STATE ——————— ZIP ———
        Allow Four Weeks for Delivery